F   Park, David
PAR

The Big Snow

AUG

2002

DEMCO

THE BIG SNOW

Oranges from Spain
The Healing
The Rye Man
Stone Kingdoms

THE BIG SNOW

DAVID PARK

BLOOMSBURY

Published by Bloomsbury, New York and London.
Distributed to the trade by Holtzbrinck Publishers

A CIP catalogue record for this book
is available from the Library of Congress

ISBN 1-58234-249-0

First U.S. Edition 2002
10 9 8 7 6 5 4 3 2 1

Typeset by Hewer Text Ltd, Scotland
Printed by Clays Ltd, St Ives plc, England

For Alberta, again and again

The North of Ireland

1963

The Light of the World

HE SPREAD THE MAP carefully over the bed-end so that it wasn't creased. There were some marbled white bruises on it, a legacy of all the times they had stretched it over their knees or on the quilt of this same bed. He wasn't sure if she could see it or not, but he had marked the route in blue ink. Coast to coast. From the grey swell of the Atlantic to the sweet blue of the Pacific. A whole continent in between. The sea is where it starts and where it always ends. He thinks there is a fitness in that, a rightness. The blue of the road runs like a vein across the shaded skin of the continent. He doesn't know if she can see it but he wants her to know that he's traced the road, followed the journey they planned to share, and maybe if she can see it and understand, there is still time to make it. It's a long way to go, for this is a big country, bigger than even his imagination is able to picture and there is no way for people like them, people who have grown up and lived nowhere other than a small place, can ever grasp it. Not until they see it for themselves. Not until they let their hearts believe it.

He went to the window and looked out on where their lives had been lived, saw the empty, wind-whipped fields stuttering and fretting into each other, and it felt as if their days had been measured and framed by these shadowy lines of hedgerows, the low seal of sky, the fixed boundary of time and place. Where you were born was just one more random twist of fate, which now for him seemed the engine that drove all human existence. So it was no good for the church spire to thrust itself skywards from the heart of the village because he couldn't believe that it aspired further than a collective need, an insistence on what it wanted the world to be like. When he turned back to the bed and looked at the ashen pallor of her shrivelled skin, the skin of which his hand had known the caress and soft beauty, he felt that what he saw was living, dying proof that there was meaning only in what could be found in the present. It was the thought that charged him, stopped him collapsing at the side of the bed and weeping in anger and rage, stopped the paralysis of self-pity. Now there were only moments – he didn't know how many – and each had to be filled with the things he needed to say. The preparations for the journey.

He smoothed the map again and made sure the angle was right for her eyes to see, eyes that drifted in and out of unconsciousness, the drug-fuelled respite from the pain. Then he opened the book of Ansel Adams photographs at her favourite – the one where the stretch of lake seems to hold up its fluid, animated face and pull the sky into it, like the embrace of a lover. And everything is open and brushed by light that feels like the light of the world. It was what she wanted to do, take photographs that were bigger than themselves, opening the moment into such light and space. It was what he, too, now had to do, and he was frightened that he wouldn't know how to prise open what was left and fill it with what she wanted, with what he needed. He had already told her that he loved her and the raw words had burned his throat with the knowledge that they hadn't been used enough in the past, so now they seemed like what was expected, a final tidying-up, of setting things in order, and that wasn't enough.

He thought best when he focused on practicalities so he stood up and looked around the room. He had to keep it warm so he put some more coal on the fire. They had never used the fireplace before, but he was grateful that they had only blocked it with a piece of painted plywood and not had it bricked up. It smoked a little but if he kept a window on its snib it wasn't so bad, and the single-bar electric fire could be used as well if the temperature continued to drop. Sometimes he was tempted to open the window wider, to let cold, clean air swirl into the room, but he knew he couldn't and he knew, too, that what he wanted was something to carry off the smell of what he couldn't recognize as her. It was as if this thing had sought to take from her all the things that went to make her who she was, the person whom fifteen years of marriage had lodged in his memory. So in its ravenous, gnawing greed it consumed the skin that she had kept beautiful only by the splash of water; the scent of her body; the glory of her red hair, which now had withered into a thin stubble and left her scalp exposed and cold to the eyes. He had tried lying with her on the bed but it didn't feel the way he wanted and he couldn't touch or hold her for fear of hurting the fragility to which her body had shrunk, so the most he did was lay his finger lightly on the back of her hand. Even there his eyes fastened on the skin, which seemed to have tightened and pushed the blue tributary of veins close to the surface. The veins reminded him of the road on the map and he remembered its importance and that all that was left for him now was the final chance to step outside his own self-pity and push aside every one of the selfish impulses that flooded his head. He almost envied those who had the comfort of faith. Right at the start, when the doctor told him, he had tried a silent prayer but it tasted of hypocrisy and the words had stumbled then fragmented into the sense of a greater futility, part of a deception that prevented the acknowledgment of the profound and inescapable truth that they were giving him back his wife only so that she could die.

He turned to another photograph. A stretch of desert, running from the eye to the dark bevel of mountains and a rim of thrown sky where striated, penumbral light seemed to slip into a memory of itself. Then, taking the damp cloth from the bedside table, he slowly traced the hollow contours of her face like a blind man feeling Braille, trying to read the memory of who she was and who she used to be. He let the edge of the cloth linger on the dried-up lips and tried to conjure the lilt of her smile, the way her eyes seemed to smile too, but there was only the flinty staleness of her breath and the open purse of her mouth, which had not uttered a word since her return. He switched on the bedside light in an attempt to chase away the tide of thickening grey light that had started to seep into the room, but it made her skin seem yellow and brittle like parchment, and the light was intrusive and illuminated what he didn't want to read until he angled the shade to the wall and she fell into shadow again. It was the light of the world he wanted for her now, the light in these photographs that would bathe and swaddle her in its warmth, stir these wintry limbs into life. If only there was a doorway into them that he could carry her through, everything might be all right. And coming home to die was only right but it wasn't right enough when it wasn't where the heart wanted for its home. She was bigger than this place with its falling mesh of narrow and mean understanding; she belonged in the space of some other world. Always.

He pointed to the map, moving the shade a little so that it was encompassed by its stretch of yellow. 'It's a long way,' he said. 'Not like taking a dander up the road, or going up to the shops. You could put this whole island in the back pocket of any one of those states and never notice it was there. A whole continent. A whole different world, too.' The closeness of his whisper to the side of her face trembled a little feather of her hair. 'It'll be an adventure all right, no two ways about it, but what a thing to do. Who around here would ever believe it possible? They'd think we were off our heads if they ever found out – maybe we should send them postcards from everywhere we go but not sign our real names on them.' The lines at the sides of her eyes crinkled a little and for a second it made him think she was going to open them and the thought that his words were reaching her made him talk faster and more intensely. 'We'll have to plan it really well, though – it'll take a lot of planning all right. It's not just like going off for a week at the seaside. There's the car to hire and the best route to work out and we should keep a diary, a log of every town and place on the way. You can draw little pencil sketches in it and we can collect things and stick them in, too. It'll be important to keep a record of everything. Your photographs of course – we'll have those and I've been thinking that I should try to write something when we come back home or even as we go. Our kind of *On the Road* but I don't know if it'd be fiction or travel writing or what. Maybe we can put everything together in a kind of journal. Maybe if we did it well, someone might be interested in publishing it. You never know.'

The doctor wouldn't return until his morning surgery was over. He'd give her more drugs, touch him on the shoulder and then they'd talk about the weather. He wished he could give her the drugs himself, avoid the embarrassment of small talk and that joint walk down the stairs and the inevitable fumble with the door. It had transmuted into a predictable ritual and only the knowledge that it was coming to an end made him accept it with patience. He turned another page and, conscious of the thickening gloom, angled the bedside lamp again so that it illuminated the photograph. 'El Capitan, Merced River, Clouds, Yosemite National Park'. The river is in white-ridged full flow, funnelling out from tall, fir-clad banks and rushing past the humped blackness of rocks. In the foreground, firs and pines scratch the darkening tumble of clouds. Behind, the sheer stretch of rock is lightened on one face by the sheen of light that seems to have travelled from a brightness further off. Maybe some nights they'd sleep in the car or even take a small tent with them and pitch it in the lee of trees. In the morning, drink from the river, let the water splash their faces and feel the tangy freshness on their tongues. He told her about it and his voice was washed by excitement as he lived it for her and in the telling he remembered about the stars – more stars than they could ever imagine – and before they went to sleep at night, before they smothered their night fire with dust, they'd lie under the stars and just stare, just stare at the great arch of sky.

Stars in her hair. Not those brittle strands that dithered and splayed their dryness across her skull. He'd kissed her first under the stars, at the end of the lane leading to her parents' farm, his heart pumping and kicking in his chest like a piston, his arms holding the whole of her so tightly that it was as if he wanted all the life of her to flow into him. And he had felt it more intensely than he had ever felt anything before or since –

the press of her breasts against him, the softness of her mouth, which took his and silently spoke her equal need. Afterwards they had laughed but held each other as if frightened either to let go or to do it again, and neither of them had spoken until she told him it was time for her to go inside again and he had stood until she vanished through the yellow square of light before he threw his face to the same stars and shouted, 'Yes, Yes!' again and again, then started to run like a boy on the first day of his holiday.

He turned to another page. 'Mount Williamson, Sierra Nevada, from Manzanar, California, 1945'. A plain of rocks and boulders stretches like a moonscape towards the mountains. A corridor of light braids one of their flanks. The two mountains are shaped like a woman's breasts, the range like the supine body. The oval rock closest to the camera becomes the secret place. He wondered why he had never seen the photograph properly before as he propped it open at the foot of the bed. But in the last few days he had realized that there were many things he had never seen properly. This was only one more. Taking things for granted was what people called it, but that didn't explain it all. He felt as if he had been sleepwalking these last few years, his senses worn dull by familiarity and complacency. Now he had come to them suddenly and terribly so that there was nothing in the moment that was not felt, nothing that did not press and print itself on his consciousness with a sear. And he didn't want it any other way, didn't want it muffled and rendered vague by the drugs the doctor had offered him surreptitiously as if trying to sell him something illicit.

He felt a pulse of shame and panic about the past. There was so much that was unrecorded, so much that had slipped into the flux and flow of time, and with a kind of desperation he sought to retrieve whatever he could, to feel vicariously what had been lost. He looked at where her camera sat on the dresser and tried to refocus on what had slipped away. But there was so much and so little time. Her head moved on the pillow and for one foolish second he thought she was going to tell him and he went to her and lightly soothed her cheek with the back of his hand. At the very start he had been angry with her secretly, as if he blamed her for letting this thing happen, for taking it into her body, for not being strong enough, but he recognized it now as part of that selfish self-pity he had determined to dispel. The doctor didn't think there was much left now. Not long. But they weren't words he had been comfortable using and he had slipped them out of the side of his mouth almost as a whisper. Her nurse told him she prayed for her and sometimes God worked a miracle and what was needed was faith. After she had gone he had burned the tract she had left.

He straightened the map on the bed and tried to adjust the light so that it caught the route he had marked. He read her some of the place names, pointed out deserts, mountains, forests, the Great Plains. Coast to coast. The blue seas of the Pacific Ocean. He told her they would enter the light of the photographs, leave this shadowy, fretted landscape behind. He turned to another photograph. 'Minarets and High Clouds, Sierra Nevada'. The mountains are patched with pockets of snow, and above them the white ridges of clouds seem to run and scatter into the sullen water of the sky. It's as if the snow from the slopes has been wind-blown and scattered skywards. There was one place he wanted to go, go while there was still time. He had remembered it while he looked at the photograph.

The boarding house where they spent their first night

together nestled under the Mourne Mountains on the edge of the resort. They had a room at the end of a corridor beside the bathroom. A room dominated by a cavernous wardrobe with glass panels on its doors and a sagging double bed which was a mountainous pyre of eiderdown and a mismatched assortment of balled and scratchy blankets. From their window they could see the grey rim of the sea, the tired stretch of a headland. It wasn't what either of them had imagined, but neither wanted to be the first to reveal disappointment or seem ungrateful for what had been a gift from her parents. Instead they told each other that if the weather held up they would be able to spend most of their time out and about. He remembered his own nervousness, the sudden flare of self-doubt when the time came. He thought she probably felt the same but was better at hiding it and, with that indifference she always possessed to what didn't matter, simply refused any show of coyness. He had watched her take off her clothes in the frosted, pitted mirror, which was marbled and stained with rust in its corners, the sudden whiteness of her breasts flitting like ghosts across his eyes. Then she had turned to face him and he could do nothing but stare at her and then only at her face until her outstretched arms held him as tightly as he had ever hoped.

Tentative, frightened of ineptitude, their lovemaking was framed by the flushing of the toilet, the tread of feet in the corridor, the groan and complaint of the pipes, and afterwards they had wondered half-aloud if that was what it amounted to and then found comfort in their laughter. They joked about being paid-up members of this exclusive club, talked as if they had just been granted life membership after having had to wait so long for their applications to be accepted. In the morning he woke to find her standing at the window and he imagined he saw disappointment in the frame of her body but when she turned to him there was no trace of it. That night they took a bus round the coast to the harbour at Kilkeel and watched as the fishing boats prepared to set sail. Everything was sharp and clear to him, the way he wanted it to be. He looked at her head lolling on the pillow, her mouth slightly open, and he wondered if somewhere hidden now to the world were the same images lodged for ever. Provisions for her journey.

The boats bobbing like a heartbeat, the oil-skimmed smear and skein of reflected light lapping against their wooden hulls. It was the first time he had known the full force and shock of desire. It mixed with the tang of the sea and the lights already shimmering on the horizon and laced his breath as he spoke. He trusted his voice less and less and so he listened silently as she recited the painted names – the *Steadfast Hope*, the *Starry Sky*, the *Climbing Wave*. He wanted to pull her into the shadows of the empty sheds, to have all of her, but the excitement and happiness in her voice made him hesitant as he tried to smother what pushed and pulled at his insides. She skipped like a girl over the splay of ropes and nets and scolded him for his silence, and he smiled to hide what tugged below his surface as she joked that they should steal a boat and sail away. He knew she didn't want to go back to the room, and the strung pearls of light which glinted in the distance seemed to be what her eyes wished for, but that knowledge did nothing to diminish his desire and as he locked his arm in hers it was his own urgency he felt.

They were given a ride back in a lorry heading for Belfast. The driver had stopped for them as they stood at the bus stop and offered them a lift. They had sat together in the narrow passenger seat and as the driver talked about his job he felt the press of her body against his own, each point of contact the fusion of need. They had been dropped right outside the door of the boarding house but both had hesitated, unwilling to enter, and then he led her across the road, down over a stony swathe of beach, across jagged tendrils of rock that led to the sea. She understood now and it was all right, and when he found a secret bed of sand that filtered between the shelter of rocks she lay down for him and with the shuck and break of the sea close by he made love to her in the way he hadn't the night before. And afterwards, when he had nothing more to give, he lay still with his head buried in her hair and she cradled him, and then, inside the rasp and shuffle of the sea across the pebbled shore, he heard her voice repeat the names of the boats – the *Climbing Wave*, the *Steadfast Hope*, the *Starry Sky* – whispering them until they ran into each other and he thought her voice must be part of the sea.

'Do you remember it?' he asked. 'Maybe we should have stolen that boat, sailed away as you wanted.' He was suddenly aware that the room was cold – the temperature had dropped in the last few hours. He put more coal on the fire and raked it into life. He was glad the drugs helped the pain but sorry that they took her so far away from him. He turned to another photograph but didn't like the one he saw. It was 'Jeffrey Pine, Sentinel Dome, Yosemite'. The ancient tree is twisted and gnarled, stunted and wind-shaped in its growth, sculpted and contorted by the elements in its exposed site. Between the frame of its lower branch and the shadow-streaked rock below it stretches a distant mountain range. He turned the page again. It was his old thought. Did where you live shape the limits of what your life could be? Did living in a small place make it inescapably small, unable to grow and expand? Perhaps if he had taken her away from this place she would have escaped this thing that had caught and twisted her life in its fist. He went to the window. It had started to snow.

That unfettered force of desire, that total abandonment of self, perhaps that was what he had tried to find again in someone else's arms. Once, only once, he told himself, trying to assuage the guilt that he had carried with him since the moment. Maybe trying to explain it was to elevate it to something that it never was, when the truth was, perhaps, that it had sprung from nothing but a sudden surge of loneliness, a momentary hunger that left as quickly as it had come. It was a weekend conference – she was a teacher, too, married like him, and afterwards they had avoided even a goodbye. And yet how could such a once meaningless thing linger and fester in his head until he thought of it as the meanest, most terrible thing he had ever done, a betrayal that shamed him with unremitting intensity? He had tried to tell her many times, but each time his fear had stifled the words in his throat and then his sense of cowardice whetted the edge of that shame so that it felt like a two-edged knife cutting them both. Of all the consequences he had been frightened of, the greatest was losing her.

He was frightened now because he knew this was the last chance for the truth. How could he let her set out on the journey while he harboured this lie? He looked at the blue line on the map, the light in the photographs and it seemed there was only room for the truth in these things, that anything else was a deviation from the route, an impure focus. Every day during her illness the lie had coiled a little tighter round his mind so sometimes it felt that unless he tore it away it would choke all the other life they had known. He switched on the electric fire and pulled the curtains, then turned another page. 'Fresh Snow, Yosemite National Park, California'. The camera looks into a dense frieze of trees and latticed undergrowth frozen into a black-and-white negative, where snow fuses and links the black branches and spindles of stems. It's like a painting by Jackson Pollock and it's cold to the eyes. Cold and beautiful. But he isn't sure, for who is it that needs the truth? And will it be one final selfishness if he tells her now? He isn't sure. Her head moves a little on the pillow, a thin brittle filament of hair kinks across her cheek. Let her sleep, and in the morning, perhaps, before the doctor comes. When he has thought of the words.

He wraps a blanket round himself and curls into the armchair at the foot of the bed. In the morning. He tries to sleep, tries to hear one more time her voice threaded with the sea. The *Steadfast Hope*, the *Starry Sky*, the *Climbing Wave*. The final leg of the journey when they see the Pacific. The night is cold, he wakes many times, tries to squirm into new respite. Sleeping under an arch of stars. Once he thinks of joining her on the bed, of trying to be close to her again, but he's frightened of hurting her and then he falls into a sleep that carries him through to the morning.

The fire is out, burned away to nothing. His neck is sore and he rubs it with the palm of his hand. The blanket has slipped to the floor. Even in the shaded light from her bedside table he knows that she is dead. As he goes to her something wells up in his throat and pushes for release but then vanishes in a stream of soft noise like the wind running through grass. Her eyes are open but they stare at the wall and he goes to close them, then pulls his hand away, frightened to touch her in death. And there is the sudden fleck of fear and anger because he knows that she has left him with the truth unshared. There is resentment, too, that she has left him, gone on the journey without him, for he knows now that it is her journey and he cannot share it. Then into that loneliness breaks the full pain of loss and he sits on the bed beside her and hugs his hurt like a child, rocking slowly back and forwards as if the motion might drain it away. After a while he stands up because he knows there is work to do and soon the doctor and nurse will come and what he has left will have to be shared with them. So he goes to the window and pulls the curtain and there is a new cry in his throat when he sees the world outside, but it is a cry of something beyond the pain of grief. The old world is gone and in its place the whiteness of snow. Its sudden brightness hurts his eyes. Instinctively he turns to tell her and then he remembers and he turns again and stares.

There isn't much time before the doctor and nurse come. The bed is old and heavy so he can only move it a few inches at a time. It scrapes and plucks the linoleum where the rugs don't cover it but the slowness of the movement leaves her still and undisturbed. As he lifts lightly and drags it, he wonders how anyone can ever think that death looks like sleep. His breathing is heavy from the effort and he glances at the window over his shoulder and goes and opens it as wide as it will go. Inch by inch he pulls the bed until it is tight against the wall below the window. The cold air brushes against his face. The breeze blows a few flakes off the sill into the room. There may not be much time. Then, touching her for the first time, he raises her up on the pillow so that her face is level with the window and she can see the snow, and he talks to her in a low whisper and his voice and the voice he remembers sound to him like the soft ebb and shuffle of the sea. A strand of her hair is disturbed by the wind and falls across his sleeve and the light burnishes it for a second into a memory of its former colour. The camera feels lighter in his hand than he can ever remember it. In a few seconds everything is ready. Her eyes are open and in them the light of the world. He kneels beside her, their cheeks touching, his eye level with hers, his hand clasping the coldness of her hand, and then he presses her finger downwards. The shutter opens and closes.

Snow Trails

HE STOOD WATCHING FROM under the trembling lattice of branches, his back pressed against the dark bark. Already the first fine eddies of snow were beginning to fall, drifting in dreamily on the sighs of wind, uncertain and vague in their direction. They flecked and salted the distance that separated him from the house and its yellow squares of light. Above him the whole tree suddenly seemed to shiver, shaking loose the scent of pine, and he pushed his back tightly against the solidity of its trunk and let his hands brush and trace the knotted surface.

There were spaces in the snow, pockets of what felt like stillness, and in the silence of its fall he sensed a mockery of his own agitation. He was conscious, too, for the first time of his own coldness. He had no watch to tell him how long he had been waiting, and he stamped his feet on the frozen earth and blew a stream of his breath into his cupped hands. The sound rushed in his ears, an intrusion into the silence, and he stared again at the distant house as if somehow it might have betrayed his presence, but it stood squat and imperturbable, its yet uncurtained windows unblinking and resolute in their indifference. He dreamed it wouldn't always be like this. The cold, the distance. And other images warmed and sparked the darkness as the desultory, languid fall of snow quickened and the wind slanted it as if it was riddling through the brindled wash of sky. He walked out of the inner shadows of the tree until his face touched the tremulous sift of the branches that veiled his presence, and for a crazy second he thought of pushing them aside and walking through the falling snow towards the light.

Then he saw her cross one of the downstairs windows, come back and stare out, her face close to the glass, one hand shading her eyes to block out the reflection. He pulled back into the darkness even though he knew she couldn't see him, and as he did so his memory painted in the blueness of her eyes, the pale softness of her skin. Painted them from his secret store. She was looking for him, waiting for him to come, and soon she would open the door and call out to him. That's how he would see her – framed in the fan of light, holding out her arms, and he would step out of the faltering folds of darkness and, shrugging off the clutch of the snow, would walk towards her open arms. Walk into the corridor of light towards her.

In a few seconds she pulled away again and disappeared but it was enough, for even a little was enough. Her face pressed against the glass, looking for him. Waiting for him. He walked forward again and pushed his face against the clumps of needles and they held the softness of her hair and what he breathed was the musk of her scent. One of the needles broke free and stuck to his cheek like a fallen eyelash and he let it linger on his skin before shaking it away. He knew it was time to go, but hesitated while he stared at the sky. Something strange was happening to it – it was as if all its dark folds, its tight seams and creases, were being slowly prised open, as if all its secrets were being surrendered and given up to this fall and flow. It was really coming down now, coming down as if all restraint had been brushed aside in a sleet and slurry of flake. Already it was beginning to shadow and cream the contours of the earth into a oneness. He pulled up his collar and stuck his hands deep into his pockets, then crouched so that he could see the house from below the branches for one last time.

Nothing had changed, but the thickening tide of snow made it harder to see and even the yellow squares of light were marbled and blurred. Some snow sifted through the spread of the branches like dust and he held out the palm of his hand and let its coldness wet his skin before he carefully raised it to his bending head and touched it against his lips. Then he was moving back the way he had come, heading across the open pasture towards the tall sentinel trees which guarded the boundaries of the estate on two sides. As the snow arrowed in on him, plastering his hair and plashing against his eyes, he bowed his head against it. Another few steps and he wouldn't have heard it, the sound swirled away into the depths of the night, another few steps and the bark of the dog would have been just another frozen particle crunched by his feet.

He stopped and turned his gaze back to the house. The sound came again in a succession of sharp, angry barks but he was too far away to see and for a second he stood motionless, holding his head to the sky, indifferent to the flurries that beat against him. He looked down at the dark sleeve of his jacket and saw it spangled and glinting, saw the spreading bruise of damp seeping into it, then walked back to the canopy of the branches. The lights on either side of the front door had been switched on and the falling, stuttering snow, flitted into brief wisps of yellow in front of them.

She was a few feet from the door, wearing a dark duffel coat with the hood pulled up so only a thin rim of her hair was visible. In front of her, the dog snapped at the strangeness of the snow and jumped in the air to bite the flakes, determined to ward off the intruder. She took a few steps forward and feathered up the settling snow, shuffling it in the air with kicks of her feet. The dog was bouncing higher, its head twisting to snap at the fall. Then she stood still again and he wished he was the snow that fell on her. The dog stopped jumping, circled itself, snuffling for some scent, then started towards him until she called it back and it retreated reluctantly into her shadow. He watched it follow her when she turned back towards the house. He stood motionless, watching through the thickening frieze of snow as she stepped into the arc of light spun from the open door. Watching as she suddenly turned and stretched out her arms, the black cross of her body transfigured by the light.

'Are you off your head?' his father asked, staring at his sodden clothes and dripping hair. 'Only someone with a screw loose would be out the door on a night like this.' Then without waiting for an explanation he turned back to his paper.

'Peter, Peter,' scolded his mother, 'in the name of fortune what's got into you? Get those wet clothes off and something dry on before you're laid-up with pneumonia.'

She fussed around him, pulling at his jacket and smoothing the damp tails of his hair with the towel that hung on the back of the kitchen door. His father snorted into his paper, a sound of disbelief, but it was unclear if it was related to his son's appearance or what he was reading: his mother took his jacket and hung it over the back of the chair, before pulling it up to the side of the fire. Soon thin snakes of steam seeped upwards from its dampness.

'You're a bit old for playing in the snow,' his father said.

'I wasn't playing.'

'Well, what in the name of God were you doing out there? Looking for Scott of the Antarctic?' He blew a thin burst of breath and flapped the paper to get a clean fold on the next page.

He stared at the fire but didn't answer his father's question. On the hearth was a row of socks and handkerchiefs. The front of the fire was an angry gash of embers.

'Go and get changed, Peter, and then come back down and warm yourself at the fire. Don't be going to your room before you get dry.'

As he climbed the stairs he heard his father call after him, 'Tonight's not the night for skulking in your den,' and then there was the soft chiding of his mother, her 'whist' and her 'easy', her 'Let the boy be.' In his room he didn't switch on the light but went to the window, lightly pressed his fingers to the glass and watched the snow's unrelenting fall. Already, their tussocky snatch of garden had been smoothed into a uniformity that made it strange and unfamiliar. It seemed as if the whole world was turning, slowly changing and it felt right for he was changing, too, leaving behind the meaningless husk of his past and becoming something new. It frightened him, the power of it, the pain of it. Not like anything he'd ever known in the past, for what few tawdry moments of feeling existed there seemed now only a foolishness in his memory. This was real, real as the falling snow layering and smoothing the world. It silted and coursed through his veins in his waking moments, came whispering home in the moments before sleep, in the warm confusion of waking. Lifting his fingers away from the glass he watched the ebb of his print, the settling of the snow on the sill, its smudge and crimped lisp against the glass. The world was beautiful, the world was strange. And there was something happening to him. At times he wanted to scream it to the sky, at others it was joy, and sometimes it was the scourge of more pain than he felt he could bear. Maybe the snow would help him. Be a salve. Maybe its fall would call her to the truth.

'Is there something wrong with us? Are we not good enough for him? Has he joined some holy order, taken a vow of silence? Well, if he wants to hide up there, it's no skin off my nose.' His father's voice, riddled with irritation, clattered up the stairs. 'And what was he doing out in the snow? Did he say?' His mother's reply was lost in the gush and drum of the kettle being filled. 'A dog would have more sense than to go out on a night like this. Is it still coming down?'

'Aye,' his mother said, 'and getting heavier.'

He turned away from the window. Under the green smoothness of the eiderdown was a small hump where she had placed the stone jar and he knew without looking that she had wrapped his pyjamas round it. She was making supper, and if he didn't go down soon she would call and there would be more from his father, so he lifted the book from the side of his bed and went down to the living room. His father folded his paper and dropped it into the cardboard box at the side of the hearth.

'I'll bank the fire up later on,' his father said to no one in particular, 'and put slack on. Keep it going overnight.' Then, partly turning his head towards him, 'Did you see many people out?'

The tone was not sarcastic and he recognized it was as close as his father would come to an offer of conciliation. He looked up from his book. Thin trembles of steam were still curling upwards from his jacket. The smell of its sodden fibres infused the whole room. 'No, I didn't see anyone. It's starting to get heavy, beginning to lie in the fields and roads.' He paused, then offered his own gesture. 'Is there more forecast?'

'Who knows? Thon forecaster boys aren't worth a spit in the wind. Never see anything coming till it hits them full in the face. Sure, you remember the time of the church fête, way last year: they said it was going to pour and we had the extra tents up and everything inside the hall and wasn't the sun splitting the trees. Not a drop of rain all day.'

His mother came in and set plates of toast on the hearth, then went back into the kitchen for the mugs of tea. Leaning forward to the fire, his father cleaned his hands by rubbing them together and stretching them towards the blue-tipped flames. 'You'd be better slipping oul Janey Thompson a few bob and asking her to read the tea leaves,' he said. 'Probably be just as accurate as those boys with their charts and their isobars. And one thing I do know is that if it falls heavy tonight, there won't be many venturing out to the shop tomorrow, for they'll all be tucked up round the fireside. So let's just hope it's a bit of a puff and a blow and thawed away by the morning.'

They both took the mugs that were handed to them and his father set his on the mantelpiece to cool before starting to eat a slice of the toast. He noticed that his mother was wearing, over her stockings, a pair of thick woollen socks which frothed out of her slippers and stretched over her calf muscles. Through the door into the kitchen he could see that she had rolled an old towel and laid it along the bottom of the door in an attempt to keep out draughts. Sometimes a spot of water dripped from the chimney into the fire and there was a sudden sizzle.

25

'Will the van be all right?' his mother asked. 'It's lucky you put it in the garage when you came home.'

'Aye, I'll go out later and cover the engine with some blankets. That'd be all we need – for it not to start.' His father lifted down the mug of tea, holding it in the pincer of his fingers, then turning it until he reached the handle. 'Snow's all right on Christmas cards or in a painting but it's a royal pain in the neck when it's real. All the same, a couple of flickers of the electric tonight and they'll be in on the morning, buying up every candle in the place. We could maybe even get rid of some of that supply I got in last October – you remember the boy who wanted me to buy the coloured ones? What would anyone want with a coloured candle that costs more? Is the snow still lying?'

His mother shuffled in her slippers to the front window and peered through the narrow gap between the wall and curtain she opened with the back of her hand. Her face pushed into it until only the back of her head was visible. The light reflected off the blue clasp that held her hair in a tight bun. A hairclip stuck out from its core like a nail working itself loose from weathered wood. There was the squeak of her hand rubbing the glass.

'It's still coming down. It's hard to see but it's lying all right. Coloured candles are nice at Christmas. Some of the younger ones like to put them on their tree or use them to make the type of decoration you see on a mantelpiece with a bit of holly or on a wooden log. Something like that.'

'Maybe I should've taken some of the red ones off him then.' His voice was edged with uncertainty, regret at having missed a possible opportunity. 'I can't be expected to keep up with every tomfool fashion,' he said, as if defending himself from some unspoken criticism. 'Remember we got took with that box of fancy furniture polish. I've sold but the one tin since the day and hour thon cowboy wiped me eye with them. And he'll not be back, for I heard he's selling insurance up in Belfast. Probably making a mint with the patter he has.' Then, taking the poker, he raked air into the base of the fire as if trying to dispel the misery of the memory.

As his father and mother slipped into shop talk, the familiar litany of accounts and ordering, of unpaid bills, he opened his book and tried to read, but his father's voice with its relentless, jarring vocabulary of commerce grated and jangled inside his head. It was *Le Grand Meaulnes* by Alain-Fournier, the book he'd been reading the Saturday afternoon she first came into the shop. It was part of his first-year reading list for Queen's and it was propped on the counter, which ran at right angles to the rows of metal shelving, home to boxes of nails and screws, bolts and locks, electrical wires and plugs, brown packets of seed, gardening equipment, the rubbery smell of wellington boots and a thousand other things, each allocated to a precise place and part of a sequence which only his father could explain. The hardware shop acted as an ordering point for coal, slack, and it also sold some small-scale farming equipment and animal feeds. There were a hearse and a limousine which served both weddings and funerals and in which, despite the most scrupulous hoovering, it wasn't unusual for mourners to discover their dark clothing blushed with tiny spots of confetti, squeezed out from the seams of the seats by their weight.

He'd read about thirty pages on that particular afternoon as business had been slow. It irritated his father to see him read in the shop – maybe that was one of the reasons he did it – and it also irritated his father, that he wouldn't wear the same brown shopcoat as he did. Said it made the shop, the service, look sloppy. But to wear the coat tainted the position with a sense of permanency and an acquiescence in the pattern of his father's life, regardless of the fact that he only worked on Saturdays and holidays in order to supplement his student grant. Occasionally he assisted at funerals, but only when the regular man wasn't available, and when he did he always insisted on the full rate for the job in the hope that he would price himself out of it.

It was the knock of the handlebars of her bicycle against the glass that made him look up from his book. His father was putting in time by stock-taking, jotting numbers and codes into a ledger with the stub of a pencil. When she came in she said hello before the bell above the door had finished ringing and her voice mingled with its peal. He guessed almost immediately who she was, although he'd never seen her before. The clothes she wore and the way she wore them said that she wasn't local, even though there was nothing special about the way she was dressed. She was probably about thirty and wore a casual woollen jacket and corduroy trousers. Her blond shoulder-length hair was pulled back from her face by a black band and the perfume she wore was the scent of wealth. Her name was Alice Richmond and she and her husband had bought the manor house and estate of Colonel Ashbury, who had been forced to put it on the market after he got into financial trouble. They said her husband was big money from Belfast, one of two brothers who had inherited their father's engineering company. He looked ten years older than her, maybe more, and they had moved in a short time earlier, spent a lot of money on redecorating and restoration, kept on the existing staff, who were the only source of information about them the village could find. They didn't mix with the village, didn't attend the church, but at regular intervals they had dinner parties when convoys of cars arrived from Belfast and for these outside caterers were brought in and the food served was described as 'nothing ordinary', as 'high-falutin''.

She came straight to the counter and her face was flushed by the cycle ride, the corners of her eyes dampened by the wind. Smoothing stray hair with the comb of her fingers she shook her head lightly to wave it back in shape, and as her eyes went to the cover of his book she smiled and asked him if he was enjoying it. He explained about his course, glad to have the chance to distance himself from his current position, and she made a joke about not expecting to find French literature in hardware stores, then on impulse he said his father was out the back reading Sartre. At her laughter his father appeared with his ledger, sticking the stub of pencil behind his ear, and asked was she being served all right. 'Admirably' was the word she used and it rang in the air like the timbre of her voice. It struck him that it was a word that had probably never been used in the shop, and at its audacious syllables his father retreated behind the shelves again but peered out at her, inspecting her, weighing her up.

She bought picture hooks, white spirit, brass-headed screws, and when he wrapped them in brown paper his hands felt clumsy under her gaze. As he made a mess of the folds she turned back to the shop and ambled amongst the displays. She picked a brush and a garden rake. 'The leaves get everywhere,' she said. 'So many trees. A lot of leaves to clear up.' She weighed the rake in her hand as if testing its balance.

'The best clear-up for leaves is a good east wind,' his father said, walking towards the counter, holding the ledger under his arm like a bible.

'You're probably right,' she said smiling, 'but they blow up round the house, get wet, then clog up everywhere.

'Would that be Colonel Ashbury's old place?' his father asked, his feigned ignorance transparent.

'Yes, that's right.'

'So you're Mrs Richmond, then,' his father said, extending his hand over the counter. 'You're very welcome to the village.'

He watched their hands meet briefly and saw the soft glint of gold on her wrist. Then his father said he couldn't possibly let her carry her purchases on the bike in case she had an accident, and when she protested he insisted, saying it wouldn't be any trouble to deliver them later that afternoon. She smiled again and thanked him for his trouble, hoped she wasn't putting him to any bother.

'No bother at all,' his father returned, 'and anything you need, just let us know, and if we don't have it here we'll order it in.'

She glanced again at the book, wished him good reading and then she turned and walked towards the door. They both stood watching her, and as she stepped into the cold winter sunlight she turned up her collar and flicked out the sudden burnish of her hair.

'Did you see her hands?' his father asked. 'Never raked a leaf in her life. And that sparkler didn't come from Woolworth's. Big bucks there all right. Put a sheet of brown paper over the rake head and tie it with string.'

After closing time his father had another delivery to complete so he dropped him off at the gates to the estate and left him to deliver the purchases, then make his own way home across the fields. The bare branches of the trees pleached across the driveway and a frost was already beginning to whiten and coarsen the grass. The shafts of the brush and rake felt cold in his hands. He had been to the house several times before but only as a child and never inside – mostly when the Colonel had opened the grounds on special occasions. The last time had been a Coronation party when they had sat at trestle tables and there'd been music and little flags. As he followed the curve of the driveway the house suddenly came into view, and in that moment he felt like a character in a Hardy novel, a poor boy delivering his message, but the house looked less grand than he remembered it, smaller, even a bit shabby in the dropping darkness. He wasn't sure whether to call at the front or the back but it was in the back that the lights were on and when he headed towards them he saw her bike propped at the side of the door.

After he knocked, it was opened by someone he knew – Jenny Chambers, his old Sunday School teacher, who was now working as a housekeeper. She seemed pleased to see him and as she chatted and took the objects he handed her, a voice he already recognized called to her to bring him in. He hesitated, frightened that she was going to humiliate him with a tip, but as he stepped into the blushing warmth of the kitchen she stepped forward to offer him only a cup of coffee. He hesitated, fumbled with the seeming weight of his hands. 'Warm you for the walk home, the kettle's just boiled,' Jenny said, and he sat at the table with its blue-glazed bowl of fruit and his cack-handed parcel of brass-headed screws and picture hooks. Mrs Richmond was wearing a blue smock, scribbled with paint. A smeared rag dangled from the corner of a pocket.

'You're painting,' he said.

'Trying to. Not very successfully at the moment.'

'A lot of rooms to paint, I suppose.'

'Not painting, decorating, Peter,' Jenny said, scolding him with a smile. 'Mrs Richmond paints. Pictures, like.'

'I'm sorry,' he said, squirming his hands across the table, relieved when he was given a cup to hold.

'I might be more successful at painting and decorating, probably make more money, too, if the bill we got for the work done here is anything to go by.'

He declined the cigarette she offered him and watched the movements of her hands as she lit hers. 'What do you paint?' he asked.

'Whatever takes my fancy, I suppose. Portraits, landscapes, interiors. Goes in phases. At the moment I'm trying to be a bit more abstract in style. Jenny doesn't like them very much.'

'Can't really make head nor tail of them, but then I know nothing about it so it's hardly surprising,' Jenny said while she washed dishes in the sink, turning her head sideways when she spoke.

Then Mrs Richmond asked him about his university course and how he liked it and what he hoped to do.

'We always knew Peter would make something of himself,' Jenny interrupted. 'The whole village knew it. When he was in primary school they called him The Professor.'

She laughed at his embarrassment, flicked the ash of the cigarette into the saucer of her cup. He saw that she held the cigarette more than she smoked it.

'It says more about the others than about me,' he countered. 'It wasn't a vintage year – if you could do joined-up writing you were considered a prodigy.' Then he asked her if she'd gone to Queen's and she told him she'd gone to art college in London, then spent a year studying in Paris. 'So you can speak French?' he asked.

'Enough to get by. But we went back a couple of years ago for a short holiday and I felt a bit rusty. Had forgotten a lot of things.'

He felt able to look at her only when she was speaking. Her eyes were blue and they never rested on anything for very long, flicking to his face and then away again, flitting about the room. When she was teasing him, as she was now, they widened, then crinkled with laughter.

'Your father didn't strike me as a man who reads Sartre.' The laughter in her eyes encouraging him to momentary boldness.

'Oh yes, Sartre, Camus, Victor Hugo – he's read them all in that shop. Never without a book in his hand.'

'The only book I've ever seen him with is his accounts book,' Jenny said, her hands pressing and plumping the water.

They both smiled conspiratorially at her confusion. 'I really like *Le Grand Meaulnes*,' Mrs Richmond said. 'I read it when I was in Paris. I cheated, though, read it in English. Too much like hard work in the original. That's probably the root of my problem – I'm a bit lazy. Don't work hard enough at things.'

There was a moment of silence and he stared at his almost empty cup. Jenny dripped a plate on to the draining board.

'Do you like the Impressionists?' he asked.

'I suppose everyone likes the Impressionists,' she said, smiling at him. 'Sometimes now I think they look a bit chocolate-box cover – maybe it's a case of familiarity breeding contempt. I like Van Gogh very much.' He searched frantically in his memory for a painting but his mind had gone blank and so he nodded as if approving her choice. 'They say he only sold one painting,' she continued. 'A sad life.'

'Alain-Fournier only wrote one novel,' he said, staring into his cup. 'Died in the First World War.'

'Maybe if he'd lived he would never have written anything else so good. Who's to know?'

'*Starry Night*,' he remembered. '*Starry Night* is a beautiful painting.'

'Very lovely – I like it a lot. What people don't understand about Van Gogh is that he wasn't strictly a great painter in the technical sense, but what he was was a great colourist. He used colour in a way that was new and original. And in the paintings he was using colour to represent human passions. So if you look at *Starry Night*, you can feel the darkness and the fear but also the beauty and I suppose the love.'

His hand tightened on the bevelled edge of the table. Her words were little splashes in his consciousness like the fall of rain on water. He tried to stop himself getting lost inside the sudden swirl inside his head. He looked again at the empty cup and it felt as if a tumbler of whiskey had hit the back of his throat, the way that it had that first time in McCullion's bar the night their exam results came through. He was walking over the thinnest sheet of ice, so fragile and beautiful, as he sat at this table where this woman, this most beautiful woman, spoke of Paris and colour and love. He held more tightly to the table, trying to anchor himself in some outward show of stability, frightened that the earlier clumsiness of his hands would transmute itself and splutter into an excruciating embarrassment of speech. So he made himself think of the contents of the shelves in his father's shop, the soiled sheen of his father's coat, listened to the clink and squeak of the plates being washed in the sink.

She was looking at him and holding the cigarette at the side of her face and he watched the smoke curl into nothing. He went to speak but stopped himself, frightened that his voice would buckle and warp in his throat, spill itself in some form that would be unrecognizable. He had to go. He had to leave before he made a fool of himself. '*Starry Night*,' he said suddenly without knowing why he'd said it or what was to follow. She stared at him and nodded. '*Starry Night*,' he repeated, looking towards Jenny for help.

The phone rang in the hall. Loud and insistent, demanding

attention. She excused herself. As soon as she had left the room, he stood up and took his cup and saucer to the sink. 'I better go now,' he said, staring into the hall, half frightened that she would return before he had the chance to leave.

'She'll only be a second,' Jenny cautioned him. 'Don't be running off before you've said goodbye. It was a treat to hear you both chattering away ten to the dozen. I didn't follow the half of all that stuff about painting and books. I had to laugh to myself when you were talking – me being your Sunday School teacher when you were a boy. Not much I could teach you now, I think.'

He remembered her sincere little lessons written out on the back of old Christmas cards, the slap of her hymn book on fidgeting legs, her warnings against the modern manifestations of sin – television, films, rock'n'roll. He was still standing with his hands on the back of the chair when he heard the phone being replaced and she returned to the kitchen.

'Brian, my husband, has to work late. Getting to be a bit of a habit. Then he drives here like a madman. He'll end up killing himself some night.' She saw that he was about to leave and stubbed out her cigarette in the saucer.

'I have to go now,' he said, and in his ears it sounded as if he had made himself a boy who had to be home by a certain time.

'It was good of you to call,' she said as she showed him to the door. 'I got a new brush and rake and a conversation about art. And all at a bargain price.'

He said goodbye to Jenny, who wished him luck with his studies, then shuffled through the open door. The cold night air nipped and tightened his face. 'Thanks for the coffee. I hope the painting goes better.' He turned to go but she called him back.

'My name's Alice,' she said, extending her hand. There was a small slender touch, but no matter how hard his senses tried to hold it, it slipped away from him like his breath in the night air. 'Starry night,' she said, smiling.

'*Starry Night*,' he repeated, not knowing why he was smiling in return, before she ended his confusion by pointing at the sky. Above their heads shuddered a cold shock of stars and while he stared at them she said goodnight and when he turned the door had been closed.

He stood for a second, then set off, glancing back at the house from time to time. None of the windows was curtained and the yellow light yawned out sleepily at the night. When he reached the first great spruce with its layered canopy of hanging branches, he hurried inside its darkness and stood very still. There was a heady rush to his breathing, a rasping dryness in his throat. He felt the glaze of the cold brush his cheekbones, touch his eyelids, seep through his hair. Looking up through the thick spokes of the tree he was able to see the broken, pitted moon and the whole night felt stretched and tautened by something which couldn't be seen and couldn't be touched, but which felt as if it sprang from somewhere inside him.

He thought of Meaulnes listening for his long-lost music. But the only sounds now were the shiver and fret of the tree as it stirred in the strengthening wind, and the ghostly echoes of her voice. There was something in her voice he had never heard before, something that drifted in the spaces between the words. Something light that carried the words but he didn't know what it was. He stared at the house and tried to capture it for his memory but just when he thought it was secure it slipped away again, leaving him with nothing but the flung fistful of stars and the rising whimper of the wind.

*   *   *

His father was worried, had already made two phone calls to the council office. Only that the grave had been dug earlier, there'd have been no chance. No chance at all. For better or worse they'd have to go ahead. The arrangements had all been made. Her sister was coming over from Scotland. They'd just have to make the best of it, hurry it along with decent haste. Her parents weren't in the flush of youth either – they couldn't be let stand in the snow for too long.

'Surely to goodness McCance'll keep it short,' his father said, toasting his hands at the fire as if trying to build up a store of heat in anticipation of tomorrow's cold. 'Surely to goodness he'll not ramble on, take the mourners to Hell and back like he usually does. The bare minimum with a bit of respect – surely that's the ticket tomorrow. If he does the full works he'll be speaking to a line of frozen bodies. Take more than a cup of tea to thaw them out.'

'I heard McCance isn't doing it – hasn't been asked,' his mother said. 'But then I don't think they were in the church from the day they married. Poor child, the nurse says at the end she was skin and bones, the flesh just fell off her. And him a widower and couldn't be even forty yet.'

'Sold a few wreaths yesterday,' his father said. 'But if McCance isn't doing it, who is?'

'No idea, but give your flowers in life – that's what I say,' his mother answered while she pressed her feelings into the weft of the cloth.

'I'm glad everyone doesn't think like you, for you need flowers at a funeral. A few wreaths, like. No flowers is like a table without a cloth or . . .' but he tried in vain to think of another comparison and as if to compensate for his failure lifted the poker and let air into the fire. A tongue of flame pushed through the widened mouth of slack. His father squirmed his back into the chair and felt on the floor for the paper he'd been reading earlier, its front page big with the news of some Belfast murder. 'Is it still coming down, Peter?' he asked.

As he prised open the curtain, he could feel the seep of cold through the glass. He knew already that it was still snowing; he had started to think he could hear its thickening silence. Pressing his face against the glass, he peered outside and saw the steady stream of flakes.

'You'd think somebody'd turn off the tap,' complained his father. 'If it goes on like this much longer we'll be snowed in, trapped like Eskimos in our igloos. But it'll probably turn to sleet soon and then the rain'll wash it away like soapsuds.'

'It's a couple of feet deep in the yard already,' his mother said. 'I had to take the shovel to it to get the coal shed open. My feet were soaking by the time I'd finished.'

'Aye and I hope you changed into dry stuff. I don't want you laid up like you were last year.'

'You needn't worry,' she said, as she sniffed and folded a pillow case. 'I've two pairs of your old socks on and I won't be going over the door again without wellies. And last year was something else entirely, as you well know.'

'Aye, aye,' his father said, pulling the paper about his face. 'But if it gets any deeper it'll be no laughing matter driving over there to collect the body and then up to the church. The roads'll be mustard, and I bet you there won't be a snow plough to be seen for love or money.'

'They can't be everywhere,' his mother said.

'Everywhere?' his father repeated. 'Nowhere's more like the case. This country's not cut out for snow – that's the long and short of it. We're just not cut out for it. Now if this was Canada they'd laugh at this – it'd be a spit in the ocean to them, for they have all the gear, all the machinery.' The lights flickered. 'Peter, there's no way there'll be buses running to Belfast tomorrow, so if you're stuck here you might as well help with the funeral.' The lights flickered again, throwing thin spasms of darkness. 'Here we go,' continued his father, 'candles at the ready.'

The electricity shuddered finally. Only the fire whispered light. There was the scratch of matches, a bleb of flame, and then the room became a little shrine of shivering light.

'They'd laugh themselves silly at this in Canada. They've so much snow there they could sell it. And life doesn't collapse into chaos like this shambles.'

'Be able to sell plenty of candles tomorrow,' his mother said, giving a little snigger.

'You may laugh but tomorrow's going to be no joke. Driving the hearse in this, making sure the coffin doesn't slide about, and then carrying it to the graveside – what a night-mare!'

His father lapsed into silence, pondering the potential disasters that might befall him, while the light from the candles silvered and thinned his hair, darkened the shadows under his eyes. He watched the constant flick of his eyes, the way his lips suddenly moved as if he was speaking silently to someone, then the silence of the snow sifted dreamily into the room, drifting into the corners and crevices, soothing but separating them into their own stillness. The thin waver of flame from the fire was edged with blue. His own hands raised to his hair were the fluttering wings of a bird on the wall.

The sudden clatter of the front door made them all start. 'Holy heavens!' his mother said, her hand holding the iron just above the board as if frozen in space. None of them moved. The tattoo of blows rumbled again, then fell silent.

'Who in the name of God is out on a night like this?' his

father asked, then, bending down, lifted the poker out of the fire. Its tip glowed red in the wavery shadows.

'I'll go,' he said, while his father stood motionless with his back to the fire.

'Be careful, Peter,' cautioned his mother. 'George, go with him.'

He lifted one of the candles in its saucer and, cupping his hand round the snuffling flame, walked slowly into the hall. He heard his father's shuffling behind him and, smelling the frizzling heat of the poker, said, 'For goodness sake, Da, watch that poker and don't be branding me.'

'Aye, aye. Lead on, Macduff, I'm right behind you.'

Then as he placed his hand on the front door his father's voice rang out, demanding to know who was there. He had deepened and roughened it, so it sounded strange as he struggled with the lock, his other hand trying to ensure the candle stayed upright. When the door opened, a thin flurry of snow coughed into the hall and the candle flickered. The man standing on the doorstep was dressed in a snow-spattered dark overcoat, his shoulders draped in a white cape. A yellow scarf hung limply round his throat, and as he stepped towards the light they could see the scowl of bruising on his cheek.

'I'm sorry to trouble you,' he said, 'but I've come off the road back there about half a mile, and I wondered if you could tell me where I can find some help to get her out of the ditch.'

'Anyone hurt?' his father asked, slipping the poker behind his leg.

'No, I'm the only one in the car. Just got a bit of a smack to the face, that's all,' he said, fingering his cheek as drops of water ran down from the plastered mesh of his hair.

'Where you going to?' asked his father, clearly determined

to find out as much as he could before committing himself to any course of action.

'I'm on my way to The Lodge. My name's Brian Richmond. I should have stayed in Belfast; never thought it was going to get as bad as this.'

'Aye, it's bad, all right. So you're in the ditch, then.'

'I lost the road just after the last bend and the next thing I knew I was sliding sideways into the hedgerow. It's in a kind of drain or culvert. Is there someone who might be able to help?'

'You'll not get anyone at this time of night,' his father said.

'We can help,' he said, looking closely at the caller. He was older than her. Too old, he thought. To save himself the embarrassment of more questions from his father, he offered to come as soon as he got his coat. When he turned to find it, his mother's voice rang out from the end of the hall.

'In the name of goodness, don't leave Mr Richmond standing out there freezing to death. Bring him in. Bring him in to the fire.'

She came towards him down the hall, waving him forward, and he nodded and offered his thanks as he followed her into the living room. 'Sit yourself down there and warm yourself by the fire,' she urged, directing him to the chair where her husband had sat a few moments earlier, while she pushed the newspaper under it with her foot. 'Are you sure you're all right? she asked, staring at the seam of bruising.

'I'm fine,' he said, 'just got a bit of a smack on the face. Nothing to worry about. Could I put you to more trouble and use the phone? Just to let my wife know what's happened.'

He stood with his father in the doorway of the living room and watched him dial the number while they both tried to look as if they weren't listening to his call. He was suddenly conscious of how small the room looked in the candlelight, of the smell of food and wet clothing that infused it. Maybe ten years older than her, even twelve, he was tall, well-built, his black hair shiny with water, and when he spoke to her his voice was reassuring but businesslike. The call lasted no more than thirty seconds. When he had finished, his mother handed him a towel and a cup of tea. She had used her best china. He balanced it on the arm of his chair and patted his hair and face.

'Maybe Mr Richmond would welcome something a bit stronger,' his father said, the poker still in his hand. But he said no, tea was just fine, and apologized for putting them to such trouble.

'No trouble at all,' his mother said, 'and isn't it that what neighbours are for. George and Peter will have you out of that ditch in no time and on your way again.'

He apologized for not knowing their names and his father introduced them all, telling him that they'd already met his wife in the shop. He nodded but showed no sign of recognition. When he'd finished his tea he stood up and pulled the yellow scarf more tightly, tucking the ends inside his coat. Having been conscripted, his father took a torch, went out to the garage and returned a few moments later with two spades and a length of rope, and thus armed they set off down the road. Almost immediately the wind-blown pelt of the snow forced them to bow their heads, reducing vision to a few yards and making conversation almost impossible. The white world swept about him, and took what he thought he knew so intimately and changed it into something that mocked and played games with his senses. Like some staid and predictable maiden aunt gone crazy, it wore a painted face that disavowed its previous existence and it danced about him with an abandon that left him dizzy but unable to turn his eyes away in case he missed part of it. Sometimes the snow slanted in towards them, at others it seemed devoid of any direction, and as they plodded on it plashed their faces and filled the prints they left in their wake.

About ten minutes later they saw the car. It was already covered in fresh snow and at first glance looked like a buttress or extension of the hedge. It was a green MG sports car and with its nose in the ditch it looked even smaller and more fragile than normal, like the discarded toy of some child too lazy to bring it inside at night. Richmond examined the wheels, crouching down on his hunkers until he had satisfied himself that they were OK, and then, taking the rope, attached it to the back end of the car. But when they attempted to pull it out they couldn't find firm footholds, and when the rope squirmed and slithered through their hands they collapsed into each other like shuffled cards. Then Richmond suggested that they should both push from the front while his father pulled on the rope, so they slid into the ditch and positioned themselves at each of the headlamps and tried to brace themselves for the push. The headlight at his side was broken and tiny shards of glass gleamed like teeth. 'We should be able to do it,' Richmond said, but he wasn't sure if it was an encouragement or an attempt to convince himself. 'If we push together, we should be able to get it out – it's not that heavy a thing.' And then he counted as if starting a race and all three of them took the strain, their groans blending with each other's and their faces lifted skyward despite the incessant fall of the snow. The car moved forward a couple of feet and then slipped back a little, but just when it seemed they would lose it Richmond gave a great shout of determination and while he, too, pushed with what strength he had left, he looked sideways and saw the momentary ugliness of Richmond's face as it buckled and creased with the strain and he thought of that face coming close to her face and a knot of sickness tightened in his stomach as the car finally shuddered out of the ditch.

'Well done, men, well done!' but despite Richmond's pleasure it sounded in his ears as if his words had turned them into employees and while he pondered whether money would now be offered to them, he was conscious for the first time of the pain in his hand and, when he stared at his glove, saw that a thin shard of glass had pierced it. He started to take it off but stopped when he saw the first drops of blood spot the snow. His head felt suddenly light and as he clasped the wrist of his cut hand to give it support, his legs buckled and he almost fell. He felt a fool and when his father and Richmond closed in on him, kept repeating that he was all right but as his father's arm tightened on his shoulder, he sensed that he was going to faint and, leaning against his father, lifted up his face to the cold dampness of the sky and let its snowy compress shock him into consciousness. The glass had penetrated his palm like the stab of a knife and the slither blinked in the light of his father's torch like ice. Inside his glove was a sticky, searing mess which was already oozing through the black wool. He wanted to pull the glass out but Richmond urged him to leave it and then told him to get in the car and he would drive him the short distance to The Lodge, telling his father that he would take good care of him and fetch the doctor if need be. His father nodded, and Richmond promised to phone with news.

His father helped him slip into the passenger seat of the car and wordlessly patted him on the shoulder. He felt as if he was sitting just above the snow about to sledge over it, and as the car growled into life he raised his good hand and waved to his father. Sometimes as they drove along the road he could feel the wheels churning and spinning the snow and then Richmond would swear quietly to himself and slow his speed to a crawl. The snow squalled and rushed headlong into the one headlight beam and watching it made him dizzy again. Richmond was talking to him, asking how he was, but the words seemed to mingle with the frantic slant of the snow and he heard himself repeating that he was all right, over and over again, as if saying it would make it so. He wanted the glove off his hand; not being able to see the cut made it worse and he could feel the blood seeping between his fingers and sticking them together.

They managed half a mile. The Lodge was only round the next corner but they couldn't make it – the snow was beginning to drift and bank and gradually the car came to a complete halt, its nose barely above the top of the snow. 'Time to bail out,' Richmond said, clambering out of the driver's seat. 'We'll just have to leave it here, maybe push it over to the side a bit so it doesn't block anything else trying to get through.' But despite both their efforts they were able to move it only a few feet and although Richmond pushed his back against it, and heaved with all his might, the thickness of the snow prevented further progress.

They set off with the snow streaming into their faces but he was glad to be out of the car and the cold helped to clear his head while their muffled tread tramped through the thickening fall. Neither of them spoke but occasionally Richmond looked back to check that he was still following, before digging his chin into the shelter of his chest again. He watched the broad shape of the man in front contract into himself as he struggled against the wind-driven fury and suddenly it felt that the world had made them small, paltry stick-figures struggling in the face of the blizzard. He glanced towards where the sharp slope of the fields met the road and only the hump of the hedgerow marked where one began and the other ended. It felt that they were being funnelled through a mountain pass where at any moment suffocating tumbles of snow might slide over them. But it wasn't that thought which hurried him on.

He paused to scoop a handful of snow and press it lightly against the pain in his hand in the hope that it would ease it and thought of her waiting in the house. The image quickened his step and he was glad of the pain. It was his ticket of admission. After all, he'd got it helping her husband. He tried to remember the timbre of her voice, the way her eyes smiled, the flow of her body, but everything got mixed into the welter and confusion of the snow and the struggle of his journey and then there was only an unsustained glimmer of memory glinting like haws in the hedgerow. He could only conjure elusive little shimmers of her physical presence – the colour of her hair, the way she held her cigarette, her hand moving through the air as she spoke – and they tantalized and drifted softly about him before being blown into the night.

Finally they reached the gates of the driveway and Richmond turned and waved him on with a sweep of his arm that seemed to saw through the falling flakes. The trees bordering each side of the drive were crimped and clumped in white, their heavy heads wilting towards them. When they rounded the curve he could see the lights of the house and their dogged plod turned into a scamper that kicked up skiffs of snow. They drew shoulder to shoulder and the heavy draw of their breathing beaded them together and hurried them on. Richmond headed for the back of the house where the blink and flaw of light was a welcome and he watched him suddenly beat his arms into the air as if flailing at flies, then heard him say, 'Thank God for that. I've never seen snow like it. How's the hand?' He started to speak but the snow was on his lips and in his mouth and in reply he nodded and forced a smile.

Richmond thumped the door with his fist and even while he was still striking it she had it opened and the light that flowed from the kitchen fought fiercely with the snowy swathe of night, but Richmond's lumbering shiver into the house blocked his first view of her.

He hesitated at the door, even in these circumstances unwilling simply to walk in, and then she was grabbing him by the cuff of his sleeve and almost dragging him inside. He blinked away some of the water running down his face and the sudden surge of heat made him think for a second that he was going to melt into a puddle on the kitchen floor. Richmond was struggling with his sodden overcoat and shaking snow off himself the way a dog shakes itself free of water. And she was behind him, shutting and bolting the door, her scent already coiling itself round his senses, the scurry of her slippered feet dancing in his ears. He didn't know what to do, so he stood there dripping water and didn't look at anyone.

'Get that coat off, Peter,' she said. 'You're both soaked. I thought you'd had another accident. I didn't hear the car.'

'We had to abandon it back down the road – the snow's too deep,' Richmond said. 'And listen, Peter cut his hand helping me get the car out of the ditch. It needs looking at – there's still glass in it.'

He met her eyes for the first time, smiled, then looked away. He had started to take off his coat but realized he couldn't get his arm out of the sleeve so it hung over one shoulder like a cape. For the first time he saw his gloved hand clearly, with the sliver of glass protruding from the matted mess of wool and blood. She gave a little squeal and put her hands to her mouth.

'It's not as bad as it looks,' he said. 'I think it's stopped bleeding. I just need to get the glass out.'

'Do we need to get the doctor?' she asked, turning to look at her husband, who stood now in his white shirt, which wore a waistcoat of damp. He had stopped towelling his hair and draped the towel round his neck, holding its ends with both hands. He looked like a boxer just finished his training. 'He'd never get here through the snow,' he said. 'Let's get a look at it and see if we can patch it up until the morning.' While she stood facing her husband he allowed himself to look at her for the first time. He was only a couple of feet from the back of her head and he stared at the strands of her hair, which tumbled over the collar of her blue dressing gown, at where her hand bunched some of it behind her ear. A strand fell across her cheek and curved forward to the edge of her mouth. She pushed it back again and he watched the slow brush of her fingers. Small, slender hands, the nails rounded and pearl-coloured. Like the colour of her skin.

She told him to sit at the kitchen table and made him stretch out his hand towards her. Suddenly his badge of honour seemed to dissolve into a disgusting mess when it drew close to her pale-blue dressing gown which was buttoned to the neck and reached below her knees. The collar and front were edged with a white piping. His hand was only about a foot away from her. If he leaned forward a little he could have touched her. A thin bead of water ran down his face from the teeming tails of his hair. She called for the scissors, but when Richmond handed her a pair from the dresser she rejected them and asked for the sharper pair that stayed in one of the kitchen drawers.

'We'll have to cut the glove off,' she said, lightly lifting his hand up with the tips of her fingers. 'Can you hold it up in the air while I cut from the wrist?'

He nodded his head. As she raised the hand holding the scissors he glimpsed the whiteness of her wrist, paler where it vanished into the blue of the sleeve. He didn't know where to look. Her blue eyes were so close. Darker than the blue of the gown. So he stared into the corner of the kitchen and tried to hold his hand still, only flicking his eyes to it for the briefest of seconds while the scissors started to snip the glove. Richmond had moved closer to the table and was staring at the operation. He had opened the front of his shirt and a splurge of tightly curled black hair tumbled from his chest. The thought of it touching the softness of her skin made him shiver suddenly and she stopped cutting and let go of his hand. 'Does that hurt?' she asked, pushing back another fallen strand of hair. Hurt more than he could ever explain, but he shook his head and forced a smile. 'Good lad,' Richmond said, 'we'll soon get it fixed up. Alice is a good nurse.' She held the scissors poised at the side of her head for a few seconds and they glinted in the light, before she lowered them and then turned and said, 'Brian, get changed out of those wet clothes and put something cold on that bruising or it'll look a sight in the morning. And look out some clothes for Peter.' Richmond nodded and disappeared into the hall. There was the sound of his heavy tread on the stairs. 'So, Peter, let's get this glove off and see the damage.'

He held up his hand and by the total exertion of his will tried to stop it shaking. He searched for something funny to say, but the sentences collapsed like felled trees and the most he could utter were meaningless expressions of surprise at the extent of the snow. She nodded at each of them but all her attention was on the cutting and he saw the way she angled her head and the thin little lines of concentration above her eyebrows and at the corners of her mouth. His black, blood-soaked hand hung between their heads and slowly the scissors snipped the sodden wool. He could feel the cold of the metal on his skin and he blinked at its touch. She had reached the base of the fingers.

'The Red Hand of Ulster,' he said and she smiled, then said, 'Don't make me laugh or I'll end up cutting a finger off.' There was the sound of footsteps above their heads. 'Bad enough him nearly killing himself without involving other people. Get yourself a good lawyer and sue him. That's the only place you can hurt him – his pocket.' Her voice sounded like water. Just below the lobe of her ear was a tiny thin white scar. He only noticed it when she turned her head and it was exposed to the light. The glove was almost cut, and to help he pulled the tips of the fingers free from his skin and she moved closer to snip the final strands of wool. Close enough to touch. He wondered what her hair felt like. He wondered what it felt to touch her milky skin and then he looked at the bloody hand that was slowly emerging from the glove and felt the flare and burn of his foolishness and he wanted to snatch it away and be gone into the hidden folds of the night.

Little bits of glove were still stuck to his skin and she got up from the table, fetched a pair of tweezers and started to pick them free. She held the tips of his fingers with hers and he wanted to flow into her across that narrow bridge of touch before it was too late and it slipped away. Then her hand slipped under his, supporting it as she worked, careful always to avoid the embedded shard of glass. He could see now that it had entered the fleshy fold of skin between his thumb and first finger and that the damage was not as great as might have been imagined. 'I'll live,' he said. 'We need to get the glass out,' she replied. 'I don't think it's in too deep.' She puddled around in his palm. He felt as if she was reading his future and he was frightened. Two lines that diverged, never to meet. Two different orbits. How could it be otherwise? He felt the weight of his foolishness again. 'Maybe it would hurt less if you did it yourself,' she said. He looked into her eyes and he saw she was a little frightened by the thought. 'It'll be all right,' he told her. 'Just try to get it all.' She asked him if he was sure and he told her again that it would be all right. Then she lowered his hand until it rested on the table and tried to get a good grip with the tweezers. He braced himself by holding the edge of the chair with his other hand. Her face was almost hidden from him by the forward fall of her hair when she brought it close to his palm. Close enough for his breath to touch the strands of hair that glinted under the light above until they shone like the gilt-edged leaves of a bible. And then there was a short hiss of pain in his lips and the sudden bubble and spurt of blood as the thin spear of glass also glittered in the light. 'Got it! she said. 'Got it!' but then she saw the new flow of blood and rushed to smother it in the folds of a towel. 'It's all right,' he said. 'It's out and it's all right. Just a bit of blood.' She was using both her hands to press the towel against the wound and nodding and then he looked up into her eyes and they smiled at each other.

'Need to get it well cleaned up,' Richmond said from the doorway of the kitchen. He was wearing dry clothes. 'Stop any infection.' He came over and asked to see it and, when she lifted the towel away, inspected it closely before saying that it might need a few stitches in the morning. 'Did you get Peter any dry clothes?' she asked and he told her that he had left some in the guest bedroom.

'That's very good of you,' he said, 'but I should be gettin' back home. They'll be worried about me.'

'You can't go back out in that. It's worse than ever by the look of it. Tell him, Brian. It wouldn't be safe.'

'She's right Peter, there's no need for you to head out in that blizzard. Stay here tonight – give your folks a ring. Tell them everything's all right and you'll be over first thing in the morning.'

She showed him where the phone was in the hall, holding the receiver while he dialled the number, then left him to speak to his mother. He could hear the concern in her voice but reassured her as best he could, telling her that the cut to his hand wasn't serious and that it was only the snow that was keeping him from returning home. She broke off to exchange words with his father, whose voice droned in the background, and when she spoke again it was to tell him that he was to ignore his father trying to remind him that the funeral was in the morning. There was more argument away from the phone and then she told him to thank the Richmonds for looking after him and after an almost embarrassed hesitation she said goodbye.

When he returned to the kitchen there was a basin of warm water on the table and the smell of disinfectant. She was cutting a length of bandage, gnawing at its stubborn resistance with the pair of scissors. He pushed back the sleeve of his jumper and slipped his hand into the warm froth of water, wincing at the sharp sting but glad to have the cleanness of it flow over the sticky mess that spread across his palm and oozed between his fingers. 'Good for it,' she said, measuring out a length of bandage and fiddling with safety pins. 'It'll clean it up, stop an infection.' He nodded but when he glanced up at her the electricity quavered and the house stuttered into darkness. 'That's all we need,' Richmond said, knocking against something before there was the click and flicker of his cigarette lighter and the whole kitchen seemed to have contracted into the tiny bleb of its blue light. She told him there were candles on the boards, that the electricity had gone off earlier but come on again, and in a few minutes Richmond had them lit and the room shuffled into a soft tremble of light that formed vague little pools which drained everything of its solidity and substance.

'Let's get this finished, Peter,' she said, lifting a candle and placing it on the table close to the basin and the light seemed to echo the sudden sheen and flush of her skin and he couldn't help but stare. He lifted his hand out of the water and patted it dry with the towel and then she took it and, holding it out towards her, began to work the bandage round it. His hand turned and moved about the light like a moth. Richmond stood supervising, bending over the table and throwing his shadow across its wavering grain. When the job was finished he stared at his white-gloved hand and thanked her and she said it would do the job until he got the doctor to look at it. Then she made them a cup of tea and Richmond offered him a brandy to go with it but he declined it and made a little joke about his mother making him a cup of cocoa most nights. He watched Richmond swirl the brandy in his glass, then jerk it to the back of his throat and he saw that there was a physical intensity about the man that only the snow had managed to subdue. It lurked under the surface of his good manners, his social ease. He remembered the way he had sought to push the car out of the ditch, remembered the momentary contorted ugliness of his face, and in his presence suddenly felt his own boyishness.

After they had sat for a while she took one of the candles and went to check the room he was to sleep in, and there was a thrill in that image as he turned it over in his mind and he let it warm him. He tried to think of something to say to Richmond but couldn't and instead stared at his cup of tea and the little spiral of steam that vanished into the soft seep of light. It was Richmond's strength that had made him the money he had, his strength that made people work for him, rather than the other way round. He was the type of man his father wanted to be. But her? He couldn't understand that. She read books, looked at paintings. Her touch had been gentle. He couldn't understand, no matter how hard he tried. It had to be a mistake, a mistake realized too late and then she was trapped with no way out. He listened for her tread above but heard nothing, then looked at Richmond and everything about him seemed to confirm his judgment. The way he held the brandy glass, the very way he sat in the chair, and as he glanced at him the bruising on his cheek seemed to have frozen into a stain on his skin.

Her voice called him from the hall, telling him to bring one of the candles. Richmond wished him good night and thanked him for his help, then lit a cigarette and its red tip swept in an arc through the air when he waved his arm in farewell. She stood at the bottom of the stairs, the candle's light drawing only a part of her face from the shadows and making her hair a part of the flame's tremble, and she told him to follow her, waiting until he was only a few steps away before she moved ahead. Pictures briefly emerged from the dark patina of wood on the stairs, then faded again into shadows. He thought of the snow on the roof of the house, pressing against its walls, filling the fields all around it, and he remembered the way it had changed the world he once knew, transforming what had been the familiar and mundane into something that he no longer recognized and the memory suddenly lifted his step and filled him with an unexpected hope.

He followed her along a corridor which had a large window at one end with its black white-webbed glass pulling the reflection of her candle towards it, until the light seemed to be outside and beaten by the swirl of the snow. And then she was showing him into a bedroom lit only by their two candles, which fluttered and echoed each other in the glass of the dresser. There were clothes laid out on the bed and he knew that if he were to wear Richmond's they would be too big on him and he didn't want the foolishness of that but she encouraged him to wear as many of them as he could against the cold.

'Bed's probably the warmest place now that the heating's off,' she said, and then she told him where the bathroom was and wished him good night. He listened carefully to her voice, trying to hear some inflection that might say something beyond the words but there was none to be heard and instead he mumbled a thank you for her care. She cupped her hand round the flame of her candle when it flickered in a draught from the open door and told him that it was him they had to thank and then she was gone, leaving behind her only the faint trace of her scent and a little whisper of smoke.

He stood looking at Richmond's clothes for a second, then moved them off the bed to a chair. There was a bowl of pot-pourri on the dresser and a set of silver-backed brushes that were cold to his touch. He wondered again how her hair felt, remembered the strand that fell across her cheek, wondered had she ever slept in this bed. He let his hand touch the cover and then he went to the window and opened the curtain. In the glass he saw the reflection of his face but it wasn't that he wanted to see and turning to the dresser he blew out the candle, its final stutters lingering in the frost of the mirror. Then he stood and watched the fall of the snow.

The bed seemed inescapably large after the narrow single bed of home and there were great pockets of cold in it that stopped him sleeping. He listened for their voices but what sounds there were seemed to have been muffled by the size of the house and the smother of snow-brindled darkness that surrounded it. He clustered little memories of what had gone before, sifting through them like coloured stones picked on the beach, polishing each with the intensity of feeling that flecked them with the grain of something precious. His hand was still sore, its smart of pain flaring at intervals, but he tried to blank that out by a new focus on something rescued from the flux of his thoughts. He had never felt like this before and it scared him a little because his control over his feelings seemed tentative and liable at any moment to slip beyond his reach and ability to impose any sense of order or understanding. He wasn't a boy, a moon-struck teenager, falling headlong Narcissus-like into the depths of his own reflection, the mere creation of his own consuming need. He had read books. Once he had drunk whiskey. He had kissed girls. He tried to anchor himself by a recognition of his own foolishness, but he felt like a vessel thrown about in a storm, his thoughts careering dangerously like loosened cargo. And what was his experience? A few scraps of nothing, the vicarious experience provided by books.

He tried to sleep but was conscious of the space in the bed for someone else. Little melodramatic fantasies played out in his mind, involving escapes in the night, rescues and pursuits, duels in the snow. And all of them involved her seeing the potential of a different world in him, of breaking free from the deadening weight of a material existence and a life subdued by the repression of money and power. There was the sound of laughter. It was as if someone had been listening to his thoughts. He pushed his head into the pillow to shut it out but it came again and through it rustled the scornful reminder of what patched together the fabric of his life. So it was his father's store he was standing in and this time he was wearing his father's coat and his fingers were brown, as if stained by nicotine, from searching in the box of rusted nails and screws. And he was writing the account of his life in the big ledger, filling in the columns and totalling up what his life amounted to, and as he struggled to do it people came into the store, setting the bell ringing angrily and asking for things he couldn't find, even though they were somewhere on the shelves. There he was again, cleaning out the wedding car for a funeral but spilling all the gathered bits of confetti and as if in a dream they floated slowly down like snow and his hands were powerless to catch them.

The door to his room is slightly open and through it slip little runs of laughter, the light flow and skip of hers, like water over stones in the stream, and then the deeper ragged timbre of his which tears at the stillness of the night. There is a sudden wince as she touches the bruising on his face. He lies perfectly still in the bed and each sound registers sharply on his senses despite their soft distance but, like the fall of the confetti, the meaning slips between his fingers and eludes him. For the first time he is aware of a thin thread of light that lingers in the corridor. Just for a crazy second he thinks of following it, winding it in until it leads to where the sounds begin but instead he raises himself on to his elbows and as he lifts his head he smells the scents of the room and he thinks of the silver-backed brushes on the dresser and wonders if she ever used them to brush her hair and what sound they would make as they move through the strands. What her hair feels like to the touch. Does he touch it now? He's suddenly conscious of the pain in his hand and for a moment he's glad of it.

He lies down again and tries to sleep and perhaps he does now, for more sounds slip into the room and this time they're not smothered by the snow but it's as if the deepening swathe that layers itself against the roof and walls of the house, pressing its silence against it, serves to magnify these sounds which scamper like mice inside. The laughter has vanished into a rush of whispers that are broken at first, then fluted into a rhythm that begins and stops, and he remembers the way the wind swirled the snow, slanting in at strange angles and the way it felt on his face. He pictures his hand when she held the tips of his fingers and sees how close it was to her face, how close it was to touching her skin, and now he stretches out his hand those final few inches but all he touches is the sound that filters through the night. And it's her voice but it has no words and at first he thinks he's hurting her and he's almost going to help her when he begins to understand that what he hears must be the sounds of love and they send a shot of what feels like fear through him, which is followed by the jolt and spasm of sickness. And he tries to tell himself he's wrong, that he's mistaken and the moan and rasp of intermingled voices are only the weary scurry of the snow-laden wind, tired of what it's had to carry for so long. But there are words, too, words he can't fully hear and which run and crash into each other and at first he squirms his head on the pillow but then there's something pushing into his head and slowly he knows he wants to hear it all and his heart is pumping and his body tightening and stirring.

Carefully he gets out of the bed and goes to the open door, rests his hand on the handle, then drops it again. He stands behind the door where a thin edge of light seams the narrow gap between it and the frame. His back is pushed against the wall, leaning into it for support, and her voice rises and curls in his head and it's his love that he's giving her, his love that's filling her, and across the bridge of touch flows all the depth of what he feels in this moment and his hand drops and tightens on the force of his desire. Her voice is fluttering like the silken wings of a moth and its coming closer all the time to the core of the flame and his senses are mesmerized by its rhythmic movement, its fragility, and then he hears the voice climb finally, before breaking into breathless pieces and he cups the warm spill of his love in the palm of his hand. His breathing is the rush of the sea in his ears but he's careful not to spill it, as if doing so would spill what he feels, leave him stranded on a solitary shore. Suddenly there is laughter and it coils and lingers in his head, breaking the spell, and then in the shadowy darkness of the room he sees Richmond's clothes laid out on the chair where he had set them and they are suddenly infused and filled by their owner's body. His hair is still wet and matted by the snow and the scowl of bruising has spread across more of his face, and as he stares at it he thinks of it pressing to the paleness of her cheek, of the printed stain it now leaves, and he feels the surge of anger and then a sudden burst of shame. Turning away from the clothes he hurries to the window and quietly opens it and lets the cleanness of the night air rush in, then he skims a thin handful from the ledge and washes with it, finally pressing a last trace against his eyes and the dryness of his lips.

His father says he's never known a funeral like it and he's seen some in his time. There was no way the cars would reach the Stevenson house to carry the coffin and the passengers to the graveyard. He'd done his very best but he couldn't work miracles and it wouldn't be fair for anyone to blame him or say he hadn't tried. It would have been dangerous in these conditions to risk the cars on roads that had all but disappeared and if anything were to have gone wrong, who knows what the insurance company's attitude would have been? He watched his father straighten his hat, brush dandruff off the shoulders of his black funeral coat – the coat he always described as a good investment. 'People don't die in the summer,' he liked to say each time he wore it. He looked at the hat his father had handed him, even though he knew he always rejected it, and for some reason put it on.

'It's a team of huskies we need this morning,' his father said as he wiped the sledge one last time. When he had returned earlier that morning from the Richmonds', his father had been cleaning and polishing the metal frame, staining the scuffed wood with shoe polish. 'Are you sure your hand's up to this?' he asked now as he stood back to give the sledge a final inspection. He nodded and smoothed the new dressing his mother had put on it. The doctor was attending the funeral and she had already phoned to ask if he would look at the cut after everything was over. Then he took the new rope his father had fitted to the front of the sledge in his good hand, and they set off for the Stevenson house with the sledge trailing lightly behind them. As they walked, his father rehearsed the arguments he had already heard since his return home. No one could blame him about the cars, and under the circumstances it was the only thing he could think of and wasn't it lucky enough that he remembered that Tommy Leeman's brother had made a sledge in his metalworks a couple of years earlier. A few spots of rust here and there but it had cleaned up a treat – he'd be getting it back in better nick than he'd lent it. He'd give him a few bob and all. It was the only way of getting the coffin up to the graveyard – without it there'd be no chance. They just had to be careful, really careful, that there wasn't an accident because that didn't bear thinking about.

There had been no new fall of snow and the night frost had crisped everywhere, making it firmer underfoot but there were still places where it had drifted into deep mounds and they had to pick their way carefully. There was a cold wind stirring which felt as if it come straight from the Arctic and it tautened and nipped his face and skimmed thin flurries of snow into the air. He was almost glad of his hat, not for the little protection it afforded but for the greater anonymity he thought it lent him. For he carried a sense of shame as he walked and sometimes it felt so strong and uncovered that it seemed it must be visible to anyone who looked at him. Keeping his face lowered, as if to pick his steps, he wondered if everything had been destroyed, rendered soiled and smirched by what he had done. His father rattled on but the words blurred, then vanished inside his deepening sense of loss. Some crows flapped away at their approach and their cawing laughter mocked his miserable plod. He thought of her voice, the sounds he had heard, and he tried to tell himself that they belonged only to him, a secret that no one else could ever know, but then in his memory he saw again Richmond's clothes draped over the chair in his room. His hand began to smart and he wanted the pain to be greater so that it might block out the shame and stream of his thoughts. Behind them as they walked, the sledge hissed over the surface of the snow.

There were already people gathered outside the Stevenson house, huddled in small groups and wrapped against the weather in bulky layers that culminated in Sunday best. All turned to watch their approach and his father lifted his head and stepped out with a more formal stride as if to compensate for the absence of the car. As they got closer, heads nodded in greeting while their gaze fastened on the sledge. His father left him holding the rope before vanishing inside the house. Along its guttering a jagged row of icicles caught a sudden throw of light and sparkled even in the weak flare of sun. Faces at the upstairs window got blanched and lost in the same light. If there was no minister as his mother had said, they'd bring out the coffin at any moment. He wasn't sure what he should do to anticipate that moment but he straightened the sledge and tightened his grip on the rope. He only knew Martin Stevenson, who taught in a local secondary school, to see, but they had never spoken. He'd served his wife in the shop a few times and knew she was keen on photography – he'd once seen her taking photographs along the river. A summer's evening when the midges had clouded above the water and the banks had been clotted by thick-headed rushes. She had red hair. The sinking sun seemed to seep into it. Skin and bones at the end, his mother had said. She hadn't seen him, she was so intent on the camera. He couldn't see what it was she was focusing on, for all he saw was the glaze of the sky on the dark shimmer of the water, but all her energy and concentration had been in that moment and he wondered how such a person could be dead.

The snow had been freshly cleared from the front steps but the concrete was blistered with white whorled spots as a rock is spotted with shells. One ridged footprint marked the top step. It might have been his father's. There was the murmur of voices and the door opened fully. He heard his father's voice slip into his familiar guiding litany of 'Slowly does it. Steady now, almost there. That's the way.' His voice had assumed a gentle authority which was reserved for these occasions. He spoke like a pilot guiding a boat to shore, someone who knew the reefs and hidden currents. He came out the door backwards, his steadying hand on the top of the coffin, his head half turned to negotiate the steps, then he paused the carriers so that they could shoulder a new assurance. Stevenson's face was inclined to the wood, his cheek brushing it and as they came through the door he turned full-face and his eyes blinked at the unexpected brightness. Then on his father's signal he stepped forward with the sledge and helped as they slowly lowered the coffin towards it, his father's eye and hand gauging the precise moment when to anchor it to the support of the wood and metal. He felt the sledge shift and settle as it took the weight of the coffin and then his father joined him on the rope and they moved it forward to the road, glancing back all the time to check that it was balanced and secure. 'So far so good,' his father whispered. 'Your mother was right. There's not any weight you could talk about – we were lucky there.' They both draped the rope over their shoulders and began the slow haul to the graveyard. Behind them processed the line of mourners, their low voices and the sound of their feet muffled almost to nothing by the swathe of snow. Along the route others waited at the end of their driveways or on corners and as they passed the men joined the tail of the cortège, leaving the women watching in silent huddles.

The sledge pulled freely through the snow but it still required physical effort to keep it moving forward and after a while the rope started to cut into his shoulder. The strangeness of this new world suddenly struck him. A different world, a different continent: even a different time. He remembered a Russian film he had seen at university and thought of the funeral scene. All that was missing now was the priest walking ahead scattering incense and someone carrying the holy icon. The wind rose a little and smoked the snow ahead. He glanced back at the procession – it was as if the whole world had transmuted into black and white. The holy icon, the only colour, with its gold and seraphic blue. The sun igniting her hair.

'I've never seen the like of it,' his father said. 'In all my days I've never seen its like. This is beginning to pull the shoulder out of me – we could've changed sides but for that hand of yours. And we can hardly stop for a rest. Bloody snow! My feet are like blocks of ice.' His father's breath clouded in front of his face as he spoke. 'And I haven't told you the half of it, about what happened in the house. Your mother was right, there's neither sign nor trace of McCance – not a dicky bird. What we're going to get at the graveside, I've no idea. I suppose the way to look at it is that it's bound to be shorter than one of McCance's sermons.' They plodded on and it seemed that his father had forgotten whatever it was had happened in the house.

'I'd like to take her now,' Stevenson said. He'd come up behind without them hearing. 'I'd like to take her the rest.' He nodded his head in affirmation of his words and his eyes were shiny and blue. His father went to say something but he stalled him with a tug at his sleeve and by handing over the rope. 'We'll be close behind,' his father said. 'Try to keep her steady.' Then with a slight reluctance he handed over his share of the rope and as the sledge moved forward he followed close to it, but keeping to one side as if to distinguish himself from the rest of the procession.

The runners hissed in the snow and the strengthening spear of sunlight struck the varnished grain of the coffin and polished the brass. 'Keep her steady as she goes,' his father whispered to himself as he slipped into his pilot speech, then, 'This man'll do us all out of a job – first he gave McCance the sack and now it's us. All that's left now are the gravediggers. But thank God the grave was dug before the snow or we'd never have managed it.' He watched his father take a hand-kerchief from his pocket and wipe his brow. 'She was like a doll in the coffin – wasted away to nothing. And I was telling you, before I sealed the lid he put things in the coffin. Seen that done all the time but never seen anybody put what he put. Keep her straight and steady. That's the way. A camera, a book of photographs and then a map. It was folded over so I couldn't see where it was.'

They trudged on. It wouldn't take much longer. The sky had clouded and closed again over the moment like ice. A map. To find her way to the underworld? To find her way back home? He thought of Meaulnes poring over ancient maps, trying to find his lost domain. They had started the climb to the church. His own hand circling and fluttering round the candlelight like a moth. What was it that brought you home? What was it that carried you into the flame and release of love? Suddenly Stevenson stopped. He still held the rope but he stood motionless in front of the sledge. Behind him the procession had also stopped. His father blew a stream of breath between the press of his lips but was unsure of what to do. They looked at each other and behind at the waiting line of mourners. His eyes followed the thin trace of the runners left in their wake, then leaving his father he walked forward to Stevenson and briefly touched his back before taking up half the rope. Stevenson lifted his head to the sky, then wiped his eyes quickly and roughly with the back of a hand and shouldered the rope again. On impulse he removed his cap and shoved it inside his coat and said, 'Not long now. Just a little further.' Stevenson nodded his head and said, 'Sorry.' They pulled together and the sledge felt weightless as it skimmed over the frozen snow. 'Sorry,' he repeated. 'I promised myself I wouldn't. Didn't think there were any left.'

'You don't have to be sorry,' he answered, his own voice suddenly wavering. 'It's us who are sorry. Very sorry.'

Stevenson nodded, then looked up at the sky. 'It's not how I imagined it would be. The snow and everything. It's hard to get a hold of it all. Maybe it's a good way. She liked the snow, said it made the world beautiful. Maybe it's as good a way as any.'

Ahead the church tower loomed into view. 'Not long now,

just a few minutes,' he said when his father came alongside and asked if he wanted to change but he declined the offer and his father faded out of sight again. He looked at Stevenson, who suddenly expelled a rush of breath which sounded as if he had been holding it in for a long time, then bit his lower lip with his teeth. The rope slipped a little. He had to say something. 'It's a good way,' he said. 'If she liked the snow, it's a good way. She was right – it does make the world beautiful.' Stevenson tightened his grip and stared at the yew trees, which had coiled into white cones, and he wondered if he had said too much, spoken foolishly, for how could anything in this world ever seem beautiful again to this man beside him. The light was slipping away. It looked as if more snow was coming. There was a new smart of pain in his hand. They both sensed the need for urgency and they stepped out with greater insistence and then almost without thinking he said, 'I saw her once – Mrs Stevenson – along by the river. She was taking a photograph. Of the river, I think.' They had reached the open gates of the church and they paused there for a moment: their burst of speed had opened a gap between them and the mourners. Stevenson ran his hand along the layer of snow on top of one of the pillars, then looked at him as if seeing him for the first time. 'She was trying to photograph light. Trying to capture the light.' Then he dropped the rope and walked in search of the open grave.

'God in Heaven,' his father hissed, 'one minute he's stopped and the next it's the race to the North Pole.' He was struggling for breath. 'We're not home and dry yet either – we still have to negotiate the headstones and get it lowered. We'll need to shoulder it now and please God don't let anyone slip. I've picked out the best of the bunch and no harm to him but her father isn't up to this – not in these conditions. So keep your eye open and be ready to put your hand to it. And put on your cap, give it a bit of dignity.'

He did as he was told and the arrival of the procession of mourners coincided with Stevenson's return. In a few moments the coffin was shouldered and the cortège fanned out amidst the almost buried headstones as they headed for the board-covered grave. The gravediggers had worked hard to keep it clear and only as the mourners approached did they remove the boards and lay them down at its sides. He watched his father in his long black coat and hat lead the coffin forward, his soft litany of guidance his incense and icon. One of the younger men stepped forward and read a short verse from the Bible and said a prayer. When he had finished the gravediggers looked at his father, in anticipation of his signal to start lowering, but then the young man invited Martin Stevenson to say a few words and the gravediggers leaned back on their spades again. Several heads turned skyward where a few slow flakes had started to drift down. Stevenson stood at the end of the open grave with a page in his hand. He was conscious again of the pain in his own hand and when he glanced down he saw that the wound had opened to seep blood to the surface of the bandage. It was some verses of a poem Stevenson wanted to read. He thanked them for coming and his voice was nervous and broken. He asked them to bear with him for a moment more, told them the poem was by Henry Vaughan. As he started to read, his voice strengthened:

> They are all gone into the world of light!
>   And I alone sit lingring here;
> Their very memory is fair and bright,
>   And my sad thoughts doth clear.

It glows and glitters in my cloudy brest
   Like stars upon some gloomy grove,
Or those faint beams in which this hill is drest,
   After the Sun's remove.

I see them walking in an Air of glory,
   Whose light doth trample on my days;
My days, which are at best but dull and hoary,
   Mee glimering and decays.

Dear, beauteous death! the Jewel of the Just,
   Shining no where, but in the dark;
What mysteries do lie beyond thy dust;
   Could man outlook that mark!

And yet, as Angels in some brighter dreams
   Call to the soul, when man doth sleep:
So some strange thoughts transcend our wonted theams,
   And into glory peep.

If a star were confin'd into a Tomb
   Her captive flames must needs burn there;
But when the hand that lockt her up, gives room,
   She'l shine through all the sphere.

O father of eternal life and all
   Created glories under thee!
Resume thy spirit from this world of thrall
   Into true liberty.

Either disperse these mists, which blot and fill
   My perspective still as they pass,
Or else remove me hence unto that hill,
   Where I shall need no glass.

Someone coughed; a gravedigger's spade clanked against his shuffling toe-capped boots. Stevenson folded the page and put it in his pocket and so they knew he had finished. Someone said an uncertain Amen and it echoed round the edges of the group until it faded into a whisper. The snow had started to come down. He looked down at the reddening palm of his hand and knew he had to find her, had to see her again.

'A star confined to a tomb, her captive flames must needs burn there' – the words ran round his head. When he went back to university he'd look the poem up, write out his own copy. He wished he still had all the words clear in his memory. Something about being set free and shining through all the sphere. But even though he didn't have all the words, their meaning seemed unclouded as he thought of her. Surely her house was that same tomb, bereft of what she wanted. He stood at his bedroom window and watched the light stretch into the snow until it edged a faint blueness to its surface. The tall trees in the next field had been dressed in a flounce and filigree of white that made them look fragile, even delicate, as if old age had suddenly been thrust upon them. For the first time he had an awareness of time, of its potential for brevity, of its capacity to snatch away what was taken for granted. He thought of Martin Stevenson sitting in his empty house trying to make sense of what had happened, he thought of the long haul to the grave-yard, of the tracks the procession had left in the snow, tracks which had already been obliterated by fresh falls, and knew that he had to try to make this thing happen before it was too late.

There were other cautionary voices in his head but he tried to stifle them and hold on to what he knew was true. If he didn't, he saw his future replicate that of Meaulnes as he pored incessantly over maps and memories, hoping that they would lead him back to his lost domain. He tormented himself by allowing his imagination to give his father knowledge of what now spun round his head and so he heard that scornful voice rattle out all the doubts he had already constructed for himself. The voice talked about class and money, about age and experience, about things over which he had no control. There were no answers to these doubts but there was something even stronger that diminished their significance when he let himself think of her. It was his father's real voice that now climbed the stairs to his room as he gave another account of the morning's funeral, talking his part up until it took on the characteristics of a military campaign, dwelling on strategies and crucial decisions made, of victory grasped in the face of innumerable obstacles. And once again his incredulous descriptions of what he had never witnessed at a funeral before – 'Never seen the like of it, in all my days,' he was still repeating while he reiterated every detail that deviated from what he thought of as the right way of doing things. Afterwards he'd asked him several times what the poem was all about, the things placed in the coffin, as if the education his son shared with Stevenson must provide the inside knowledge. His curiosity made him dissatisfied with the answers he received and he had started to talk about it the way he spoke of the Masonic mysteries and rituals, that if only you had access to this inside knowledge everything would make sense and some desirable power would be shared.

He tried to obliterate the voice by concentrating on something else and he tried reading but the words swam round his head like a shoal of fish where each one was indistinguishable from the next. He knew his father was about to leave and open the shop again. Despite the snow there had been a steady stream of customers, earlier that morning, mostly looking for the same things – candles, gas cylinders, bags of coal, spades. He had wanted to keep the shop open during the funeral with his mother holding the fort but she had refused on the grounds that it would look disrespectful, ignoring all his arguments about special circumstances and his claims to be providing an emergency service.

Then there was a phone call and a few minutes later his father's pleasure-laden voice calling to him. 'I'm going to have By Royal Appointment painted above the shop – it was the Duchess asking if I was open today. She's looking for under-coat, says she needs buckets of it.' He knew he meant Alice. 'Says that if she's stuck inside she might as well get some more work done to the house. I said you'd run some up to her right away.' And then to anticipate arguments that never came he added, 'You know I can't leave the shop when there's so many looking for things. There's some out in the shed, you don't even have to come to the shop – you could use the sledge to run them up.'

There seemed something disrespectful about using the sledge for commerce so soon after it had carried a coffin but he had tried lifting the tins on his own and knew they were too heavy and too awkward to carry with only one good hand. So the eight tins sat in two cardboard boxes with a piece of cord securing them as he set out across the fields. His father waved him off with a chorus of 'Good King Wenceslas' before the sound of the van's engine rang out across the space he had put between himself and the house. It wasn't how he imagined himself returning to the house but the thought of seeing her again shaded out hesitations about his message and into his step slipped a run of anticipation that sent him scurrying and kicking through the snow with as much speed as he could muster. Sometimes he plunged almost to the top of his boots and he had to wade as if through water with slow deliberate steps and pull of the sledge. It felt as if he were making the journey for the first time, seeing the foreignness of the landscape as if it was a stretch of tundra transported from some distant empire. Fresh drifts and humps of snow had rendered even the most familiar fields both confusing and intriguing in their unfamiliar sweep and contour. There was a glittery throw of iridescence that overlaid everything and touched even the most humble of objects, making him feel that in this world the doubts he had spoken to himself in his father's voice were stripped of their full power and replaced by the force of something else. And it felt, too, as if the landscape belonged to him alone, for apart from a couple of inky crows and a solitary rabbit emerging from a hedgerow, he had seen no other signs of life. Once he stopped for a rest and sitting on the sledge watched as the wind powdered the trees ahead so it looked as if they were shivering the snow off their black branches. Then he pushed on again, driven forward by anticipation of who waited for him.

About five minutes from the house he saw a figure in the distance, zigzagging down a slope beyond the estate boundary of fir trees. He stood on the sledge to gain a better view and realized it was someone on skis. There was a smooth lightness in the turns and curves and a speed that he envied as he glanced at the plodding, heavy path he had left in his own wake. For a few seconds he told himself that it was her but as he watched the figure drop below the top of the firs he saw from the frame and size of the skier that it was Richmond. He headed on, trying to infuse his steps with greater lightness, trying not to press so much of his weight into the snow, but he felt clumsy and slow. He remembered

Richmond's clothes laid out on the bed for him to wear and he wondered what it would have felt like and what it took to be the person who wore them. There was an edge of fear, too, in the thought that there must be things below the surface of the man that he had been blind to, things that had attracted her to him in the first place and that maybe these things were too powerful to be broken. And what did he know of what passed between them or what existed unseen and unknown to the rest of the world? What had anyone known of the life that Martin Stevenson shared with his wife or what the words of the poem had really meant? So now his arrival at the house was shrouded in doubt and by the image of a man skiing effortlessly down a slope.

He was greeted by the dog's barks as it fretted and sniffed at the snow from a cleared area round the back door. It was Jenny who opened the door to see what the noise was about. As always she was pleased to see him but when she glanced at the sledge she said, 'It's been put to some use today,' and he felt anew his original disquiet at using it so soon after the funeral. 'It was my father's idea,' he said, 'and he's a hard man to change his mind.' She nodded and opening the door invited him into the kitchen. His eyes hunted the room and hall but there was no sign of her when he sat down at the table where he had sat the night before. Jenny offered him a cup of tea and while he wondered if she was out skiing with her husband, she came into the kitchen wearing a paint-smeared smock and denim jeans. Her hair was pulled back sharply from her face.

'I wondered who you were talking to Jenny,' she said. 'How's your hand Peter? Looks like someone more expert than me has done your bandage.'

'The doctor dressed it this morning, said it'll be fine. Won't even need stitches. Thanks for looking after it for me,' he said, aware of his face flushing with colour.

'The least we could do, seeing as we were responsible for you getting it in the first place. And thanks for bringing over the paint. I thought I'd heed my own words and take a break from my work and try painting walls instead. The last work we had done wasn't so wonderful, so I'm thinking of slapping some undercoat on and then trying something different myself. Maybe a kind of frieze or trompe l'oeil, something like that – I'm not sure yet. Haven't really convinced Brian yet but if it saves him money he should go along with it in the end.'

'It's going to be in the big room that's used for entertaining and parties,' Jenny added while she poured tea for all three of them.

He watched her sip the tea, her skin paler than he remembered it but her eyes the same blue. There was a fleck of white paint on her forehead. 'Brian found his old skis packed away in the garage and he's out there somewhere trying them out. Probably break his neck. He didn't like her hair pulled back so tightly – it made her face seem thinner, took away some of its mystery but it also made it more open, less remote. She stood up and, going to the back door, saw the sledge for the first time. 'So that's how you brought the paint. All you need now is a team of huskies to take all the work out of it. I haven't been on a sledge in years, maybe I should give it a try, put one over on Brian.' He hated the name on her lips. He watched her standing with his back to him while she stared through the glass. Her clothes made her shapeless but, like her pulled-back hair, less elevated into a higher world, far beyond his reach. He found himself wishing that Jenny wasn't there but was glad for the break her presence put on the swirl of words in his head and then shamed by the knowledge that he wasn't brave enough to shape what it was he felt into those same words. She opened the door and the light streaked the side of her face. 'I'm going to bring in this paint and get started again,' she said, setting her cup in the sink. He hurried to help her but she insisted he finished his tea and after she had brought the last tin inside she lifted one and held it up to read the label as if reading the name on a bottle of wine. 'Do the job,' she said and then, reaching for her purse, she asked him what she owed him but he refused payment by saying that his father would put it on her account, desperate to avoid her handing him money.

There was nothing to delay his departure. Jenny was rinsing the cups and wiping the top of the boards. The back door was still open and the dog wandered in and out, leaving its damp prints on the stone floor. 'I'll help you with the painting,' he said. Maybe just being close to her would be enough. Maybe all the rest was nothing but foolishness. 'I couldn't take your time like that,' she said. 'I'm sure you've studying to do or maybe your father needs you in the shop.' Jenny was looking at him. He hoped it wasn't so obvious.

'I've nothing else planned, I could spare a couple of hours,' he said, frightened that she was going to refuse.

'Well, only if you let me pay you for your time.'

He wanted to refuse the offer but he saw that it was the difference between helping and having to go and reluctantly he accepted, determining that when the time came he would shrug it off, offer the help as a sign of his friendship.

The room she was working in was the main drawing room and all the furniture was wreathed in white cloths so that for a second when he entered the room it seemed that there had been a fall of snow inside the house. She had started on the end wall and covered the lower part in a thin wash of white, leaving the area above head height untouched. 'The walls seem to soak in the paint,' she complained. 'It's going to need a couple of undercoats before the top colour and then the actual painting. At the speed I'm going at, it'll take about a year. I'll probably end up bringing in someone to get it done.' He offered to do the top bit and she went to fetch step-ladders. Then he heard Jenny's voice in the kitchen saying that she was off and after a brief conversation there was the sound of the back door closing and with a kick of his heart he realized that they were alone in the house. The wooden ladders were old and rickety and she fussed about him being careful and not having another accident while helping them out. He tried to think of amusing stories to recount but struggled in vain and instead concentrated on painting and listening to what she had to say as they worked.

'I'd like the room to be different,' she said, 'from what you might expect to see in a house like this. Something a bit original and surprising. Just haven't worked out exactly what, though. We're keeping the ceiling the way it is – I really like all that moulding and plasterwork. Have you any ideas?'

'Why don't you put some of your own work straight on to the walls?' he offered.

'I don't think you'd say that if you saw the abstracts I'm currently producing,' she laughed. 'Don't think people are quite ready for them yet. They'd probably spill their glass of sherry on the carpet in shock. Jenny's face is a real treat when she sees them for the first time. I was toying with the idea of doing a Chinese theme, painting the walls red and then adding traditional designs – cherry blossom, herons, calligraphy, that sort of thing. Mostly red and black. What do you think?'

'Sounds good,' he said, thinking of his own living room and cringing at the thought of her ever seeing it. With a quiver of embarrassment he remembered that her husband had sat in the same room, ameliorated only by the knowledge that he had seen it by candlelight. The memory distracted him a little and he watched his brush run a thin drip of paint. 'The Chinese invented gunpowder, writing and fireworks,' he said suddenly without knowing why. He had to lean from the ladders to mop up the escaping drip.

She laughed. 'Thank you, Professor. Watch you don't fall off those ladders!' He felt foolish and turned his face to the wall and hoped she couldn't see the flush of colour that filled it. 'And what about kites?' she asked. 'Did they invent those as well?'

'I don't know,' he said, pretending he was concentrating on painting.

'I think they invented opium as well,' she added, 'and talking of drugs I could do with a cigarette. Let's have a break.'

He watched her slump to the floor and he knew that already she had lost interest in painting and he remembered the first time he had come to the house and the way her eyes flitted from object to object, never resting on anything for very long. In that moment he knew that she would spend time and money fixing up the house and then a short time later probably get bored with it and move on to somewhere else. Resentment seeped into his body as he continued to paint.

'Why did you come to this village?' he asked. 'Why not stay in Belfast? Where your friends are.'

'It was Brian's idea, really – I think he had this vision of himself as a country squire with a bit of fishing and shooting thrown in for good measure. And property is always a good investment. This place was a snip – old Ashbury had let it go to seed, hadn't spent a penny on it in years. When it's done up it'll look nice and turn a pretty profit as well.' She inhaled, then angled her head to let the smoke stream through her lips. 'We don't actually have that many friends living in Belfast, more

77

business associates than anything. Most of our friends are in London now and Belfast is an awful place – all that smoke and noise. People spitting in the streets.'

'Money's important to Mr Richmond,' he said as he stopped painting and sat on the top of the ladders.

'Peter, money's important to everyone. Makes the world go round. Do you like living in the village?'

'Not particularly. I was thinking that maybe next year I could stay in digs up at Queen's.'

'That sounds like a good idea. Probably improve your social life as well. Have you told your father yet? Won't he miss you helping in the shop?'

'I haven't mentioned it yet, haven't finally made my mind up. But I won't miss having to work in the shop,' he said. 'It's not much fun.'

'You met me there,' she said lightly, brushing ash off the knee of her trousers.

'That's right,' he answered. 'I owe it that.' He wasn't sure if he should have said it or not, aware how different the tone of his voice was from hers, and to distract attention from it he went on talking. 'The village is so small; everyone knows everyone else's business. I wouldn't want to live here all my life. And anyway there isn't much call for jobs that need French.' He stared down at the side of her face, saw again the light, thin scar. He wanted to touch it, to run the tip of his finger along its seal. 'Maybe I should do what you did and go and live in Paris after I get my degree.'

'You should,' she said but she was staring into the distance and he imagined that he heard indifference in her voice. He wanted to pull her back again to the moment. 'I think I'd like to live in Paris – it would be like the other side of the world to my parents, though. Walking along the

Seine, going to look at paintings, sitting with a drink or coffee at one of those cafés.'

'You'll have to learn to smoke,' she said. 'Everyone smokes in Paris.' She reached her cigarette up to him. He looked at the pale stretch of her underarm as he took it. It looked white and perfect as paper before it's written on. Her scent was on the cigarette as he smoked it. 'See, it's not so hard. Makes you look very intellectual.'

'Like a professor?' he asked.

'No,' she laughed, 'like a young Camus or Sartre. There was a funeral in the village this morning, wasn't there? Jenny said something about it.'

'Hannah Stevenson. Thirty-seven years old: she had cancer.' He handed her back the cigarette.

'How terrible,' she said, smoothing her hair flat. 'Makes me shiver just to think about it. I hate to hear about people dying young, it always scares me a little.'

But as he listened to her he knew that she wouldn't think about it very much, or think very much about anyone beyond herself and, despite this knowledge, he knew it didn't matter to him or change the way he felt. He knew, too, that she would be interested in things or people only as long as they amused her and when she became bored she would discard them as speedily and lightly as they had been taken up. He looked at the unfinished wall and wondered how soon that moment would come for him. He started to paint again, his brush scratching at the silence that had settled.

'Let's leave this, Peter, it's going to take forever. We need bigger brushes. I think I'll get someone in to do the preparation, then I can concentrate on the important stuff.' She splayed what was left of the cigarette into the ashtray and went to the window. He watched her stare at the snow and as she did so she took out the band that held back her hair in a pony tail and shook it loose. 'I wonder how Brian's getting on with the skis. Hope he hasn't broken his neck. Why don't we go out and have a look – we can bring the sledge. I haven't been on a sledge since I was a girl.'

'What about the brushes? Shouldn't we clean them?' he asked.

'Leave them, we can do it later,' she said, already on her way out of the room and searching for her coat. He balanced his brush on the side of the tin, then did the same with hers. She put on a black duffel coat with a yellow scarf and pushed her hair under a black velvet hat. 'How do I look?' she asked. 'Lovely,' he answered, but injecting his voice with lightness and trying to avoid looking at her. 'Why, thank you,' she said. 'But staying warm and snug's the ticket today. Now where's those wellies?'

Outside a pale, washed-out sun was shouldering the sloped fields behind the house. There was no sign of her husband as they set off across the grounds at the rear of the house. She laughed and played through the snow like a girl and he wanted the sledge to have wings, to hear himself say, 'Come away with me from this place. Fly away to somewhere better.' He thought of them walking in Paris, sitting in the shadowy corners of bars where famous people met to discuss paintings and politics. Come away with him and know that something purer than money and wealth could hold people close, that what he felt for her could carry them beyond any obstacles the world might throw in their way. Come while life still gave them time. He remembered the evening he had seen Hannah Stevenson beside the river with the sun in her hair. The world could change, change as quickly and suddenly as this snow had transformed the earth.

They passed through the screening hedge of fir trees and into the slope of what was open pasture. She took the rope as they started the climb, and walked shoulder to shoulder with him, harnessed to the task, and only the cold stream of air against his face stopped him stuttering into speech. The sun was sinking slowly into the hollow of the afternoon as sometimes her shoulder touched and rubbed against his. She spoke in little running trills of words about the snow, about holidays she'd had as a child, but the words only touched the edges of his consciousness. The light on the slope caught tiny nuggets of ice and made them shine so that as he walked he wanted to scoop them with his hand and offer them to her as diamonds. He saw the tracks of Richmond's skis but turned his head away and she didn't notice them in her self-absorbed pleasure of memory. Where the climb steepened, her words got lost inside the run of her breathing, the rise of her laughter, and they reminded him of the sounds he had heard her make, but now she made them for him and each one strengthened the force of his desire.

Standing at the top of the slope it looked much steeper and further to the bottom than they might have imagined. He looked at her and sensed her hesitation. 'We can always walk back down and look for somewhere else,' he said. She pointed out her husband's ski tracks curving in perfect symmetry down the slope and disappearing through the fir trees. 'If he can do it, so can we,' she said, pulling her hat tighter on her head and clutching at his sleeve. 'The worst we can do is break our necks.' He asked her again if she was sure and she answered by climbing on to the sledge, resting her feet on the runners, and handing him the rope. She wanted him to steer and when he sat in front and shortened the rope in his grasp, he felt her push up closer with her arms resting lightly on his shoulders. 'Are you ready?' he asked, tightening his grip on the rope. 'Yes, yes,' she called and patted his shoulders as a starting signal, but when he tried to push off his foot merely sank into the snow and nothing happened. Her laughter rippled behind him and he shoved again and this time the sledge started down the slope, barely moving at first but gradually gaining momentum until it rushed into a surge of speed which drew a cry of fear and pleasure from her as they flew over the frozen snow. She was tight against his back now, her arms round his waist and her breath fluting and singing against his neck. Picking up speed all the time they hurtled forward and her body pressed hard against his, while for a second he tilted his face skyward and let the air flare past his face. Down below he saw Richmond emerge from the trees to wait their arrival at the bottom. They were rushing towards him but he no longer cared for he knew this was his moment, nor did it matter that in a few seconds it would be over. The rope was cutting into his sore hand as he tried to keep the sledge on course but nothing mattered now because he knew that he had the whole of her. He lifted his face again to the speeding sky, imagined he felt the sun's rays on it. Felt the sun on his wings. She was shouting something about her hat but he was oblivious of everything beyond himself. Everything was falling away. He suddenly felt free of it all, so light he was almost weightless.

They were reaching the level now; slowing down and heading towards the snow-seamed trees where Richmond waited leaning on his ski sticks. Suddenly the sledge angled against a drifted bank of snow, and sent them both tumbling into the snow. He heard her peals of laughter as she rolled in a tumble of flailing arms and legs. He gathered himself on to his knees and brushed snow from his face while she did the same. Her hat had come off halfway down the slope and she shook her hair free of its sprinkling of snow, laughing all the time with the sun in her hair and in her voice. Then she saw her husband, called his name and waved her arm in elaborate circles. He watched her stumble to her feet and set off to meet his advance. When they got closer then stumbled into each other's laughing arms, he raised his hand to let the flakes fall into his palm, watched as they faded into nothing at the touch of his flesh and wondered if it must always be so.

The Wedding Dress

SHE GLANCED AGAIN AT the clock. Each tick was edged with her own impatience. The boy was late again: he couldn't be relied on. Even now he was probably dandering along somewhere, stopping to jaw with some of his mates, or breaking off his round to kick ball or throw stones at cats. Surely Fitzimons could find a better boy to deliver his papers. You'd think the cold would make him hurry. Thinking of the cold made her shiver and pull more tightly the extra cardigan she had draped over her shoulders like a shawl. It was cold enough for snow. She went to the window and peered out into the dropping chalky gloom, then listened for the bang of a gate or the jagged-edged whistle that might mark his approach. She thought for a second of putting more coal on the fire but decided against it, knowing that she had to be strict in her rationing. Before it got dark she would fill the coal scuttle and there was a broken deck chair in the shed that she could take a hatchet to in order to build up a store of firewood. There was an old armchair as well, its upholstery spotted with mildew, which could be broken up. And if she put a layer of slack on the fire maybe she could keep it in all night. Better the extra expense than the cost of a burst pipe.

Where was the boy? She remembered with resentment the shilling she'd given him at Christmas; he'd taken it with barely a thank you and it was soon obvious to her that the gesture had failed to establish any kind of contractual arrangement or greater respect. Sometimes he left more of the paper on the outside than through the letterbox. Once he had come early and the rain had wet two-thirds of it before she realized it was there. She had thought of complaining to Mr Fitzimons but was nervous that it might only make things worse. And it would be difficult to complain about the variation in time of delivery. Fitzimons might wonder why it mattered whether the paper arrived at one time or another, so long as it actually arrived and wasn't unreasonably late. 'What did it matter?' he'd think and he'd brush his chin with fingers grimed by print and the dirt of money. Well, it did matter; it mattered to her as much as anything did during her day. She was waiting for news, for the right one; not the news on the front page because she never read that much, or much else on the rest of the pages. If only that boy would hurry. If it hadn't been so cold she might have gone and waited at the gate as she sometimes did, disguising her impatience by pretending to be looking at the garden or brushing the path. The thought of the coldness made her shiver again. After the paper had come and she'd searched it, she'd chop some more sticks as she'd planned. Before it got too late.

She went into the kitchen and set the kettle to boil. It was important to keep warm. She'd make a cup of tea, then fill the stone jar. She could sit in front of the fire and heat her feet on the jar – not so close of course that her legs would get all measled and blotched. It was important to look after herself – it wasn't every day you got married. She had to look her best. The date hadn't been fixed yet but probably around Easter would be best. When the weather was warmer. A lot of people got married at Easter. The papers were always full of wedding photographs then – sometimes a whole page. It was hardly likely that there'd be a photograph in that evening's paper, for who in their right mind would get married in February? None but those in a hurry and they'd hardly want their faces published in the paper. Weddings in February? All pinched faces and trains blown ragged. No, Easter was about the right time or even the summer but the summer was too long to wait – she's be a bride long before the summer.

Everything had to be sorted, everything had to be ready. That's why she needed the paper. Where was that stupid boy? If this kept up she would complain to Fitzimons; he wasn't the only shop in the area. And he was prompt enough in giving the bill. She walked into the hall to check it hadn't plopped silently on to the carpet when she was boiling the kettle. But she knew already it hadn't come – the clumsy clod of a boy always made enough stir to fanfare his arrival. There was no way she could have missed him. The air in the hall was cold, but not settled and stained with dampness the way it sometimes was. She'd have to take the electric fire to her bedroom, half an hour before she went to bed, just to take the coldness out of the room. And it'd be a question of putting more things on not taking them off.

In another couple of weeks she'd be sleeping with her husband, his arms round her to keep her warm and safe. She coloured a little at the thought because it wasn't something she allowed herself to think much about. Still, it was a fact of life, something that couldn't be denied, and when she considered it in those terms there was nothing unseemly or vulgar about it. Of course it wouldn't be easy, sharing her bed with someone after all these years, but she knew he was considerate and gentle and, well, if things didn't work out they could surely come to an understanding. It wasn't such an important thing anyway, not half as important as people liked to make out and there was far too much talk about it – people making a show of themselves, talking about things that wouldn't have been dreamed of years ago.

She'd nothing to reproach herself about and she was glad. Nothing to be ashamed of, and if the papers were to be believed there weren't many could say that any more. In her day girls knew how to behave and those who didn't soon had their families reminding them. When she'd been old enough to go to the dances in the village hall she'd still been thought young enough for her father to collect her outside the door, the moment it was over. The way it should be. For a second she thought of her father, saw him standing cap in hand beside his bicycle, the yolk of light from the hall's open doors touching him in the shadows. He'd have been so proud of her now if he'd been alive to walk her down the aisle. If truth be told, a little jealous, too. She was sure about that, there was no denying it. She'd seen it in his eyes when a boy's name was mentioned or he'd noticed her talking to some lad. A few words in passing, that's all it ever was, but it'd be enough. 'There'll be time enough for that,' he'd say as if he didn't need to say any more and he didn't, for she'd never argued, never sought to cross his will. Time enough.

She glanced at the clock. It was already after six. What if he didn't come? What if he was sick or hadn't turned in? What if there was no one else to do the round? A little pulse of panic spun her to the window. The grey tide of light seemed to rush towards her, swirling and encompassing every part of her. She tried to raise herself above it by painting pictures which were tinged and shaded by hope, the hope that this would be the night she would find something very beautiful. The one she was meant to have. Moving away from the cold square of the window she practised the slow steps of her walk – that slow walk down the aisle – keeping her head high, acknowledging with a smile the faces turned towards her. Careful not to trip, careful not to step on the train. Careful to be on time. She wouldn't make him wait – that was only a foolishness. Not for a second would she make him think she wasn't coming or that she'd changed her mind. It was beyond her how any man or woman could do that, a cruelty that could brook no forgiveness.

Maybe it was the stern defiance in her father's eyes that had kept the callers away. Maybe they weren't brave enough to challenge his dominion but if they weren't brave enough they weren't deserving of her. A man had to struggle for the woman he loved, had to pay a high price, for if his claim was too easily granted he would hold what he had gained too cheaply. She turned to the mirror and traced her fingers over her cheek. Maybe it hadn't been her father's face. Maybe it had been her own face. Never beautiful the way a few women were blessed, but surely there was beauty there if someone had wanted to find it. Angling her head, she smoothed away some of the lines with both hands. It happened for other women, happened every day the world turned, and not all of them were beautiful. It was hard to understand, hard to bear. But time enough.

She remembered the day the photographer came to school, his great box of a camera balanced on spindly wooden legs. The line of excited children standing under Mr Simpson's stony gaze, trying to suppress the bursting, exhilarating desire to laugh. And when it was her turn, the sudden splash of apprehension, her unwillingness to look in the camera's eye. He'd asked her name, then told her her face was as good as anyone else's face. And wasn't he right. Afterwards her father had sent the photographs back – there was no need of them, he'd said, for didn't they have plenty of their own.

Of course, when she was older she'd had lots of boys interested in her – if she'd wanted she could have had any number of suitors but she was never that type of girl. She had standards and some of those who might have come calling didn't share all of them. A girl had to be careful, a single mistake could ruin you for ever. She'd known plenty of those along the way and felt no sympathy for their shame. She prided herself that she was entitled to wear white, wear the white dress, even after all these years. No one could deny her that, no one could take it away from her.

Going to the sideboard she took out the photograph album, handling it carefully because it was precious. Before she sat down by the fire she went and checked again in case she hadn't heard it, but there was still no sign. She stared at the fire and thought of someone who wrote you letters and sent you all his love. Someone who walked with you down the country lanes where spring hedgerows were loaded with blossom. The warmth of his arms. Someone who told you you were beautiful, his breath warm against the tremble of your skin. She turned the pages, looked at the faces. Young, linked by their smiles, the closeness of their bodies pressing into the lens of the camera. And the dresses, of course. White and crisp as that spring blossom, billowing and flowing round the slender shapes of their bodies.

As always, she paused at her favourites – the one with the little lace cap and veil; the couple so young and so alike that they might have been brothers and sister; the couple standing under the trees with the breeze flustering her dress a little. Soon she would add her own photograph, cut it out more carefully than she had ever cut one from the newspaper and paste it into the album. And who could say that it wouldn't be the most beautiful of them all? They'd have it taken not on the plain stone steps of the church but in the grounds of the hotel, where there were trees and flowers. At Easter the daffodils would be in bloom. That would be the thing to do, have it taken against a spread of yellow flowers, amidst the trees.

He'd always brought her flowers. Her first real love. Sometimes John, sometimes Peter or Andrew. For some reason Bible names seemed best. His face changed, too, for sometimes he was blond and others dark, his brown eyes fixed in the flux of her memory. But what did any of that matter, for he always brought flowers. Sometimes he picked them from the hedgerows or meadows on the way up to the farm – once he'd brought her bluebells and she'd pressed one later between the pages of a book. That was the type of thing lovers did: they gave each other secret things, little private tokens of their love. She imagined some of the things she had received. A book of poems, a little red Chinese purse, a ring, and of course the letters. He couldn't send them to the house so they must have had secret letter boxes. Like a film. Like a story in a book. She saw them clearly – a hollow in the big oak tree with the spreading branches under which she sat to read the declaration of his love; beneath a marked stone – the one with the weathered whorls of yellow and white in a dry-stone wall near the lower pasture. In the little graveyard of the church. That would be a good place. She saw herself slipping surreptitiously through the black iron gates and past the yew trees, then looking under the base of an urn.

All those words of love. She recited them to herself with tenderness, putting different faces to the speaker. And then she spoke aloud, touching herself with the soft brush of the words, letting them caress her with the gentleness of the love they bore. Her voice rose a little, fell into a whimper and then grew silent as the newspaper rattled in the letter box and dropped on to the carpet.

She'd be a bride soon. The thought warmed and comforted her as she scurried on through the morning's sharp snatch of cold which squeezed the features of her face into a tight immobility. The people who passed her were plumped up like fat parcels, all trying to protect themselves from the plummeting temperature by additional layers of clothing and sometimes with scruffy, belted overcoats. No one went bareheaded. She didn't want to arrive too early and give the impression that she was desperate, but neither did she want to run the risk of arriving too late and missing it. It had been a long wait; such ads appeared at regular intervals but she didn't want an address which was either too far away, or too close to her own home and which might lead to future awkward encounters. Now she had the right opportunity and she was sure this was the best way. Of course, it would have been nice to have picked her own but there was the expense to consider and going to a shop presented too much potential for difficult questions.

Occasionally as she walked she checked the wording of the ad, which she had carefully transcribed on to a small piece of cardboard. The price seemed reasonable. She turned the words 'Never worn' over and over in her mind and sometimes she felt sympathy for the sadness of them but then told herself that she was too soft. Probably for the best. Some slip of a girl who'd rushed blindly in without weighing up everything, some foolish young girl whose head was full of nonsense off the television or cheap magazines. Well, better now than later and wasn't it only right that someone older and wiser who had waited longer for love should wear it? But she tried not to let herself dwell too much on the dress because she didn't want to build up her expectations, to hope for too much and then be disappointed. And even if she liked it and decided that it was right, there was still the business to be done and for it to be completed successfully it would be better not to appear too enthusiastic.

The road felt lengthened by the cold and there weren't as many people about as usual. Was it just her growing anticipation or was there a feeling of expectancy enfolding everything? As she passed the bakery the sweet smell of bread perfumed the air in a sudden surge that stirred her senses. Perhaps she was wrong, perhaps there wasn't something foolish in the house she was going to but something tragic. The type of tragedy that had touched her own life. She shivered as she thought about it, sifting through the memories until she stumbled into the image of the boy who had loved her lying in a hospital bed, his hand holding hers until the final vestiges of love drained away and the nurse putting her arm round her before gently separating them. His final whisper of love, the same words he had engraved on the ring he was to put on her finger in the church. What would the words be? She tried to think of them, to construct a line or verse in her head, but they got confused and frittered away again.

She looked again at the number on the card, matched it up with the house then walked slowly by, fleeting it only the slightest of glances. It wasn't grand but quiet and tidy – a respectable terrace house with careful paintwork and neat blinds and curtains. Then despite the sudden press of panic she stopped and walked back until she stood at the front door. If things didn't feel right or the dress was wrong she could always make an excuse and leave. But she had to stay calm, not do anything foolish or say anything that might arouse suspicion.

The knocker was cold to the touch and as she let it drop, its sound clattered deep inside the house. The woman who opened the door wore a blue pinafore over a jumper and black slacks. One of the buttons was missing.

'I'm sorry to trouble you,' she said, 'but I've come about the dress – the one in the paper.' The woman stared at her, her eyes not appearing to register any understanding. 'Am I too late? Is it still for sale?'

'The dress – yes, it's still for sale. I wasn't expecting anyone this soon. I wasn't with you for a second. I was just getting rid up.' Then she hesitated, looking out past her into the street.

'It's for my daughter,' she said, peering into the hallway. There was the smell of cooking.

'Aye, right. Well you better come in then. No point standing out here in the cold.'

She stepped into the hallway and the woman closed the door behind them. The house was quiet except for the sound of something simmering on the cooker. The lid of a pot rattled slightly.

'I've some broth on,' the woman said. 'They'll all be needing a hot meal when they come in after a day like this. It's bitter cold. Have you come far?'

'No, not too far,' she replied, looking round the living room she'd just entered. It was nothing fancy but it was clean and tidy. 'Up the road a bit.'

'So it's for your daughter, then. Will she not need to see it for herself? To see if she likes it.'

'No, it'll be all right,' she answered, staring at the family photographs on the mantelpiece, 'I know what she likes – she's happy for me to choose.'

The woman excused herself to turn the soup down. She sat on the settee, listened to the movements in the kitchen and looked at the photographs while the voice filtered through to her.

'You're lucky to have a daughter who trusts you that much. I never know what's going on in the head of mine and any time I guess I get it wrong. Sometimes there's no fathomin' them.'

'We've always been very close,' she said, 'always very close. And we don't want too much of a show, nothing too grand. Just quiet, like.'

'Sure isn't that the best way,' the woman said, returning to the room. 'Would you like a cup of tea?'

'No thanks, I don't want to put you to any trouble. I'm sure you're busy.'

'It's no trouble. I had the kettle on. Won't take a second. I think we need it on a day like this.'

'Well that's very good of you,' she said, 'but don't go to any trouble now.'

'Sure take a cup and then you can have a look at the dress, see what you think.'

The tea was a delay but she didn't want to rush things and it would keep her calm, settle everything down. It came in a china cup with a saucer. She looked at the rose pattern and thought she recognized it. She'd have nice things in her new home – delicate, beautiful things but they wouldn't just be ornaments, they'd be for everyday use. She wouldn't be one of those women who stored everything away in china cabinets or in drawers for an unspecified future date. Her wait for the future had been too long and now that it was nearly over she was going to live for the moment, make the very best of things.

'Your daughter's getting married, then?' the woman asked.

'At Easter,' she replied, balancing the cup carefully on the saucer.

'That's when Shauna was set for. Everything arranged – church, reception, the lot.'

'It's a nice time of year,' she said, then wondered if she'd said the right thing. Roses, red roses, she'd have in her bouquet and the softness of the petals and the sweetness of their scent stirred her with pleasure.

'Depends whether Easter's early or late what weather you're likely to get. But it hardly matters now one way or another.'

'You must be disappointed,' she ventured.

'I've got over it. Shauna hasn't but I suppose that's only natural. For the best, really.' She hesitated, stared at the fire then towards the window. 'Better finding out now than later when it's too late.'

'Things not work out?' she asked, nodding in sympathy, her question prompted not by curiosity but by a desire to know if the dress was stained with something sordid that would make it impossible for it to become hers.

'We never really took to him – Alex thought he was a waster from the start – but you know how it is with young girls. What can you do? Say anything bad and it's you who's the worst in the world and it just makes them more determined. So I bit my tongue and next thing they announce they're getting married. Afterwards when I'd the house to myself I cried my eyes out. But she never knew – I never let her know, so she can't blame me for anything.'

She watched the woman smooth her hair flat with a jerky, nervous flutter of her hand. She didn't think the colour was entirely natural – it was too dark.

'So your daughter's getting married,' she continued. 'Well, it's an expensive business, that's for sure. Maybe you can save a bit on the dress, then, and after all when all's said and done it's only worn the once and then left to hang in the back of a wardrobe. Your daughter's got more sense than mine by the sound of her.'

'She's a good girl,' she answered. 'Just wants things done quiet and simple. No fuss or anything and she could have anything she wanted. Within reason, of course.'

'We had everything booked – the church, the photographer, the reception. Everything. 'Money down the drain,' Alex called it, but I told him whatever we paid was cheap at half the price, for what price can you put on your own daughter's happiness?

'And he was no good?' she asked.

'No good – that was one thing Alex was right about. Said he could read it in his face. I don't know about that but I never took to him, either. I couldn't put my finger on it but there was always something about him you couldn't warm to. And he was never reliable, no matter what way you look at it he was never reliable. Some nights she'd be sitting where you are now and she'd be waiting half the night for him to turn up. And good with the excuses he was, too, but I bit my tongue, said nothing. For say anything and you're the worst in the world.'

The woman offered her a top-up out of the teapot and she accepted. Sometimes it was important to listen.

'To tell the truth, I'll be glad to see the dress out of the house. It's a reminder, isn't it? I've caught her looking at it a couple of times and there'll be tears. I tell her he's not worth it but it'll take a while, I suppose.'

'It can't be easy, for any young girl. Can't be easy. But she'll get over it in time – I'm sure she will.'

97

'And your daughter, has she found anyone nice?' the woman asked.

'Very nice. He works in a bank. Has his own car.'

'You're very lucky. And he won't mind about the dress? Not being new, I mean.'

'No need for him to know, really, and I'm a widow – you can only do your best. He's happy with a small wedding,' she said. 'And like you say, it's only something you wear the once. No point pushing the boat out when the money could go to other things.'

'That's right, and anyway it's a nice dress. It was her choice but I thought it was lovely.'

She felt her impatience now and she set the cup and saucer down on the side table beside her chair. She wanted to see it.

'Well look, thanks for the tea – it was very good of you – but I'll not keep you back any longer, I know you're busy.'

'I'll just bring it down,' the woman said, standing up and lifting both cups and saucers away. As she listened to her footsteps on the stairs and in the room above her head she felt the shiver of her heart and for a second it was almost too much to bear and she thought of running into the street to escape the moment. But the woman was coming back down and she forced herself to straighten in the chair and assume a composure she did not feel.

She returned with the dress draped over her arm, its hem almost brushing the carpet, and carefully hung it from the top of the living-room door. Standing up she walked towards it, trying to steady the tremble of her hand as she lightly touched its whiteness. White as snow. She had never been this close before, and even though the woman was talking to her the words blurred and faded in her head as she stood staring at it. She touched it lightly again as if to make sure it was real, touched it gently with the lightness of love. It was more beautiful than she could ever have imagined.

'Yes it's nice, right enough,' she said, fingering the filigree of lace and bead on the bodice, then tracing the tips of her fingers down the flow of the sleeves.

'Would it fit all right?' the woman asked, staring at it as if she, too, saw something beyond the dress.

'Yes, it'll fit all right – I can tell by looking at it. Is there a veil?'

'I'm stupid – I left it upstairs.'

As she listened to the footsteps hurry up the narrow stairs she encircled the dress in her arms and slowly buried her face in its folds.

'There it is,' the woman said, shaking her head at her own foolishness. 'Don't know how I forgot. It just sets it off, doesn't it?

The veil was fastened to a silver comb and reached to waist height. It bore the same pattern and print as the dress. She was given it to hold in her hands.

'The price is what was in the paper?' she asked.

'Yes, that's right – I couldn't really let it go for any less now. We lost so many of our deposits.'

She didn't try to haggle, for arguing now over a few shillings would demean the dress and her impatience could no longer be resisted. She was reluctant even to set aside the veil for the few moments it took to count out the money. When it was done the woman produced the white cardboard box the dress had come in and she watched her lay it flat then carefully smooth and fold it in.

'I hope it brings you more luck than us,' she said as she tied it shut with string. Will you be able to manage all right? It's quite heavy.'

'I don't live too far,' she said. 'I'll get a bus at the stop.'

And then she was gone, clutching the long box under her arm ever tighter, as if at any moment the falling swathe of sky might reach down its nipped and blanched fingers and try to wrest it from her grasp.

She wasn't sure what time it was but she knew it was early and she was glad. The time was precious – there wasn't a moment to waste, not with so many things to be done. Everything had to be right, just everything. She took the brush from the side of her bed and started to brush her hair. Soon her mother would come and take it from her hands and start those long patient sweeps and she'd whisper to her as she smoothed and separated the beautiful tresses. She'd always had beautiful hair – her crowning glory, that's what everyone said and she'd smile and blush at the words. Almost a pity to hide it under the veil, but it, too, was beautiful – so light and fine that she could almost forget it was there and when the silver comb caught the light it looked pure as ivory. Careful, Mother, there was no need to rush, for didn't they have plenty of time. Time enough. And it was sad for both of them, too, that they would never do this again, never share these moments of intimacy. But they said nothing of this to each other and there was only the swish of the brush and the whisper of her mother's voice in these secret moments.

Her mother had already checked the weather, and everything was just the way she had imagined it. Nothing was going to spoil this day – she could feel that knowledge flow through her and the strength of his love course and pulse in her veins. Her mother's incessant babble started to irritate and frustrate her because now she felt the need to be alone with the words he had written to her the night before. The letter lay on the table beside her bed, its careful folds hiding the strength of his love. Words came so easily to him and in the rattle of her mother's gossip she constructed a little clearing and wove the words that meant so much more to her.

Of course it hadn't been easy for her father – to him she would always be his little girl and giving her away would be the most difficult thing he had ever done. She knew that and so she was glad and grateful that finally he had given her his blessing. A blessing in his own way and so not in words, but when she looked into his eyes she no longer saw the stern refusal to countenance a rival. And she knew that love could be expressed in many different ways. Don't worry, Father, there'll always be a place for you in my heart, she'd say. A special place. And when you see me in the dress you'll be so proud.

She walked to the wardrobe door and stood in front of the mirror. It seemed misted and she peered more closely at it, then stretched out her hand and squeaked the glass. But it didn't clear. She felt tired, as if she hadn't slept. She stared back at the bed but couldn't remember if she had made it or not. What time was it? There was something she was supposed to remember but it wouldn't come to her. What time was it? Maybe it wasn't as early as she had first thought, and she felt the first beat of panic. Lifting the cardigan she had worn the night before, she started to scrub and polish the glass, desperate to see her face in it, and panic rushed through her as she searched to see the face she remembered. Too many faces and all of them falling into a crazy spiral and slipping further away from her. She stretched out her hand and tried to grasp one and pull it close but her fingers touched only the coldness of the glass. Someone was calling her name. She spun round and there in the light of the open doorway was her father standing waiting for her. The light flickered on the silver spokes of the bicycle and for a second she thought the wheels were spinning but then she saw the rigidity of his arms and the immobility of his face. Maybe she had been too long in the dance, maybe she had made him wait too long for her, but she knew that she was one of the first to leave and that as always she was missing the final dances – the ones where invitations were offered and promises given. I'm coming, Father, I'm coming now. His face is glazed and pinched by the cold moonlight. He turns away before she reaches him, and begins to push the bicycle, and in her head mix the whir of the wheels, the clack of his heels and the fading flutter of the fiddles in the hollow of the hall. They walk in silence and the silence is the price she has to pay for something about which she isn't sure.

She went to the window and looked out. There was something strange about the world. Something she didn't understand. Was it the wash of moonlight? Was it the silvery blossoms of the hedgerows as she followed her father home? Maybe if she hurries on and walks beside him he'll speak to her and ask about who was at the dance, but as she skips her steps he strides on and there is only the angry glare of the dynamo and the whir of the wheels.

Silence is important. He tells her that. Asks her if she understands. She nods while she looks up into his frightened eyes. There is no need – she doesn't think she will ever use words again. No sounds can shut out what she has heard – the storm of his breathing, the grunt and then something that sounds like his sobs. Strange, broken little gasps that fill her ear and stream into the broken splay of her hair. Silence is important. It's so important that he tells her again and again, and she believes him because he is a man who says things only once. And when he leaves her he pats her on the head as if she's been a good girl, so she can't spoil anything by letting him hear her cry and so she hugs the pain in the silent embrace of her tears.

Now it's time that's slipping away and her mother returns from her stay in hospital and everything is the way it always was, but sometimes she gets confused and when she looks in the mirror it's her mother's face looking back at her. And it's her mother's voice now telling her to hurry, that she's got no time to dilly-dally, so she turns away from the window and begins to get ready. When her mother goes quiet, she thinks she knows the secret, but nothing is ever said and the moment fades again into the rush of words and work to do. When you're dirty your mother tells you to wash your face but she does this without being told – scrubs and scrubs until the flesh is red and raw. Her mother tells her to hurry again and it's as if she understands, understands that only something as pure and white as this will take away the stains.

The dress is spread carefully on the bed – it is the beauty she will put on, it is the love that time has finally brought. He will be waiting soon and when she walks towards him on her father's arms he'll turn to see her and she'll smile at him. She must hurry – she is determined not to be late. Her mother has gone to help her father and it's better that this moment should be hers alone. So she stands at the mirror and lets her night-clothes slip to the floor and in the mottled and frosted glass looks at her body, which only her father has wanted to love. She cries a little as she caresses the withered emptiness of her breasts, then traces the ragged and ridged girdle of her ribs. The grey strands of her hair are brittle to her touch and she shivers a little as she stretches out her fingers and brushes the reflection of her face. Then, turning away, she looks again at the dress and a voice whispers that she is beautiful, that everything will be all right. This is her face. This is her face, untouched by the hand of time, and she sees the milky clearness of her skin and the lightness of love in her eyes.

Everything is ready now. Impatient voices are calling to her. She must hurry. The sheath of the dress is cool and clean against her skin – it fits her as perfectly as she knew it would. It salves and burnishes her as she takes her first careful steps. There are no shoes – she will wear only the blue-veined whiteness of her feet. This is the moment. She descends the stairs slowly, her hand on the banister steadying herself, her father and mother, eyes wide with wonder, unable to find any words. Her fingers fumble with the lock on the front door for a few seconds. There is no time to lose. She must hurry.

She almost gasps as the whiteness of the world dazzles her. It holds out its arms to her and at first she hesitates, then she steps towards it, knowing that for the first time she is part of its beauty, part of its untainted purity. So it is love that calls her now, and as she hurries towards it the sky opens again and turning her shiny eyes to look, her veil flutters behind her in the breeze and the snowflakes dance about her like confetti.

Against the Cold

TERENCE PEEL WAS NOT happy to see two dozen or more of his pupils arrive for school. He considered it most unreasonable behaviour under the circumstances and he greeted their arrival with an appropriate expression of wordless exasperation. It irritated him even more to see how they smiled up at him as if to claim his commendation for having struggled through the snow. But when he inspected those who had turned up, he saw not an admirable parental enthusiasm for the fruits of education, but rather a despicable desire to pass the responsibility for their children on to him. And what could he do with them? The only other members of staff who had turned up were Mildred Lewis and the caretaker, Norman. He should have felt grateful to her but he took her presence for granted: she lived only a few streets away and was the type of person who, if an atomic bomb had just been dropped, would have turned up to see if the floor needed mopping or shelves tidying.

He watched her shepherding the children into the closest

classroom, heard her trying to shush their excited squeals of anticipation of a day which promised them a release from the straitjacket of predictable pattern; then returned to the sanctuary of his office. The other staff had already phoned in to excuse their absences, blaming the conditions for their inability to get to work. Mrs Armstrong had even claimed that the radio had told people to stay at home unless it was absolutely necessary to venture out. He had listened to all their calls with the same neutrality, neither bestowing his approval or criticism. When Mrs Foster had enquired about whether they would have pay deducted for their absence, he had declined to offer a personal opinion, saying that it would be up to the department, although he did mention to Miss Morgan, who in his view took days off at the drop of a hat, that he believed it was the department's policy that in such circumstances teachers should endeavour to report to their nearest school. He took pride that this would take some of the shine off her unexpected holiday but the sudden image of her snuggling down under her eiderdown, with only her pert little nose and dark brown eyes visible, stirred a shimmer of pleasure which determined him to punish her for it by inspecting her lesson plans on her return and criticizing her for them. He went to the open door of his office and watched Miss Lewis collecting a couple of new arrivals and was struck by the question why useful, dependable things in life were never as attractive as the flighty and unreliable. A bit like medicine, he thought, mostly unpalatable but necessary for the body to function properly. She was wearing a red woollen jumper which seemed to have increased her bosom to twice its normal size, a heavy brown skirt and grey calf-length fur-lined boots. Her hair was pinned up in a beehive, held in place by a plethora of shiny pins. He supposed, with some reluctance, that due consideration must be given to the climatic conditions but wondered if she couldn't have found clothes that did more for her shape.

He tried to phone the Board again but it was still engaged. He supposed every school in the city was on the line trying to get instructions. It was also important to him that those in power should know that he was at his post, that he had walked five miles through the snow-filled city to reach his desk and that he was there, in his normal dark suit, ready for their orders. As he stood at the phone he stared out at the white playground where only a narrow ribbon of scuffed and printed snow revealed that children's feet had tramped to the front door. This reminder of the children refreshed his sense of irritation. If the snow got any worse they'd never get them back home again. And just what was he supposed to do with them? He'd no staff, the heating and the electricity could go off at any moment, and a journey outside to the toilets took on the arduousness of a trek to the Pole. A sudden bang made him jump as it echoed through the empty corridors. Clattering the phone down, he charged into the corridor and caught a glimpse of red hair about to vanish up the stairs.

'Thomas Blain, come here!' he shouted and then repeated it even more stridently. Two boys emerged from the stairwell. 'Ah, Leeman as well.' There was a vague smell of caps. He stood with his arms folded across his chest, rising on his toes as the two boys reluctantly drew closer. 'So it's not enough for you that we have problems with the snow but you think you'll take advantage and act like a pair of hooligans.' The two boys glanced briefly at his face, then at the tiled floor as if unable to understand what he was talking about. 'Give me the caps, Blain,' he said, extending his hand towards the boy's face.

'I don't have any caps, sir,' the boy said, assuming a look of pained innocence, his shoulders almost rising into the impression of a shrug.

'Give me the caps,' he said, but this time his voice menaced into a sharp whisper and, after waiting a few seconds for its effect to sink in, he grabbed a tuft of hair above the boy's ear. 'Now!'

'They're not mine,' Blain said, as if this plea might diminish his guilt, then squirmed a small round packet out of his pocket. The top was off and they coiled in a pinky-red spiral, like a spotted snake.

'And the gun.'

'Don't have no gun, sir.'

He repeated the demand and simultaneously twisted the tuft of hair.

'Honest, sir,' Blain protested, pulling out his pocket linings with the smooth skill of a seasoned suspect.

'Give me the gun, Leeman,' he said and this time his voice assumed a weariness that said he was now bored with the escapade and it would be best if it were over quickly. Leeman gave an apologetic glance to his comrade, before handing over the small black revolver. 'So it's the Lone Ranger and Tonto, is it? Well, it's "Away, Silver", and get yourselves home: tell your mothers that the school has to close and they'll have to look after you.' The boys' eyes lightened into smiles before extinguishing again in the glower of his face. 'And if I ever find you in school with caps again, I'll be warming your hands so much that you'll never need to wear gloves again.'

Still holding the tiny gun he escorted them to the front doors and in his own mind stood like a sheriff escorting two desperadoes out of town. Blain looked at him for a second as he thought of asking for the return of the weapon but he answered the unspoken request by a slow shake of his head and a point of his arm into the snowy distance. As the two boys rode away he raised the gun and shot them off their horses, then slowly blew the smoke away from the barrel. He liked cowboy films. He thought of John Wayne in *Rio Bravo*, of *The Alamo*. This was his Alamo and he'd been called to defend it against impossible odds. This was where people of character showed their mettle, what they were made of. He closed the front door and went back to the phone – it was important that Academy Street knew he was here and in control.

As he stood listening to the engaged tone he heard the caretaker's kettle whistle and knew he was brewing up yet another cup of tea in his cubby-hole which passed as a store. For a second he thought of going down and instructing him to clear a path from the school gates to the front door, but, knowing the man's reluctance to assume responsibility for any task that wasn't laid out in black and white in his schedule of duties, decided that it wasn't worth the probable dispute. He looked at the tiny gun still in his hand and envied the world of films where a raised eyebrow, or the glisten of sun on the slowly uncovered handle of a pistol, was enough to accomplish whatever was needed. He thought of his staff's desertion, of Academy Street's indifference, and suddenly he felt emasculated, stripped of his sheriff's badge, and after flinging down the phone he set off to bully Miss Lewis.

His footsteps hammered the anvil tiles of the corridor and echoed round the almost empty building in a way he found vaguely disconcerting. Pausing at the open door of her room he inspected the pupils clustered round the desks in varying age groups. She had given out paper and crayons but there was little sign of concentration or serious industry. She sat on the radiator at the window, her black hair suddenly blacker against its frame of white. The room smelled of wax and wet. Little puddles formed on the floor under the pupils as if they had wet themselves, while at the tables heads bobbed up and down like seals. He straightened himself to make his entrance, irritated that he couldn't formally announce his arrival by the sudden opening of the door. When he did enter, only Miss Lewis acknowledged his arrival by standing up and although he glanced meaningfully at the pupils he could detect no frisson of apprehension or interest, no matter how hard he strained.

'Miss Lewis, did you allow Blain and Leeman out of the room?' he asked, fixing his stare at her eyes. Then without waiting for a reply: 'I've just taken a cap gun off them and sent them home.' Her face hadn't changed expression. He tried again. 'They're not the sort of boys we can let wander round the school.'

'No,' she said, holding the end of a strand of hair, 'they're not indeed. Blain and Leeman? They haven't been in here this morning.'

'Not at all?'

'No,' she said, twirling the strand as if it was a piece of string.

'Right,' he said, unable to think of a suitable riposte, then turned to face the children as if the conversation hadn't taken place. Some of the older ones were looking at him now as if he might be about to announce something really important but the younger children continued with their play. For a moment he entertained the idea of turning this siege, this crisis, into something special, something that the children would remember all their lives, something that Miss Lewis would recount to all the other staff and they would be eternally afflicted by regret at having missed it. He would gather the children about him as if round a campfire, and he would give them a series of lessons they would never forget. He'd take them down the paths of history and geography, on perilous journeys to foreign countries where he'd regale them with tales that would make their eyes pop wide with wonder. He'd lead them in a campfire sing-song that would keep spirits up whatever blizzards raged outside, and when it was time to go home the children would cling to him and ask if he'd come back tomorrow.

He stood still for a few seconds, smiling to himself and letting the thought warm him before deciding that he didn't know how to do any of those things and so instead decided to return to his office and try the phone again. This time he got through but was immediately disappointed to hear that he was talking to a young woman and when he tried to get passed on to someone else, she said that all the lines were busy and she could help him with his query. Giving his full title, in the hope that she would realize who she was dealing with, he asked what were his instructions, only to be told in a most casual way that he should try to get all the children home safely and then close the school. She used the phrases 'Use your own judgement' and 'depending on local conditions' several times, and he knew the ball was being passed back to him. It was typical, he thought as he put the phone down. He had made a valiant and conscientious effort to keep his doors open, to deliver the education he was entrusted with, and at the end of the day no one gave a monkey's. He allowed himself the luxury of a silent curse – a single 'bloody' (he tried never to go beyond that except in the most extreme of conditions) – as he nurtured the suspicion that the top men themselves were at that very moment ensconced at some fireside with a hot whiskey in their hands.

Well, if that was the way they wanted it, so be it. But getting the children home wouldn't be so easy – he'd have to make a list of names and addresses and deliver them to their doorsteps like parcels in the post. Suddenly the electricity went off and there was an excited squeal from Miss Lewis's room. That settled it. It was Abandon Ship time but he knew too, that it was his duty to remain on board. Others who got more money than he did might have different sets of values but no one would ever be able to say that Terence Peel didn't know how to fulfil his duty. After the last child had gone he'd return, sit in his office and man the phone. At the end of school he'd phone Academy Street again to let them know he was still there, then sign off. His imagination flared with images of Scott's expedition to the South Pole, Captain Oates's brave self-sacrifice and he knew that he, too, was such a man. His eyes moistened at this acknowledgment of his bravery and he savoured the challenge of the long trek home. Only the thought that there would be no one there to garland him with the wreaths of victory, or to listen to his tales of hazards overcome, diminished his pleasure.

Returning to the classroom, where the noise level had risen considerably, he took a list of names and addresses, then in the quiet of his office worked out a route. Most of the children lived within a few hundred yards of the school and it seemed a relatively simple circuit to make. A couple of them had phones and he contacted their mothers to tell them what was happening, telling each of them that he was reluctantly closing the school as a result of higher instructions. He was glad that most of his pupils came from a better class of home where the mother didn't work, so it looked as if he would be able to unload each child safely. Then after putting on his wellingtons and clambering into his overcoat, stopping briefly to tell Norman his plan, he made his announcement to the pupils. Adopting his gravest tones, which he usually reserved for bereavements and heinous misdemeanours, he outlined the course of action and the detailed rules of engagement. Pupils would walk in twos and stay strictly together. They would line up in the sequence of their homes. He would lead and Miss Lewis would follow behind. There must be no straggling, no silly behaviour – unelaborated dangerous consequences could result. But he conjured up for himself pictures of lost and frozen children buried under squalls of snow, of himself carrying a small child to safety. Of his picture in the paper. Some of the children smiled in return, thinking that he was smiling at them.

When the line was eventually formed in the right sequence and everyone had fastened coats and shouldered bags, they set off. Before the last pair of children had even left the steps to the front door, he heard Norman locking the school. It was starting to snow again, slowly, almost like an afterthought, and some of the children held up their hands to catch the flakes, squealing with excitement and frustration. He tried to silence them into conformity by a stern glance but the power of the snow was greater than any repression he could generate. All that was in his power was to get them home as quickly as possible and he strode out with his head held high and an admonition to the children not to dawdle. It reminded him of a scene in a film he couldn't remember the name of, in which the wagon-train had been trapped in a valley by the first snows of winter and they had been rescued by the hero, who walked them to safety through a secret mountain pass. And as the children followed him up the middle of streets where the snow had been flattened a little, he felt proud of himself again and conscious of his impeccable devotion to duty. He had been irritated recently to hear of several appointments to principal-ship of disconcertingly young men, but it was a comfort to reassure himself now with the thought that, when hardy came to hardy, there was no substitute for experience and a cool head. A cool head under fire – that was the ticket. He glanced back at his train of children. Young men still wet behind the ears with long hair and pointy shoes. He called to some stragglers to keep up and gestured with his hand – a slow stylized sweep that he remembered from the film. They didn't understand style. Not at all. Screen images flowed in and he illustrated the concept to those same young men by showing them how to hold a cigarette, how to light it then extinguish the match with a double shake of the wrist; how to give a sign-off salute with a flick of the fingers; how to spin a coin to a child or beggar.

'Orange Peel! Orange Peel!' The cries came in young voices from somewhere to the left, perhaps from behind one of the tall garden hedges, but he didn't turn his head or let his stare deviate from the road ahead. 'Orange Peel! Orange Peel!' It could be some former pupils emboldened by a couple of years' distance in secondary school, or even a few reprobate refugees from his own school. He let the voices swirl round his head, trying to recognize the source, like a wine taster trying to establish the precise location of a particular flavour. When the voices called again he knew it was Blain and Leeman and he allowed himself a double 'bloody' as he repeated their names. He should have finished them off when he had the chance. He cursed himself this time and tried to increase his speed, to hurry the children on, but when he turned to signal them to greater speed he saw the smiles spreading across their faces and out of the corner of his eye he caught the first snowball arcing through the air. It broke a few feet short, ploofing silently into the bed of snow, but the second was more accurate and he had to use his hand like a tennis racket to beat it away. One of the children laughed loudly but he didn't wait to see who it was before he called to Miss Lewis to take pole position and, like a traffic-control policeman, waved the column of children past him, urging them to hurry. Then as the last pair of children passed him he turned to where the unseen assailants lurked, and stood impassively with his hands on his hips. Cool under fire. Looking the enemy in the eye. It was the only way. The good shepherd protecting his sheep. He took a step forward and then there was the sound of scurry as the ambushers broke for better cover. He caught a glimpse of red hair through the thinning screen of privet and knew it was Blain. 'Snow doesn't last for ever!' he shouted. 'See you when it melts.'

Satisfied that he had retrieved some of his dignity he set off again. Life was a permanent state of war. A cold war. He was pleased by how apposite the phrase was, encouraged by his ability as a wordsmith. As an antidote to his simmering irritation he constructed witty ripostes to the mandarins of Academy Street, devastating verbal put-downs which crushed their lily-livered spirits and sent them scurrying to their inner sanctums for shelter. He wished the powers that be could see him now, out in the field, on the front line. In charge. So by the time they had left off the last child and he had received a pleasing display of deference and gratitude from most of the mothers, his spirits were somewhat restored and despite the fact that it had started to snow heavily again, there was a satisfaction that he had discharged his duties honourably.

'Right, Miss Lewis,' he said, his tone jaunty and congratulatory, 'we've done our bit. I'm returning to school now but I don't think anyone would object if you were to head on home.' He paused to accept an acknowledgment of his generosity.

She looked at him from under her woollen blob of a hat and he noticed how flushed the walking had made her face, how shiny her brown eyes were. A flake of dampness glistened on her cheek. The wetness of her coat, the damp ends of her hair where it protruded from her hat, suddenly gave her a liquidity that flowed over the normal image he held of her. She told him that she would collect her things from school before accepting his kind offer and so they set off the way they had come, their heads bowed against the blown flurry of snow. Neither of them spoke and he touched her elbow to direct her by a different street when they approached the scene of their former ambush. Sometimes she moved slightly ahead of him and he found himself sneaking a fleeting glimpse of her nylons through the narrow vent in her coat, in the little gap between the top of her boots and the hem.

When they reached the school he found the door locked and when he tried his key he realized that Norman had snibbed it on the Yale lock, for which he had no key with him. He stood on the steps, then shuffled round with exasperation. They were locked out and there was no way that he was trudging off into the blizzard to Norman's house to try and retrieve it. There was nothing to be done but start the long trek home. He'd have to forgo the phone call but tried to calm himself by predicting that he'd get no further than the nobody girl he'd spoken to earlier. At the end of the day it was clear that no one gave a tinker's curse. So why should he? People – dependable people like him – were always taken for granted, always passed over when it came time to dish out the big jobs. The snow was coming down in big feathery flakes as if the fat pillow of sky had been slit open and shaken empty. Well, there was nothing else to do but make the long journey home in the full face of the furious snow, so he wasn't quite sure why he lingered a little on the steps, occasionally staring into the school.

'I'll see you get home,' he said to Miss Lewis, clapping his hands together as a prelude to setting off, and refusing her grateful demurring by insisting that it was on his route. A principal's responsibility didn't end with his pupils. He reminded her of the morning's news on the radio and its story of how a young woman's body had been found. 'Foul play is suspected' – that was the phrase they had used.

He thought of thanking her for turning up but the idea felt too undesirably personal and he replaced it with a swing of his arms and a steady saunter forth. The snow seemed thicker by the moment and in his mind the distance home grew with each step until it took on the demands of a polar expedition. If the electricity was off it would take him hours to get any heat into the house and he wasn't sure if there were any candles. His spirits started to sag – there was little purpose to struggle if it wasn't recompensed by reward or recognition. As his feet scrunched and pressed the snow he realized that this was the very thing that flawed life and made it so unfair.

'Hard going, Mr Peel,' Miss Lewis said, her head bowed and her hand holding the ends of her hat. She slipped a little and on impulse he offered her the crook of his arm, holding it out from his side like the handle on a cup. It was the duty of the strong to look after the weak. She took it and he felt the sudden weight of her on his shoulder. Together they plodded on, their eyes lowered to the ground for respite and he only realized that they had arrived at her gate when she disengaged her arm from his and began to fumble in her handbag for her key, holding the open bag at an angle so that the snow wouldn't get in. 'Hard going,' he repeated, without really knowing why.

'I've never seen the like of it,' she said as she put the key in the lock. Thank you for seeing me home – it was very good of you.'

'The least I could do in the circumstances,' he said, touching the brim of his hat with the tip of a finger. The gesture was the most he had ever given her. He believed she would treasure it, remember it. Then he turned and shivered his shoulders against the renewed onslaught but before he had taken more than a few steps he heard her call, 'Won't you come in for a few minutes, Mr Peel, have a quick cup of tea, before you set off? Maybe give the snow a chance to die down?'

He hesitated, torn between his lack of enthusiasm for the journey home and his reluctance to enter the personal world of one of his staff. The snow swirled between them. A few flakes entered the hall. She wouldn't hold the door open much longer. Abnormal circumstances. A hot cup of tea suddenly assumed a strong attraction. What harm could it do? Better to be fortified against the struggle ahead, better to be prepared. And at the back of everything was the image of his own empty house, an image that had increasingly assumed a rather forlorn quality. Loneliness was not a word that he would ever admit to the descriptive profiles he liked to construct about himself, but over the last year he was more ready to acknowledge the absence of something. He told himself it was something to do with turning forty, with knowing that he had all the requisite skills to achieve something higher, with a momentary succumbing to frustration. Home was also solitary and, while there were times he appreciated that, it was without the audience that was required if he was fully to catch his own reflection, to portray the man he really was.

So now the idea of a shared cup of tea developed an appeal and for the moment papered over the thin little crack in his self-esteem. It was true that it would have been garnished with a greater sense of anticipation if Miss Morgan with her pert little nose and dark curls had offered the invitation, and if Miss Lewis's sepia wallpaper hadn't harboured all the appeal of a morgue. He hesitated again. A shift of wind wiped snow across his eyes and for a second it felt as if he was crying.

'Thank you,' he said, blinking. 'The snow is getting heavier, perhaps it would be more prudent to take shelter until it eases.' Special circumstances. A bit like the war, when people had to hang together, and it wasn't as if she was the type who would assume an undignified familiarity or seek to gain some future advantage. He could tell that by the very way she held open the door for him and self-consciously ushered him in, bowing her head briefly as he passed, then squeezing past him to show the way to the living room. Not for the first time he observed that she wasn't really any type at all. Thirty-six years old – he knew that, as he knew all the personal details from their files – and there in the school since coming out of college. Part of the fittings. Efficient, reliable, colourless – he had never once heard a parent express either praise or criticism. She never had much to say and wasn't part of the inner circle of women. He watched her shuffle ahead like a geisha and had a sudden impulse of pleasure from the remembered punishment that he was to bestow on Miss Morgan. He might even make her cry if he was in the mood, then be nice to her. He was vaguely aware of Miss Lewis apologizing for something but he wasn't really listening and instead took off his hat and entered the room to which she had brought him.

The walls were covered with red wallpaper woven with white flowers, and in every available space hung pictures of various sizes and types. For a second he wondered if he had come into the wrong room and when he glanced over his shoulder his sudden disorientation was increased by the glimpse of her shaking her hair free of her hat, little beads of water bursting free as if broken from a string of pearls. 'Keep your coat on, Mr Peel,' she said, while she quickly bundled into her pocket a pair of nylons that had been drying on the fireguard. Before they disappeared they seemed to sieve the air like the fluttering tails of kites. 'At least the electric's back on. I'll get the kettle on before it goes off again. Have a seat there.' She switched on the two-bar electric heater for him that sat in the tiled hearth. It smelled briefly of burning dust as she disappeared into the kitchen.

He stared again at the pictures. He had never seen so many in one room. Alongside small framed landscapes were larger prints of what he vaguely recognized as Pre-Raphaelite work and scattered between them were assorted postcards and pictures cut out of magazines. He wondered for a second if he had stumbled into a secret manifestation of mental instability and then the picture above the fireplace caught his eye. The sound of running water confirmed that she was still in the kitchen, allowing him to examine it more closely. It was of two young people kissing: they were from a much earlier period, perhaps even medieval. He wasn't sure if it was entirely seemly. As a man of some knowledge of the world, he gauged that the kiss was either a prelude to something about to happen or a postscript to something that already had. '*Roman de la Rose* by Rossetti' was printed below it. The lewdness was what might be expected from an Italian. But as he sat down again he wondered what possessed Miss

Lewis to hang such a thing on open view, so he found it reassuring to hear her familiar voice calling to him to enquire whether he wanted tea or would like a nice cup of Bovril. He plumped for Bovril and in the seconds before she brought it in gazed round the rest of the room, looking for anything that might confirm his initial suspicion of festering instability. But although he disapproved of the number of books on the shelves and the brightly coloured cushions strewn across every chair and the settee, there was nothing quite as disturbing as the paintings.

When she appeared, carrying two cups whose contents' sweet, meaty smell infused the room, her concentrated gaze focused on preventing a spill, he was able to glance briefly at her and confirm that she looked as she always did. Perhaps she had inherited the room from a previous owner, perhaps it was merely some harmless eccentricity, and he resolved not to allude to the pictures or even indicate that he had noticed them. He was a tolerant man and after all, he told himself, what people did in the privacy of their own homes was their own business, so long as it wasn't illegal or subversive. With a sudden pang of guilt he remembered the set of modestly mucky photographs that he had confiscated from a former pupil and that now lodged at home between the pages of his *Encyclopaedia Britannica*, volume 18. There was, too, the deck of nude playing cards, acquired in his youth on a holiday in the Isle of Man, with which, purely from nostalgia, he occasionally played a game of Patience. All human beings had their foibles, their moments of private weakness, but he resolved to remove both offending articles to the bin on his return home. No one should ever have the opportunity to rebuke him for a lack of self-discipline; it was up to him to set an example to others. He sipped the Bovril and let its taste linger on his tongue. But still, he'd had the cards for a long time. He liked the waxy feel of them in his hands, the soft flitting sound as he dealt them to himself, and when he glanced at Miss Lewis sitting opposite him he couldn't help reflecting how different she looked from the fabulous creatures of those cards.

Her face was featureless, unremittingly plain, like a page that hadn't been fully printed so there was no story to be read, no mystery to be explored. Like the rest of her body it had started to slide into plumpness and it was obvious that, if nothing intervened to stop that slide, before long she would grow fat, her present nervous gait transformed into a waddle. He nodded at her over the rim of his cup to show his appreciation of the Bovril, then tried to block out the sudden image of her on the back of a playing card. She smiled politely in return and he noticed for the second time how brown her eyes were and that they hadn't lost that earlier moistness. It gave the impression that she had been crying and it pleased him: he liked tears in a woman and derived a pulse of pleasure from imagining how Miss Morgan's beautiful almond eyes would glisten when he berated her for the inadequacy of some aspect of her lesson plans. But he'd be well prepared and be able to offer her a pristine white handkerchief, neatly folded, with which she could dry them and afterwards he'd keep it until the final traces of her tears and scent had vanished. Best, too, to have a back-up in case he needed one for his own use. Two handkerchiefs in separate pockets – important not to get them mixed when the appropriate moment arrived.

'Would you like a biscuit, Mr Peel?' she asked, offering him a plate of digestives. As she leaned forward the electricity went off and the bars of the electric fire snuffed into a brief memory of brightness. 'Dear, dear, there's no end to it,' she said, shaking her head resignedly. 'I'll light the fire – I set it this morning before going out.' And indeed she had, for a mound of scrunched paper and sticks bristled in the grate and there was a scuttle laden to the brim with great, grainy knobs of coal which glinted when she struck a match. She had removed the fireguard and was down on her knees at the hearth as she lifted pieces of coal with tongs and placed them carefully on the sticks. He thought she was a little premature with the coal and would have considered it more prudent to have let the sticks catch first, but he said nothing and, holding the cup of Bovril in both hands and staring over its rim while she set up a little rhythm in the work, he studied the posterior presented to him. It was a full one, but not, he had to concede, unshapely. 'Cushioned' was the word he would use if he were asked to describe it. He felt a sweep of tiredness wash over him and he had to resist the impulse to get down on his knees and rest his weary head on that soft pillow.

'Having trouble, Miss Lewis?' he asked, glad to distract himself from the impulse with the sound of his voice. 'Perhaps the sticks are a little damp.' She had started to blow air into the base, in a steady and confusingly unnerving stream of air. His pulse rose a little and he pushed the remainder of a digestive biscuit into his mouth. He liked them better when they were buttered and pressed together. But beggars couldn't be choosers. Not that he was a beggar. Not by any stretch of the imagination. 'I think there's some snow coming down the chimney,' she said, squirming her body into one final blow. A few flames sniggered into ragged life and then some of the sticks caught and started to spark. 'Well done,' he said, resisting another impulse to lean forward and pat her on her rump. 'It'll soon get going now,' he added, intrigued by his own benevolence. He had almost finished his Bovril and knew it was the right time to go, but he was infused with a tiredness that robbed him of impetus.

'I should be going now,' he said, draining his cup but making no attempt to get out of his chair. More life appeared in the fire. It held his gaze like a magnet. She stood up and went to the window. 'It's still coming down,' she answered as she touched her cheek with a black finger, leaving an inky smudge. 'Why don't you wait a little while longer and see if it eases off?' He pretended to consider the offer before letting himself be reluctantly persuaded. 'Perhaps, just a little while,' he said, settling back in the chair and letting his fingers absorb the final vestiges of heat from the cup.

She stoked more coal on the fire and in a short while it broke into a blaze of pleasurable proportions. She had taken her coat off and he had followed suit. She had advised him to do so in order that she could place it close to the fire and try to get it dried before he set off again. For a few moments she had disappeared from the room and on her return she was wearing slippers. They were red and embroidered with gold thread and they made him think of something vaguely Eastern, and, while he watched her set a series of stunted candles along the mantelpiece, his thoughts wandered to the world of harems and potentates. Of Miss Morgan, the most recent acquisition, on nightly request. But as he watched her arrange the final candle and then sit down in the chair opposite his, the exotic edge of his imaginings floundered and then faded. Then while they both stared at the fire he felt the moment take on a new ambiance – that of the domestic – and as he gingerly savoured its flavour he found himself forced to admit that it wasn't entirely unpleasant.

'Your journey to school this morning must have been

terrible,' she said, smoothing a cushion. The black smudge still nestled in the dimple of her cheek.

'It wasn't easy. And there was hardly a soul about: most people obviously didn't relish the challenge of the conditions. In some stretches of the road mine were the first steps in the snow.' He paused to let the image sink home. 'But when you're responsible for children, you have to put other considerations second. Once or twice it got a bit hairy but the conditions weren't entirely unfamiliar to me so that was an advantage, I suppose.' He paused again to wait for her to ask why that was, but she merely nodded as if she understood. He paused also because he wasn't sure why he had said it and didn't know the answer he would give if she did. He stared at the climbing flames of the fire and said: 'I used to do a bit of mountaineering in my younger days – went on a few expeditions – and often climbed above the snow line.

'I didn't know,' she said. 'Sounds very dangerous.'

'There's always danger but if you are well-prepared and don't take foolish risks, then . . .' He didn't finish his sentence but still stared at the fire, where Hillary and Tenzing made the final ascent to a blue-tipped summit. 'In climbing you work as a team but one of the hardest things is not always being able to make the final push to the top – but that's the way it works and you have to accept it.'

'And you took part in expeditions?

'A few in my time,' he said, but then sensing that the conversation might lead into difficult terrain, added, 'I lost a good friend once – I owed it to him to go on living. I've never climbed since.' He glanced at her and saw her eyes widen. 'Don't like to talk about it.'

She nodded and said nothing for a while before offering him another cup of Bovril. He declined and shook his head slowly, lost in the tragedy of snow and crevice. She took his cup from him and carried them both into the kitchen. As he heard her rinse them, his eyes drifted to the painting of the couple kissing. Such a thing to have hanging on your wall! The holding of hands, their closed eyes, the way their heads seemed to fit together – he took it all in. What possessed her? He felt a skip of panic as he pondered the possibility of her being some fifth columnist, a Trojan horse he had brought inside the gates. Did he really know what went on when she closed her class-room door? But no matter how hard he tried to stir his sense of unease into something stronger, it subsided in the moment he watched her predictable, unaltered self return to her seat at the fire.

'It's coming down like there's no tomorrow,' she said. 'Absolutely no end to it.' It was getting darker but she made no move to light the candles. 'I've never seen the likes of it.' He smiled as if to say that she mightn't have, but he most certainly had. 'Can I get you anything else, Mr Peel?'

'No, thanks,' he answered, stirring a little in the chair, thinking that maybe she was giving him a signal that it was time to go. 'I suppose I should be going, not sitting here inconveniencing you like this.'

'There's no inconvenience – I wouldn't be going anywhere or doing anything that I'm not doing now, and you can't venture out in that blizzard, no matter how many expeditions you've been on.'

He glanced at her quickly to see if there was any trace of irony in her face but it was as open and uncalculating as always. She put some more coal on the fire and in a short while the flames sent feathery flurries of light into the falling shadows. 'These are the only candles I have, so I need to save them for later,' she said. 'I'm afraid I'm not very well prepared – I used most of them in January. Thought we'd seen the back of the snow then.'

'Well, if you're very sure I'm not keeping you back, perhaps I would be better holding on until it eases a little.' He sank back in the chair and felt the heat massage his shins. Close to where he sat he caught a glimpse of a picture in which a young woman garlanded in flowers appeared to be drowning. It was all very peculiar. He had a picture of his own house, filled with shadows and the snow pressing down on it, the fire dead in the grate and cold seeping into every corner. He looked again at the painting. How was it women got themselves into such situations again and again? The woman lay on the surface of the water as if waiting for a prince to rescue her. He listened to Miss Lewis prattle on about a burst pipe she'd had in January's cold snap and thought that she would wait in vain for such a rescue. He noticed the slightly uneven edge of her teeth, the little gap that made certain words lisp a little; the way the firelight flared her cheek into a blush.

He prided himself on knowing women, of understanding the way their minds worked. After all, he had worked with them for many years and considered he had good insights into their thinking. It was true, he had to concede, that his acquaintance with women in the full sense was rather limited but he told himself that this was more by choice than by any failure on his part. There was an early, not entirely successful, episode with a girl he'd been to college with, and in more recent years a brief liaison with the landlady of a boarding house in the Isle of Man, though the relationship had not survived two holidays. In that particular respect he considered it fortunate that he had extricated himself from what might have led to a most unsuitable marriage and a future tied to catering for the ravenous appetites of Belfast holidaymakers and the provision of cheap cabaret. He stretched his legs closer to the fire and allowed himself a smoulder of pleasure while he remembered the one and only frantic coupling on a bed whose springs squeaked, and in the afternoon sky outside the squeals of the gulls plucked at the sky. And as always he thought of water – the slop of the tide against the keel of a boat, the oily transfer of lurid colours in the harbour, the scraping shuffle of the sea over a bed of shingle. He glanced again at the picture of the young woman sinking into the water. Spots of snow plopped into the fire, making it hiss and spit like an angry cat. But even though his memory tried to keep the moment warm, it was over ten years ago and as time passed it became more difficult. Some day he might turn to it and find nothing left, find it all used up.

'Would you like a piece of toast, Mr Peel? I could do it by the fire, now the electric's off.'

A piece of toast? Yes, he'd like a piece of toast. There was something a shade undignified about it but he hadn't eaten since his breakfast and, after all, special circumstances . . . She lit two of the candles before going to the kitchen and returning with a toasting fork and four rounds of bread and a packet of butter, then set the butter on the hearth to soften. 'Allow me,' he said, taking the fork from her and spearing the bread. He hunched forward on the chair, glad of an excuse to pull closer to the fire and happy to display his expertise. This was camp-fire stuff, real campfire stuff. When he had it toasted he passed it to her on the end of his fork and she transferred it to one of the plates and covered it in butter. He had never known a bit of toast could taste so wonderful. This must have been what it was like in the Blitz – people pulling together, people sharing things. Now it was the elements, rather than Nazis, they were fighting against but the principle was the same. She hadn't pulled the curtains but all he could see outside was a settling greyness and an occasional spit of flake against the glass. Looking at it only served to increase his feeling of snugness and he lingered over the final piece of toast.

Sometimes the candles flickered for no apparent reason and when they did the clatter of pictures seemed to come alive and for a second it seemed as each one of them was an eye looking at him, taking him in, before it blinked closed again. She still had the smudge of black on her cheek and he saw too the spreading web of measles on her legs. The fire was warm but at the back of him he felt a wash of cold pushing off the street and into the hall and he knew that this was the only tolerable place in the house.

'Have you always lived here?' he asked, stifling a sudden shiver.

'Since I was a child. My mother died last year so the house is mine.'

'Last year?' He couldn't remember a death or a funeral. 'I don't remember . . .'

'It was during the summer. She had been ill for some time.' She shuffled her feet and his eye caught the embroidered slippers. 'I haven't had time to get the house done up yet. She didn't like change and now I've got the opportunity I seem to have run out of steam.'

'So these pictures are your mother's,' he said, his relief rushing to the surface.

'No, the pictures are mine. I started putting them up the week after the funeral. Running out of space now. Something to brighten the place up. Something to make the house mine. My mother was very fixed in her ways.'

'Right,' he said, nodding as if he understood when he didn't. He felt a certain resentment that she had kept her mother's funeral private and so robbed him of one of the social obligations of his post, of the opportunity to bestow appropriate sympathy. But as he pondered the pictures he was at least able to attribute them to the destabilizing force of grief. No doubt with the passage of time she would come to her senses and see them as an embarrassing aberration. After the deaths of his own parents – barely a year between them – he, too, had felt a momentary uncertainty, felt subject to a new and unsettling lack of focus. Still, it had passed and so, too, would these pictures. He tried to think of a new conversational direction.

'Any plans for the summer holidays?' he asked.

'No, I haven't really thought about it yet. Have you?'

'Nothing fixed yet,' he said, trying to smother the raucous images of that moment in the Isle of Man by resettling himself in the chair and staring into the fire. Compared to Miss Lewis she was a rather bony, sharp-featured creature, rodent-like round her mouth and teeth. He'd had a lucky escape there: another burst of weakness and she'd have sunk those same teeth in so deep that there'd have been no shaking them off. The chair was very comfortable. He glanced over at Miss Lewis and wondered what it would feel like to be with a comfortable woman. Someone soft and cushioned. Like sinking into a feather bed. The thought made him feel a little sleepy. He tried to stir himself. He'd have to be going soon: he couldn't put it off any longer.

'My coat must be nearly dry by now,' he said. 'I really should be going.' He stood up, knowing that if he didn't stir himself into physical activity he'd never make the move. 'It's been very good of you to put me up like this.'

'It was the least I could do,' she answered, also getting out of her seat. 'Your coat's still a little damp,' she said feeling it

with the tips of her fingers. 'I was about to make a little tea –
nothing hot, I'm afraid, and nothing terribly fancy – just
something to get us by. Would you like to have that before
you set off?'

'That's very kind of you but I feel I've imposed on you long
enough and I suppose there are lots of things I should be
getting on with at home,' he said with no idea as to what those
things would be other than shutting out every draught and
trying belatedly to kindle as much heat as possible. It was an
increasingly forlorn prospect. Special circumstances. 'If you're
sure it's not putting you to any trouble?'

'No trouble at all,' she said, scampering towards the kitchen,
then returning for one of the candles. 'It's getting dark: I'll
have to get more candles tomorrow.'

'I'll keep the fire going,' he called through to her, as he
started to stoke it with more coal. 'It's a real life-saver.' There
was the clink of plates and the thin tinkle of cutlery. In a few
minutes she returned carrying a tray with a plate of corned
beef, a little cheese and two slices of brown bread, apologizing
for its paucity when she handed it to him. He accepted it
graciously but had to fight hard to prevent the hunger churning and tumbling in his stomach from making him shovel it
down. Something to wash it down would have been nice, and
even as he had the thought she returned to the kitchen and he
heard a rummage in a cupboard and the clink of glasses. It was
a bottle of whiskey, its swirling golden content glinting like the
coins in a treasure trove. She held it nervously in both hands,
pressed against her stomach, and for a second he thought she
was going to return it to its cupboard. He knew he had to help
her.

'What's that you've found?' he asked, squirming sideways in
his chair.

'It's been in the house for years. I don't want you to think that I'm a secret drinker or anything like that. The only time I've ever touched it was a thimbleful once when I had a toothache.'

'It has a lot of medicinal qualities, all right. Normally I don't really myself.'

'I don't know what I was thinking of,' she said, shaking her head as in reproof of herself, and about to carry it back.

'But under the circumstances,' he ventured, 'under these very special circumstances, well . . . Maybe we need all the fortification we can get.' He stood up to show his willingness to be fortified and watched while she set two glasses on the mantelpiece, then carefully poured two small measures. When she handed him his glass, the flames from the fire seemed to be inside it and he gave them a swirl, then stared at what he was about to drink. He knew he should sip it, that it would look bad to knock it back like some hardened drinker but the fire that burnished it into life made him spurn any attempt to slowly ration it and he tilted his head back and wasn't disappointed. The heat slipped down the back of his throat and then spread like a rip-tide through his insides until it felt as if it pushed into the very pores of his skin. He blinked as some of the same heat pushed its way back out through the rush of his breath. Flames suddenly spurted in the hearth and for a second he thought he was a dragon breathing fire. 'That'll put' – he was going to say, 'hairs on your chest', but caught himself just in time and after a second's hesitation completed it with 'a lining on your coat'.

She sat with her glass, sipping from it and grimacing a little. 'It'll be a very cold night,' he said, to help her. 'It'll help keep out the cold.' Then like a child taking unpleasant medicine she took her punishment. He laughed as she fanned her mouth and blew a stream of air. 'Strong stuff,' he said, 'but under the circumstances, maybe just the ticket.' He leaned forward to the fire but his head swirled a little and he pulled back into the support of the chair. A few minute later she gave him another glass, but this time he sipped it very slowly. He wasn't an experienced drinker and he hadn't had a great deal to eat all day. Enough was as good as a feast. He always knew when he'd reached his limits in anything. Moderation was always a virtue. Staggering off into the wintry wastes while under the influence would not be a good idea and might lead to disaster. This time the fire in his throat slid into a more mellow glow – it made him think of a turnip lantern where the hollowed inside turned golden and flickering. He wondered if that was what his face looked like as they sat in silence and stared at the flames.

'What do you see in the fire?' she asked.

'See in the fire?' He didn't understand. He searched it for something unusual, something that shouldn't be there.

'It's a game you play. I played it all the time with my sister when we were children. You look in the fire and have to tell what you see. Except she was always better at it than I was – she had so much imagination – and when she told you, she made it so real you felt you could see it yourself. Palaces, caverns, secret rivers – she always saw something different and then she'd make up a story about it with a cast of characters.'

'I didn't know you had a sister,' he said.

'Florence. She lives in London. With her husband and two daughters. Sometimes I go to see them. Not very often. He's an architect. She teaches music.'

'Did they come over for the funeral?' he asked.

'No,' she said, hesitating, 'she didn't come. Florence and my mother didn't get on, didn't part on good terms. She never came back after she left. My mother didn't like me visiting her, wouldn't even look at a picture of her grandchildren.'

'Strange things, families,' he said, standing to pour her another drink.

'I shouldn't.'

'Against the cold,' he said as he handed her the glass. 'So what do you see in the fire?'

She smiled over the rim of her glass and he tried to imagine her as a child peering into the very same fire.

'A house on the side of a black mountain and a candle burning in every window. An inn where travellers call to break their journey. They keep the lights lit all night long. Can you see it?'

'I think so,' he answered, increasingly sure he could and conscious of a little shiver of sentiment washing over him. 'So she never came back when your mother was ill? Even at the end?'

'No, she wouldn't come.'

'That's a pity.' He imagined himself as a weary traveller, almost exhausted by his long journey, ready to give up the struggle, and then seeing the distant flicker of one of those lights. 'Family falling-outs can be very bitter things.'

'She wasn't really bitter – it was just she was never prepared to sacrifice anything of her own freedom or happiness for someone she didn't really love.'

'But duty, Miss Lewis, is an important thing,' he said, hearing a call to arms. 'We can't all just follow our own desires to the detriment of others.'

'I'm sure you're right, Mr Peel,' she said, but her tone was unconvinced. He tried to persuade her. 'We wouldn't have seen the children home this morning if we'd just concerned ourselves with our own interests. We wouldn't even have turned up at all.' An image of Miss Morgan, snuggling below her eiderdown sneaked past his defences but he banished it – this was not a time for self-indulgence.

They sat in silence again. They mightn't always show it but people were glad of those who made the effort to keep those lights at the windows. Without them there would be only darkness. In a little while she asked him again what he saw in the fire. It felt like a test and he wanted to rise to it but it was difficult because in reality he saw nothing at all. 'I see blue-topped mountains, mountains to be climbed. Tiny men roped together, having to trust one another.' And now he really could see it. Slippery lower slopes gave way to blue ice-faces and hidden chasms. Danger all around and only experience and a cool head could pull you through. The trouble was that his head didn't feel cool at all. It had started to whistle like a kettle and even now she was pouring him another drink.

'And your own family, Mr Peel, was it a happy one?'

'Yes,' he said, wondering if when the time came he would be one of those chosen to make the final attempt at the summit. 'My parents were quite strict in their religious views: I think my mother would have been happier to see me go into the ministry than teaching.' He sank back into the chair, hiding in case his late father looked down and saw him with a glass in his hand and the smell of whiskey on his breath. He rasped the back of his hand across his mouth and cringed with anger and shame as he thought of his father's buckled belt lathering into his bare legs as they tried to skip and high-step away from its swinging arcs. And after whatever sin he had committed had been purged, there were the interminable prayers to salve his soul while the skin on his legs still flared and burned. He felt his eyes moisten. He took a gulp of the whiskey, hoped its swirl and sear would cauterize the pain of memory. They wouldn't choose him to be one of the elite: he knew they wouldn't. Never in his life had he been the one chosen. Now time was running out. He had turned forty, and when he thought of the empty house that was his home he stared more deeply into the fire in the hope that he might see some better future.

The candles were burning down, the room more shadowy as each hour passed. He should have been on his way hours ago. He suspected Miss Lewis was a little tipsy. Sometimes she giggled at the things he said, sometimes she hummed a little tune to herself. She was humming now, her head moving in rhythm with the tune.

'You have a nice voice,' he said. 'Does it run in the family?'

'Florence had the musical talent. But then Florence was the one who seemed to have everything,' she said, and he thought her voice was edged with bitterness.

'You have a nice voice, too,' he repeated. 'Let me hear you sing.'

'I couldn't. I'm sure it's a very poor thing.'

'Nonsense,' he insisted. 'Just a little song and then I really must be on my way. I think I've overstayed my welcome.'

'No, you haven't at all. I'm sure it's been nice to have company.' Then she straightened her back and started to sing, softly at first so that he had to strain to hear but then her voice gradually rising until it started to skirmish with the shadows and fill the room. 'Speed, bonnie boat, like a bird on the wing . . .' He closed his eyes and let the song wash over him. Such a beautiful song, about a prince returning, or was it leaving? It didn't matter. Opening his eyes he saw her face transported by the music and her voice was so light and delicate that he wondered where she kept it hidden and her face, too, had changed, changed even though she still wore the black smudge on her cheek. It had sharpened into focus, had lost some of its flaccid lack of definition. When she finished he applauded gently and she fluttered her hands in the air in embarrassment and his gaze turned to the picture of the couple kissing and he was filled with remorse for having judged them so harshly.

He rose from the chair and reached for his coat. He had to go. He felt a little dizzy but he lumbered into the dark overcoat as he thanked her once again for her hospitality. They made their way carefully down the dolorous hall and she struggled with the door. He had to help her and their hands briefly skimmed against each other. When the door opened they both gasped at the sudden shock of snow that pelted against their faces and stretched before them like a terrible tundra.

'You can't go out in that, Mr Peel,' she declared with an insistence that he had never heard from her before. 'I would never forgive myself if something was to happen to you. It would be really dangerous to try to make it home in conditions like that. There's nothing else for it – you'll have to stay here.'

'I've been out in worse,' he said, 'but I did have the benefit of the right equipment. But I can't stay here – how would it look? You know how these things get out and misunderstood.'

'No one'll be any the wiser and you can head off early in the morning. I'll make up a bed for you on the settee. You'd be risking life and limb to venture out in that.' She shut the door and he offered no further opposition. Special circumstances. Relief rustled through him.

They went back to the living room and she drew the curtains. There wasn't much left of the candles. Taking one, she climbed the stairs, returning a few moments later with some blankets and a green quilt. 'I'll put some slack on the fire to keep it going, keep some heat in the room.' He nodded and felt embarrassed without fully knowing why. 'Will you be all right there, Mr Peel?' she asked, pointing to the settee. 'It might be a bit uncomfortable.'

'It'll be just fine. Don't forget you're talking to a man who's slept on a ridge strapped to the side of a cliff,' he said. She smiled and he was pleased.

'Goodnight, Mr Peel.'

'Goodnight. But my name's Terence. Call me Terry.'

'Call me Milly.'

'Goodnight, Milly.' The word tasted strange on his tongue.

'Goodnight, Terry.'

He sat on the end of the settee and felt the return of his sadness. In a few minutes the candle would flicker for the last time. Undressing to his vest and pants, he curled on the settee under the blankets and quilt. The blankets scratched his legs and he couldn't get his head comfortable no matter how hard he tried. After a while he got up and spread the blankets on the floor in front of the hearth, rolled his coat into a pillow and pulled the quilt over himself. His face was only a few feet from the smear of embers at the fire's base. He could hear the wind murmuring in the chimney in broken little sobs of air. He had started to feel sleepy. His thoughts turned to the couple above his head and he felt a voyeur of their passion, an intruder into their nightly privacy. Suddenly something touched him on the shoulder making him start. She was holding a pillow out to him. She had forgotten to give him one. He sat up.

'Thank you, Milly,' he said, reaching his hand into the shadows. She was wearing a dressing gown and as she bent down to him he glimpsed the white rise of her breasts. He thought for a second of the two snowballs that had curved through the air towards him. White as the snow and blue-tinged like ice. 'You're very kind.' She kneeled down at the side of the quilt. Flames pushed through a crack in the slack, illuminating the side of her face with its smudge still nestling on her cheek. He stretched out his hand to brush it off and as he did so she pressed her own hand against his as it settled on her skin. She hadn't understood. But special circumstances: the unexpected welcoming flicker of lights in distant windows, the promise of rest and shelter. Never in his life had he been so weary. He held out his thin, hairless arms and as she came towards him he repeated silently to himself the words that made everything all right: 'Against the cold. Against the cold.'

The Big Snow

EACH TIME THE OUTER door of the barracks opened, the draught made the fire smoke. It didn't matter how tightly they wedged the inner office door closed, or jammed the lock with cardboard, there was still a regular puff of grey smoke which seeped silently into the corners and crevices of the room. Spidery filaments of smut hovered and rested on the Coronation picture of the Queen above the fire, landed on the wooden cupboards and settled on the sagging tiers of fat-bellied, string-tied files. Some drifted aimlessly, then fell on the high table where fingerprints were taken, to disappear amidst the hundreds of smudged whorls. Some fell, too, on the large frame of the figure hunched over a typewriter and speckled the white shock of his hair or vanished into the dark wool of his suit. In another corner of the room the younger man looked up and fanned the air with his open book.

'Sergeant Gracey, do you think we should open the door and let some of this smoke out of the room?'

'What smoke's that, then, son?' Gracey said without looking

up. He narrowed his eyes in a little effort at concentration and pinged the keys with two fingers. 'I'll tell you what you can do, though, get your arse out round the back and get that coal bucket filled. And listen, let's make it your most important duty of the day to see it's never empty. I don't want caught out like we were in January. Two days without a soddin' piece – ended up having to burn whatever was in the lost property cupboard. And when you're going past the desk, ask Maguire if he's ordered some. Half the time I think he's wheeling it home to keep his ma warm.'

Swift stood up and went over to the bucket. He hesitated, watched as an inky mote landed on the soft brown hat sitting beside the typewriter, then asked, 'Do you think we'll be going out later?' As Gracey lifted his head for the first time to look at him, he added, 'I was just wondering, like.'

'What in the name of all that's holy would anyone want to go out in that weather for? Believe me, son, any criminal worth his salt is sitting beside the fire, same as we are. Just concentrate on keeping the coal bucket filled. And can't you see I'm trying to write this report – and making a pig's arse of it in triplicate. There's something wrong with the ribbon again. Listen, son, fill the bucket, help me type this thing and we'll take a spin out later. Now I can't say better than that.'

'Can I drive the car, Skipper?'

'Get that bucket filled and you're in with a chance. But stop calling me bloody "Skipper", son – a skipper is someone who sails a boat.'

As Swift left the room he almost collided with a man carrying a brown parcel under his arm. 'Watch where you're going, son,' the man said. 'And don't bring that bucket anywhere near this parcel.' Gracey nodded almost impercept- ibly at the new arrival, then bounced the keys of the typewriter with his fist, tore the page out and scrunched it into a ball.

'See you've got the lad doing something useful. How's he shapin' up?' the newcomer asked.

'Keen as mustard,' Gracey said. 'Put your head away havin' him hangin' on your shoulder all day. When he's not takin' notes he's readin' some book or other. Grammar-school boy he is. Doesn't know his arse from his elbow yet.'

'And will you be able to train him up? Will he make it in the end.'

'Probably will – I'll say whatever he wants just to get rid of him.'

The man set his parcel on the table, close to the typewriter, then moved it slightly as if worried about the possibility of damage. It was tied with string and neatly bowed in the middle.

'Found the Crown Jewels, then, have you?' Gracey asked, prompted by a desire to have the inevitable explanation over and done with, rather than by curiosity.

'Next best thing,' Burns said, lifting the parcel and carefully pulling the bow open. He whisked the brown paper away with the flourish of a magician doing a trick. Gracey stared impassively at the roll of green tweed that bounced on the table and said nothing. 'Well, what do you think of that?' Burns asked as he skimmed the cloth with his fingers.

'Very nice,' Gracey answered. 'So what's it for?'

'A suit – I'm going to get Nugent to run it up for me.'

'Where did you get it?

'Let's just say it was a thank you for services rendered,' Burns replied. 'Make a crackin' suit, that will.'

'Wear it any time you have to go up the Falls – the colour'll go down well.

'What do you mean? There's nothing wrong with the colour.'

'Never said there was,' Gracey answered, going over to the fire and spitting into the flames. There was a sudden sizzle and then the door opened and a lop-sided Swift struggled into the room with a full bucket of coal. Burns started to wrap the cloth, smoothing wrinkles in the paper with the palm of his hand.

'Get your coat, Swifty boy, we're going out,' Gracey said. 'Can't hang around here all day.' As Swift clanked the bucket to the floor, some of the top coals slipped over the rim but when he bent to retrieve them he heard Gracey say, 'Leave them, son, we don't have all day. Leave them.'

Swift hurried to grab his coat, stuffing his book in the jacket of his pocket. 'Reading your Sherlock Holmes again, son?' Burns asked, his tongue lolling out the corner of his mouth as he concentrated on tying the bow. Swift paused to answer, then saw Gracey's head beckoning him out of the room. He walked into the corridor where Gracey was brushing the smut from his hat and heard him say, 'Get Nugent to sew a bit of silk into the seat of the breeks, for there's nothing like tweed for itchin' the arse off you.' Then there was the slam of the door and the press of Gracey's large palm in the small of his back, pushing him forward.

Swift thought the car wasn't going to start at first and Gracey, sitting in the passenger seat, drummed his fingers on the dashboard in irritation. Much of what he did irritated Gracey and sometimes he brooded on his bad luck in being placed with someone who regarded him with at best indifference and at worst disdain. His awareness of those feelings in his mentor served to make him nervous, cack-handed, assume a clumsiness that was instinctively foreign to him. At first he had tried humour, then deference, but nothing he did was able to make any impact on the older man so now he had retreated into a kind of neutrality.

Gracey sat beside him but the bulk of the man seemed to fill the whole car. He had a habit of sitting slightly angled on the seat and holding the passenger strap as if bracing himself for a collision, and because he had pushed the seat back as far as it would go the few words he spoke always seemed to come from behind Swift's head. But for the moment he had nothing to say and when Swift asked for directions he was told just to drive.

It was almost Sunday-morning quiet, and through the windscreen of the car the world appeared sharp-angled and starkly defined by the cold. Those people who were on the road looked bent and diminished in their scurry to their destination. Swift thought of attempting conversation and sifted possible topics in his head but plumped for the safety of silence. But as the almost empty road unwound before him he drifted into imagination and played out sterling little scenarios of bravado, shaped by half-remembered snatches of films. When he felt Gracey's sudden prod in his ribs his first reaction was to blush as if he had been discovered in something shameful and it took him a second to absorb the fact that he was being told to slow down. When he glanced at Gracey he met his eyes staring at him, his head angled away from the road. 'Slow down, will you,' he hissed out of the narrow slit of his suddenly toothless mouth. 'See thon boy coming towards us? That's none other than Jackie Brown – must have just got out. The bastard! If there was any justice in this world they'd have thrown away the key on him long ago. Don't look at me, son, watch where he goes. Over my shoulder. I don't want the weasel to see me.'

Swift watched the tall, spindly figure pause to look in a shop window. He was wearing a leather jacket with the collar turned up and jeans. His hands were shoved into the pockets of the jacket, leaving his long arms sticking out like handles to his body. As they passed him, the man took out a cigarette packet and searched in his pockets for something to light it. Gracey was watching him in the wing mirror, the leather seat squirming and squeaking under the weight of his movements. 'Take the next left,' he said, pointing at it as if Swift might not see it, 'then turn back on the road and keep him in sight.' Swift felt a little rush of excitement and in his haste clanked the gears. When he turned into the side street a group of boys were playing football against the gable wall and he had to slow down. Gracey leaned across and pumped the horn, then rolled down the window and shouted for them to 'bugger off' before he had their names and the ball as well. As he reversed the car he rasped the gears again and Gracey looked at him with renewed exasperation. 'You wanted to drive the car, didn't you?' he asked. Swift didn't reply but concentrated on making the right turn. However, when they headed back down the road there was no sign of the man. Gracey spat out of the still open window.

'What was he in for?' Swift asked.

'Never bloody enough – he's a slippy bastard. Always squeezes himself to the edge of the frame. But nothing happens on this road without his hand being in it. He did the O'Kane job – they beat the old man to a pulp for a case of cheap watches and a few trinkets.'

'There he is,' said Swift, pointing him out as he left a shop with a paper under his arms.

'Going to pick his runners.' Gracey answered, peering at the man's back while he headed towards Madigan's bar. 'Obviously got some money already.'

Swift stopped the car round the corner from the pub as Gracey ordered, then watched him swivel sideways as he lifted himself slowly out of the car. He didn't know if he was supposed to stay or accompany him so he sat clutching the wheel with both his hands while he tried to make up his mind. 'Are you for sitting there, then, or you wantin' to learn about being a detective?' Gracey said, bending down so that he filled the whole of the open door. There was a thin wheeze lining his breathing as if the sudden burst of cold had tightened his throat. 'And don't forget to lock the doors – I'm not walking back in this weather.' Gracey was already pushing open the green-glassed door of the pub as he hurried to catch up. On impulse he grabbed the back of Gracey's coat. 'What are we doing? Are we going to arrest him?'

'Arrest him? How can you arrest someone who's just out of prison? We're going to do what you do in a pub – have a drink.'

Inside they were hit by the sudden mottled fug of cigarette smoke and the sweet stale smell of beer. The electric light seemed to oscillate with the swirl of the smoke and the light that filtered through the squares of coloured glass. Some heads turned slightly on their entry, then narrowed back to their drinks. Swift was aware of eyes watching them in the mirrors behind the bar and for the first time felt some comfort in the size of Gracey as they sidled into a corner booth and slid along the shiny smoothness of the wood.

'Well, as it looks like you're not goin' to offer, what'll you be havin'?'

'An orange juice please.'

'In the name of all that's holy, son, I can't be going up to the bar in a place like this and asking for an orange juice. Have a wee Bush with me.'

Swift hesitated and started to mumble something about being on duty but stopped when he saw the expression on Gracey's face.

'Listen, son, if it helps you, think of it this way. We're in disguise in a place of hardened drinkers, the only way we have to maintain our cover is to blend in. An orange juice would run the risk of blowing that and put our whole mission in jeopardy.'

'And what is our mission?' he asked.

'I need to have a wee word with Jackie boy, sort a few things out.'

'Wouldn't the station be a better place than this?'

'No, this place will do just fine, just fine. For sure, what's better than a quiet word over a friendly drink?'

He watched the broad stretch of Gracey's coat as he ambled to the bar, then tried to look nonchalant by running a hand through his hair and slumping back in the seat. He glanced round but couldn't see Brown. Perhaps he had already gone out after seeing them enter. At the bar Gracey was leaning over it, the way a farmer might drape himself over a gate. Swift could see in the mirror that Gracey was talking to the barman but getting only nods or a shake of the head in return, then while the barman turned to the optics Gracey turned sideways to peruse the bar, his white hair undimmed by the grainy striations of light. He had pushed a hand into his trouser pocket, revealing a glimpse of shirt and green braces under his opened coat and jacket.

Swift straightened as Gracey returned from the bar, the two small glasses almost lost inside the cup of his hands. 'Get that down you, boy, and chase some of this cold away,' Gracey said when he handed him the whiskey.

'I don't see Brown,' Swift said, staring at the glass in front of him.

'He's skulking over there in the snug,' Gracey answered, without lifting his head. He, too, stared at his drink but it was with an obvious sense of anticipation, an unwillingness to rush the pleasure. 'The best part of a drink – thinking about it,' he said, lifting the glass and holding it up to the grimed brush of light. Then just as he raised it to his lips his eyes angled across the bar and he set the glass down again.

'Listen, Swift, I'm going to the toilet to join Mr Brown in a leak. I want you to stand outside the door and not let anyone in. And if I want you to come in I'll shout for you. Have you got that?' Swift nodded and then in an afterthought asked what he should say if anyone wanted to use the toilet. 'Tell them it's broken, tell them it's a fruits' convention – tell them anything you like, but just make sure you do what you're supposed to.'

Gracey levered himself up from the bench by pressing both hands down on the table. As Swift went to follow he was told to wait a minute, enjoy some of his drink before he took up position, and while Gracey headed towards the toilet he took his first sip of the whiskey and felt its slow burn in his throat. He timed the minute on his watch, then walked as casually as he could towards the door. Sticking his hands in the pockets of his trousers the way he had seen Gracey do, he fluffed out the sides of his coat in the hope that it made him seem broader. There were heads along the bar turned towards him and he half whistled a thin little stream of air in response, then inspected the nails on his right hand. Already he had heard the first shout but he wasn't sure if it had been Gracey's or Brown's because it had been shrill and twisted out of shape by the fierce force that drove it. It was followed by banging and the clatter and scuffle of feet. There was a scream of swearing and more banging, loud enough for everyone in the bar to hear, and what must be Brown's voice shouting a tangled string of obscenities that rose and fell on an ebb and flow of sudden pain. Swift glanced at the door, shuffled his feet and folded, then unfolded, his arms. He was aware of a man coming towards him and he squared himself while stroking his chin with his fingers. He needed a shave. The man went to walk round him without acknowledging his presence until forced to by Swift's outstretched arm.

'Is it against the law now to have a slash?' the man sneered.

'You'll have to wait,' Swift said, tasting the whiskey on his breath and wishing it was courage.

'What right have you to come in here throwing your weight about?' the man asked, assuming a bristling aggression, but Swift could tell that whatever violence the man could muster would be confined to his words and the knowledge gave him confidence. There was another stream of strangled abuse from behind the door.

'Nobody's throwing their weight around – Mr Gracey's just having a friendly word. He'll be finished any second now and then you can slash to your heart's content.'

'It doesn't sound too friendly to me,' the man said, screwing up his eyes and angling his head to one side, 'and if our Jackie gets hurt you're in big trouble.' He tried to push past Swift but it was half-hearted and easily repulsed. But over his shoulder he could see two other men getting up from their seats – he wasn't sure, but he thought one of them had lifted a bottle off the bar. A sudden image of an old man's face beaten to a pulp shuddered against his senses.

'Listen, friend,' he said, inflating and edging his voice, 'in case you don't know, Detective Sergeant Gracey's a man who doesn't like being interrupted in the line of his duty and he'd take it poorly, very poorly indeed. Now go back and sit down and keep your nose out of what doesn't concern you.' He saw the two men hesitate, before taking their seats again. The man closest to him stepped backwards and leaned against the bar, only his head jutting out and jerking towards him. He had done what Gracey had told him – he had kept his end up – but now he looked at the door behind him with rising impatience. There was the sound of a door being slammed inside and a muffled thud. Perhaps something had gone wrong, perhaps Gracey needed help. He hesitated. Everyone was looking at him. He turned and edged the swing door open with the outside of his left foot until there was a gap of about nine inches. Through the gap he saw Brown on his knees, his long thin fingers holding on to the rim of the wash basin, an open razor glinting like a grin in the grime of the floor, and his eyes fixed on Gracey staring back at him as he raised his wooden truncheon high in the air above his head, then without breaking their locked gaze brought it drumming down on Brown's hand. Swift moved his foot but before the door could slip closed he heard the breaking of bones, the split of enamel and a scream that sounded like a wounded animal. A sour whiskey sickness surged in his throat as Gracey came through the door cleaning his hands elaborately with a white sail of a handkerchief.

'I told you not to come in,' he muttered from the corner of his mouth. A silver strand of hair had fallen forward across his brow and he smoothed it back into place. Without looking round Swift knew someone was going into the toilet, but Gracey seemed in no hurry and as they passed their table he was grabbed by the shoulder. 'Never waste a good drink,' he said and, lifting his glass in a salute to the eyes giving him their hate, threw the contents to the back of his throat, then wiped his mouth with the back of his hand.

'I told you not to come in,' he said again as the car moved off.

'I thought you might need help,' he answered.

There was no answer, just a slow, throaty laugh that seemed

to come from behind his head and rolled round the inside of the car like the dankest of fogs.

That night as Swift lay in his iron-framed bed in the cavernous barracks and finished his crossword, he tried not to think of what he had seen. He took comfort in the way his mind could unravel the cryptic clues, the anagrams. That was what it should be like. Thinking. Solving clues, seeing the connection between things – how they fitted together. Joining small parts together to complete the full picture. That would be the future. The likes of Gracey were dinosaurs, headed for extinction. He tried to hold on to that idea as he pulled the sheets and blankets around him more tightly and squirmed in search of a pocket of warmth. Then he closed his eyes and hoped that dreams were silent.

It was after nine and there was still no sign of Gracey. The first burst of snow had fallen through the night and it was being reinforced by fresh falls. In the Detective Sergeant's office the fire had been lit but there was little sign of life about it. Swift sat down at the typewriter and started to type the report Gracey had left for him. He found some pleasure in correcting the spelling mistakes and unravelling the confusing knots of sentences that spewed across the page in copperplate. It began with the required 'I beg permission to report . . .' and continued in a deferential voice that bore no resemblance to the writer's own. Swift drew consolation from the fact that the awkward expression made Gracey seem smaller, less at ease with the world, less sure of himself. He conjured an image of Gracey raising his bulk on to his toes and gingerly taking tentative, diminutive steps across the thin ice of words. For a second he thought of inserting something ludicrous in the report, but contented himself with the pleasure of the idea.

Gracey didn't trust him to do anything right and that included typing a report, so he was bound to check it.

When he was finished he went out to the main desk. Maguire was writing up something in a ledger. 'Nothing happening?' Swift asked. Maguire didn't lift his head as he said no. Swift swivelled the Occurrence Book towards him and scanned the events of the night. A drunk and disorderly, a minor collision between a car and a cyclist, a missing dog. Not much more. His eye caught an entry at the bottom of the page. Maguire saw him looking at it. 'Don't ask me what that's all about. Forsyth found this old biddy wandering the streets in a wedding dress – in her bare feet and all. Off her head. To get her in the car they had to tell her they were taking her to the church.' Swift righted the book and looked at the front doors of the barracks as if inviting a customer. Suddenly both doors bumped open and the front wheel of a bicycle appeared, followed a few seconds later by the rest of the bike and the snow-spattered bulk of Gracey. There was a rim of snow on the top of his hat like icing on the top of a bun. Maguire and Swift smiled instinctively, then blanked it out as Gracey looked up at them. His face was red and shiny with water, and the dark weft of his overcoat was spangled and starred by snow. His shoulders wore white epaulettes as if he had been enlisted in some army.

'Is it still snowing, then, Sergeant Gracey?' Maguire asked.

Swift tried to stifle his snigger as Gracey quivered like a huge jelly and shook the snow from his shoulders.

'You're wasted behind that desk – it's the bloody head of Detectives you should be with a sharp mind like that,' Gracey said as he took out his handkerchief and dried his face. 'Bloody snow – it's comin' down in buckets. Detective Constable Swift, don't stand there with your two arms the same length, take charge of this bike and get it dried off.'

'The bike should be in the yard,' Maguire said while he stared at the dark patches forming on the wooden floor. 'Regulations.'

'Bugger off,' Gracey said, still drying his face. It had started to shine like the skin on a fresh red apple. 'I'm not leaving it outside in that, the saddle's already soakin'. Swift, stick it down the corridor near the store.'

The metal of the bicycle was cold against Swift's skin and as he wheeled it he left a thin snail-trail of damp across the uneven boards. Big as the bike was, Swift struggled to imagine it bearing the weight of Gracey. When he returned to the office Gracey was drying his backside against the fire. Snaking little tendrils of steam rose up from the cloth. His soft hat had changed from its normal brown to black. 'Soddin' snow,' Gracey repeated to himself. 'Did you rub that bike dry? I don't want it rustin' to hell.' Swift nodded. As the damp burning smell of Gracey's clothes leached into the room his own spirits sank. Gracey was in a foul mood: he would hardly want to stir out of the barracks unless it was an absolute necessity, and that created the prospect of a long and unpromising day. He tried to think of a possible route of escape but he was too tied to Gracey's direction to act independently. Without being told, he went to get two mugs of tea.

When he returned, Gracey was standing reading his report. He saw him glance at him. 'You're a bright boy with words, all right. I'll give you that.' He looked at the report again. 'Do you never think you might be better off pushing a pen somewhere? Some nice office job with sensible hours – that sort of thing.' For a second he thought of telling Gracey how much like his parents he sounded but instead he shook his head and handed over a mug of tea. 'Two sugars?' Gracey asked before he started to drink.

Outside at the desk the phone was ringing. Gracey made a disparaging remark about the fire as some snow came down the chimney and made the coal hiss. A few minutes later Maguire came into the room with a scrap of paper in his hand. 'There's some woman just off the phone, says she's worried about the girl next door to her. There was some shouting during the night and she sees no sign of her this morning. The woman's cat's sitting on the window ledge lookin' in.'

'In the name of God, you don't expect me to be headin' out in a blizzard because some cat's lookin' in from the cold,' Gracey said, stamping his feet on the floor. Maguire shrugged indifferently, and for a second it looked as if he might crumple the paper and throw it into the fire.

'I could do with a walk out,' Swift said, stretching his hand out for it. 'If you don't need me here, can I take a look, Sarge?'

'Didn't know you were an animal lover,' Gracey said, turning his face to the fire. 'Go if you want but you'll need a bloody pair of snowshoes.'

Swift nodded his gratitude and scampered out of the room before there was a change of mind. The address was a couple of miles away and he decided to walk rather than take a bicycle. Maguire got a pair of wellingtons for him from the store. They were a size too big but it was the best on offer. 'If you're not back in a couple of hours I'll send out the huskies,' Maguire said as he watched Swift head out through the doors.

There was a lull in the snow but already it was lying thickly on the roads and pavements. He held his head up and felt the joy of the coldness on his face. He kicked up little flurries of snow like a schoolboy and took pleasure from those moments when his footprints were the first to press on a virgin stretch of pavement. Sometimes he glanced behind at his crinkled and ribbed trail. The boots were uncomfortable and he hoped he wouldn't have to run. As he walked one of his socks slipped down and once he stopped and, holding on to railings, hoisted it up.

But when he got closer to the street his spirits sagged a little. It was probably a domestic dispute, and experience painted an unfolding scene in which a woman with a split lip or a blackening eye would cry, then tell him that it was out of character and the neighbours had no business sticking their noses in. If the husband was there, and mostly they weren't, he'd be either a sullen silence in the corner of the room or else a sobbing repentant, making a welter of promises. He didn't know which was worse. And they'd look at him with his boyish face and think of him as a double outsider; someone who came from another class and so didn't know what it was to live in the ordained mesh of their lives; and someone unmarried and ignorant of the eternal conflict that raged inside every attempt of men and women to live together. Then he'd confirm their evaluation by uttering some platitude, some patronizing little homily. For a second he wondered if Gracey wasn't right after all and imagined himself taking the man out into the yard and grabbing him by the throat, or somewhere worse, then threatening him with a slew of curses and an 'If you ever lay another finger . . .'

He checked the number of the caller's house against the piece of paper. The rustling curtain confirmed it was the right one. It was a mid-terrace house, solid and dignified, with a name plaque that said 'Bethany'. Even the imposition of the snow's uniformity couldn't prevent the house proclaiming its pride in its respectability. She had the door open for him before he had pushed the gate through the resistance of snow. A smallish woman with auburn hair pinned up in a bun and held with black metal clips Her pink framed glasses with thick lenses made her eyes seem large and milky.

'Mrs Graham?' he asked, smiling at her.

'That's right,' she said, staring at him but not returning his smile.

'I'm Detective Constable Swift.'

'You don't have a uniform,' she said, inspecting his face.

'That's because I'm a detective. You phoned the barracks earlier. About your next-door neighbour.' This wasn't going to be easy. For a second he thought almost affectionately about the office back at the barracks.

'You look a bit young to be a detective,' she said.

'I'm still training,' he answered, 'but I am a detective. Now, would you like to tell me what the problem is?'

The woman told him to come in but her swimming milky eyes watched him with suspicion as he knocked the snow from his boots. He thought of taking them off but decided there would be no dignity in interviewing her in his socks. Once inside he talked about the snow and tried to set her at ease. But his heart dropped again when with no warning she quoted the Bible at him. 'Though your sins be as scarlet they shall be white as snow,' she said, smiling. He smiled back and nodded, repeating 'white as snow'.

'So, Mrs Graham, you're worried about something – your next-door neighbour. What's her name?' he asked.

'Calls herself Simons, Mrs Simons,' the woman sniffed, 'but she doesn't wear a wedding ring and as far as I can see there isn't a Mr Simons. There's men all right, but they come and go. Who knows what's what?'

Swift watched her tighten and squirm a little on the chair as if she felt the repugnance of her own words. Her mouth was a tight little purse untouched by lipstick or colour and out of its meanness slipped the kind of statements that told him he had met the type before. God-fearing, people-hating, confirmed in the knowledge of their election by something more primitive than Swift cared to think about. And if they didn't break temporal laws, he always felt it was against something deeper, something essentially profound, that they transgressed. He wanted to get the business done as quickly as possible and be back out in the unfettered freedom of the snow.

'So you heard voices arguing last night,' he said, wondering what other voices this woman heard on a nightly basis.

'There's always noise, never a moment's peace and quiet since she moved in, what with her music and television going at all hours and comings and goings. I'm not a person to complain or pass judgment but sometimes you have to wonder about it all.'

Swift could imagine the hours of vicarious pleasure it must have provided, but he resisted the temptation to smile and asked her why she was concerned on this particular morning.

'Well, there's been no sign or sound of her all morning and she's hardly likely to've gone out on a morning like this. And, well I'm not exactly sure but I thought I heard a bit of a fight going on – shouting and the like. You wouldn't believe the language comes through those walls sometimes, and out of a woman's mouth as well. Her cat's been squealing to get in all morning – she always brings it in, sometimes before she's even half dressed.'

'Might she not just be having a lie-in?' he ventured.

'Could be, she doesn't live like the likes of us.'

Swift shifted on the seat and felt uncomfortable at being so quickly assimilated into this woman's world. He wondered why it seemed to happen so readily in relation to worlds to which he didn't aspire and so tardily to those to which he did.

He glanced towards the snow-spotted window and felt a vague sense of being an outsider, without fully understanding what it was kept him outside.

It wasn't a very complicated business and he was glad that he didn't need to sit any longer, breathing in the stuffy vapours of the room. Something about it reminded him of the wardrobe in his mother's bedroom. The same smell of must, the feeling of shadow and of clothes that would never see the light of day. He had wanted to clear it after her death but his father had reacted with horror, as if he had proposed something obscene. So it was allowed to sit untouched like a mausoleum, its double doors with their swirls of walnut inlay permanently sealing the silent decay within. He stood up and thanked the woman for her time and concern. He'd go next door and check that everything was all right, then come back and let her know. Probably nothing to worry about, but he'd check it out just to put her mind at rest.

Outside the snow was falling in lazy spirals of puffy flakes, like drawings done by children. The flakes looked so big he felt that if he was to stretch out his hand and catch one it would reveal its inner structure complete, like the photographs he had once seen. Mrs Graham came to watch as he stepped over her little fence and went next door. There was no gate to negotiate, and as he walked the few steps to the front door he saw that all the curtains were drawn, but through the thinness of those in the front room he could see that the light was on. He was aware of Mrs Graham watching from her doorway and was glad the snow had prevented her from coming out. There was no answer to his ring or heavy rattle. Standing back from the step he called out the woman's name and watched the upstairs window for response. When none came he walked to the end of the street and down the entry that ran behind the row of houses. For a few moments he was unsure which was the back of the house until he saw a number painted on a door. The entry was an undisturbed trench of snow, a valley formed by the brick on either side. Already the top of the walls had started to scab and blister in white.

He double checked it was the right door and got himself ready to shin over the wall and into the yard, before, as a kind of afterthought, he pushed the wooden door and found only the resistance of snow. A couple of shoves with his shoulder opened it wide enough to slip sideways through. There was a light in the kitchen and on the window ledge a black cat whined and squirmed against the glass. It paused to look at him with its green eyes before returning to its self-pity. Through the window he saw a narrow kitchen but no sign of anyone. He knocked on the back door and called her name without response and as he looked up at the back window the snow feathered his eyebrows and trickled down his face. He wondered if his luck could be in twice and tried the handle of the door. It turned smoothly and cleanly. His new shout echoed through the house and returned to him unheeded, and as a whisper of snow sidled into the kitchen behind him he pulled the door behind him.

In the sink was a clatter of unwashed plates and there was a bundled pyramid of what looked like unwashed clothes in a basin. A hybrid smell of stale food and kitchen drains, mixed through with cigarette smoke and sickly perfume, laced the air. It seemed intense after the clean blankness of the outside world. His boots dripped water on the linoleum when he moved tentatively towards the hall, his sense of intrusion into somebody's home making him call out again. There was a phone on a glass-topped hall table and a brown carpet with a swirl of yellow flowers. The entrance to the living room was close to the front door and as he glanced up the stairs he called again to dispel his sudden nervousness.

The living-room door was partly open and as he paused before entering he could see a television set in the corner and a radiogram with its lid open. He knocked on the door and when he entered, the first face he saw was his own, in the winged mirror that hung above the fireplace. She was lying on the blue vinyl settee in a black satin-style dressing gown, her head hanging backwards over the padded end, her open bulging eyes staring at the ceiling. He didn't move. For a second he looked again at his reflection in the mirror as if to confirm that he was really there in this room, really there in this moment. He was glad he didn't need to touch her to know she was dead. Already he had seen the belt, probably from her own gown, that had been twisted round her neck and choked the life out of her. But it wasn't that, or even the sliver of tongue lolling from her blue bruised face – it was the frozen frenzy of her body. No living thing could have maintained that terrible posture, in which every sinew was tensed and twisted into a ferocious resistance of what sought to choke the life out of her, squeeze by squeeze. She hadn't been a ready victim. He knew that by what he saw. Her legs were wide apart – the one jutting off the settee had been used as a lever in an attempt to throw off whoever pushed on top of her, the other was bent at the knee, with the foot jammed partly down the gap between the white buttoned cushion seat and the settee's back.

He stepped closer to her, smelt the scent again, the dark stain of her urine and something else he didn't know the name of. His brain was racing now, desperately trying to stop his slide into panic. He had to think. He had to think calmly. There was a sudden tumble of sickness in his stomach. He spun round, letting out an involuntary shout as he did so, aware of movement behind him, his arms instinctively rising to protect his face. The cat jumped onto the settee, its slinking blackness giving a momentary illusion of movement to the body lying there. He grabbed it and lifted it away while he tried frantically to remember the schools of instruction, to turn the pages of the training books that before this moment he could almost quote. Behind the blur of his confusion and the in-rushing flow of extraneous and irrelevant images he struggled to fasten on to what precepts he could remember. He had to preserve and protect the scene – that was the priority – preserve the crime scene intact. The cat's body was warm and pulsing between his hands as he carried it to the kitchen door, which he hadn't closed properly. Thin fringes of snow had filtered in through the open door. Conscious for the first time of fingerprints and unable to remember what he had and hadn't touched, he slipped the cat into the entry and closed the door with his shoulder in the middle of the wood.

He didn't want to go back inside the house. The newly whitened world held itself unsullied and pure. He didn't want to exchange it for the smell of the house, the sight of her face bruised dark and dinged like the damaged skin of a plum or rancid fruit. It felt as if life was laughing at him. Wasn't this what he wanted, wasn't this the very thing for which he had been desperate? Something for him to pit his wits against, something to bring thought to, the search for clues, the construction of the final picture. He hesitated at the kitchen door, then went to the corner of the yard and was sick, hiding the traces under kicked-over snow and wiping his mouth with a fresh handful which burned his hand with its coldness.

As he stepped back into the kitchen the silence of the house seemed to press down heavily on him, making him intensely aware of the rustle of his clothing, the murmur of his breathing. He stopped stock still at the end of the hall – he had been a fool, a complete fool. For all he knew the murderer was still in the house – he hadn't checked anywhere and he imagined the danger that might lurk inside. The taste of his sickness was still in his throat. His issue Webley was back in the barracks – Gracey had already made clear his disdain for firearms, calling them toys for little boys – and now he felt naked and vulnerable. There was a tray of cutlery on one of the boards and momentarily indifferent to fingerprints he lifted a bread knife and held it in front of himself as he moved slowly down the hall. He prodded the coats hanging under the stairs, separating their lifeless forms with the blade of the knife, then moved to the foot of the stairs. As he hesitated he shouted out, 'This is the police. Is there anyone there?' and immediately felt the foolishness of his action.

However, when he climbed the stairs he strained his full weight into the squeaking boards and kept the knife at full arm's length in front of him as if he was shining a torch into his fear. There were two rooms and a bathroom. The box room was empty except for a few off-cuts of carpet and cardboard boxes. The bathroom was tiny, incapable of affording a hiding place, and decorated in pink and purple that jarred his senses. He turned to the remaining room, where he found only an undisturbed bed, a dresser and a skinny wardrobe which he opened with the knife still stretched in front of him. Now he needed to phone the barracks, but going back down the stairs he first went to the kitchen and pushed the knife to the bottom of the cutlery pile. He thought he should use the phone next door but couldn't bring himself to report it with the woman listening to every word, so, taking out his handkerchief, he lifted the receiver by the mouthpiece. It was Gracey he asked for and after what seemed a long delay he heard the familiar thin wheeze of laboured breathing and his initial irritation at being disturbed.

'A woman murdered?' Gracey said, the disbelief in his voice barely disguised. 'Are you pulling my leg, son? You just went out for a wee walk and you're telling me you've got a woman murdered? We had one six months ago – we're not due one for a good while yet.'

'She's dead and unless she choked herself, then someone murdered her,' Swift said, no longer prepared to hide his own impatience.

'Right, then, we better take a look at this murdered woman of yours. We'll be over in few minutes. God in heaven, it's not still snowing is it? Where did you say the house was?'

All Swift had to do now was sit and wait. He thought of starting to look for evidence. For clues. But the tautened, twisted presence of the woman's body seemed to drain his will and overpower any inner energy he could muster, and so he slumped into the armchair facing her and did nothing but wait for Gracey and the others. At first he tried not to look, but then he found himself glancing furtively at her, as if her eyes might suddenly meet his and rebuke his intrusive gaze. She was probably in her early thirties and her face had once been pretty. Her hair was too black to be completely natural, and her fingernails and toenails were painted the same strong red. Maybe he should have closed her eyes, ended that fierce scream of a stare, but he couldn't bring himself to touch the body and so he stayed slumped in the chair.

He tried to pull himself together before Gracey arrived. It wasn't as if it was the first dead body he had seen – there was the man who'd had a heart attack at work, the old woman they'd found dead in her bed, and there was the boy. He didn't like to think of the boy, for the image never lost its power to gnaw at his insides, quivering away like the oily slime of water they'd pulled him from. He hadn't been so old himself – it was his first month in his first posting and the boy had been missing for three days when they found him. Four years old and no bigger it seemed than a big fish as he helped the boy's uncle haul him from the Lagan. Twigs and scummy green trails of plants trailing from his hair, the print of his face smeared and running like a piece of paper crumpled and blotched by incessant rain.

Swift stood up and wiped the back of his hand across his mouth. He thought of going outside and being sick again but was afraid that Gracey would discover him. He tried to kick himself into gear. Keeping busy – that was the best course. Start with the easy things, like who she was. There was a bill on the fireplace for coal which gave her name as Mrs Alma Simons, but no personal correspondence. He looked around the room, tried to take it in, aware as he did so of his distaste for what he saw. There was a sheen of vulgarity that seemed to coat everything, a cheap sentimentality that had prompted the choice of every object. And everything looked new, from the shiny blue vinyl suite to the sideboard and the radiogram. He went and looked at the record on the turntable – it was 'Lovesick Blues' by Frank Ifield – and then at the dozen or so other records that nestled in what looked like a giant toast rack. There was an LP by Alma Cogan: he wondered if she had bought it because of their shared name. He glanced at her and thought that she looked a little like the singer. It suddenly dawned on him that there would be next-of-kin to find and inform, then he hoped to God he wouldn't get the job as he remembered with a shiver the look in the mother's eyes after he'd helped pull her son from the river. During those days he was missing she had held on to the hope that a miracle might happen, that if she prayed hard enough, life might give her some reprieve. He had felt the hatred, the anger in her eyes while he stood taking that hope away with his fumbling, clumsy words. She had tried to hold the child in her arms, as if the slow, rocking cradle of her love might coax him back to life.

He stood at the end of the settee and forced himself to look. From there he could see the dark triangle of her hair and then he moved her dressing gown slightly to cover it. It was all he could give her now, all he could allow her before the others arrived. Two of her nails were broken, probably against the face of her killer. There were no other signs of struggle in the room – it looked as if all the violence had taken place on the settee – and there was nothing to suggest that robbery was the motive. He scouted round the carpet, the hall and the kitchen but there was nothing that revealed any trace of whoever else had been in the house. There were lots of questions he wanted to ask Mrs Graham but they would have to wait – he couldn't leave the body – so he slumped back into the armchair and waited for Gracey. A song filtered into his head, the tune only half remembered – it was from a long time ago. By Alma Cogan. He thought it was called 'Sugartime'. He tried to recall the words but they had faded into the past and couldn't be recalled.

He had expected that the sound of the car would indicate Gracey's arrival so when the front door was suddenly knocked he jumped from the seat and stared through the frosted glass before opening it. Gracey almost pushed past him in his hurry to get inside, followed a few steps behind by Burns. A uniformed constable took up position at the door.

'We had to leave the bastard car at the end of the street,' Burns said. 'It's snowing like there's no tomorrow.'

Gracey threw a brief glance at the corpse, then collapsed into the armchair Swift had been sitting in. He bent over, taking his hat off to reveal the white hair that looked as if he had brought a fall of snow into the room, and started to remove his rubber boots.

'Me feet are wringin',' he said. 'The snow came over the top of them – it's bloody waders you need on a day like this.' He started to shake snow from them and wriggle his toes. 'Put the kettle on, Swifty, and brew up – we need some heat in this place.'

As he went to the kitchen he watched Burns walking round the settee as if weighing up what he saw, the way a golfer might measure up a putt. 'Well?' asked Gracey. 'She's definitely dead,' Burns said, 'no doubt about it. And if you ask me, young Swift's theory about this being a murder enquiry might just be spot on.'

'Do you hear that, son?' Gracey shouted into the kitchen, 'All those books you've been reading must be paying off.'

While he looked for matches to light the gas, Swift heard the two men laugh. He stayed in the kitchen until the tea was made, then carried the cups through. Gracey asked if he had remembered the sugar. The two men slurped the tea and Burns complimented him on its quality. After a few moments Gracey set his tea on the hearth and, looking about him, asked him what he knew. After he listened to the little that he had to offer, he nodded as if satisfied, stood up, still in his socks, and perused the corpse. Burns came and stood at Gracey's shoulder, the smaller man like a mahout with his elephant. Gracey lifted the covering of her dressing gown from where Swift had placed it and asked Burns what he thought.

'Unless Detective Constable Swift took advantage of the situation to have sex with this unfortunate woman, I'd say the murderer did the business shortly before he killed her,' Burns said.

'Not a bad-looking lass, either,' Gracey said. He opened the gown higher up partially revealing the white swell of her breast, then went back to his chair and lifted the cup of tea. 'While we're waiting for the doctor and the photographer, go next door, Burnsy, and get all the gen. Comin's and goin's etcetera. Get a full statement.' After Burns had left, Swift mentioned the broken fingernails but Gracey's only response was to lift up his cup and stare at the writing on its base. Without taking his eyes from it, he said, 'Listen, Swift, this is a good opportunity for you to learn things but before we start you need to clear out all that gibberish swimming round that head of yours. So do me a favour and don't be running round here sniffin' for clues like a bloodhound. Clues are what you get in books, or those bloody stupid films they show on television. Listen while I tell you how we'll catch the boy that done this. It's not very complicated, so grab a hold of it. This is called, as I'm sure you know, a crime of passion – there's no forced entry, apart from maybe the one Burns referred to, there's nothing stolen – so that narrows the field nicely. All we need to find is the person who felt passionate enough about her to do this. That shouldn't be too hard, when if what you say is right, her next-door neighbour is God's accountant, keeping careful mental record of everything that goes on in here. And when we find him we squeeze his balls until he coughs and signs on the dotted line.'

When he had finished speaking, Gracey started to massage his feet, then stamped them on the carpet in a silent tap dance. 'I'm liable to get my death of cold out of this,' he said. 'The girl's face is familiar to me. Can't think where. She looks a bit tarty – maybe there'll be more than one sniffin' round her.

Wonder if her name's really Alma? The wife was always fond of her – Alma Cogan. Used to play that song all the time – what was it called? – 'Dreamboat', that was it. Hell of a lot better than what they're churning out now.'

Swift didn't reply but stood in the doorway watching Gracey. Sometimes he glanced up and caught his own reflection in the mirror, but when he did he looked away quickly.

'The cat bit your tongue?' Gracey asked, turning his head to stare at him. 'Don't be paying any heed to Burnsy – he doesn't mean anything, like; just a bit of fun, that's all. When he first started, he got some stick I can tell you. And if you think you're hard done to, spare a thought for Johnston out there. By the time we've finished he'll be lookin' like the abominable snowman. Any more tea left in that pot?' Swift shook his head, even though he knew there was. 'Aye and one other thing, soon there'll be reporters round here like flies round shite. Under no circumstances are you to tell them anything. Got that?' Swift nodded. 'And listen, while we're waitin' for the photographs and the doctor to tell us she's dead, take a quick reccy and see if you can find an address book, phone numbers – that sort of thing.'

'What about fingerprints?' Swift asked.

'Forget the fingerprints. Forget all that sweety mice stuff about clues. All we're lookin' for is a name. Just a name, that's all we need.' Swift opened the sideboard drawers and started to rummage in the clutter. 'And another thing, we need a next of kin – presumably a Mr Simons. If he isn't the bugger that done her in.'

'There were no men's clothes in the wardrobe or bedroom. No shaving stuff or anything in the bathroom.' Swift said.

'So then, maybe there isn't a Mr Simons after all. She's not wearing a wedding ring, either.'

Out by the phone he found a tiny piece of card with the words 'Dad's work' and a number. As he looked in vain for others he heard Gracey say, 'The boy Beckett who does the snaps is a great character – he has a collection of shots from all the cases he's ever done. Get him to show you them some time but on an empty stomach, for some would make your hair curl. That's for sure. And he does homers, too, so any time you need a family photograph or something like that give him a shout. But then you're not married, are you, son?' Swift dialled the number. Before he had finished Gracey was standing at his elbow. 'You're not goin' to tell them on the phone – you can't tell someone something like this over the phone,' he said taking the scrap of paper from his hand.

'I wasn't going to,' Swift said. 'I was just finding out where it is.'

'Right, right,' said Gracey. 'And if it's her da, we need him to identify the body.'

'Does he have to see her like this?' Swift asked.

'No, by then we'll have her down the morgue. Cleaned up a bit.'

Someone answered the phone. It was a factory on the Castlereagh Road. Swift asked to speak to a manager. As he waited he realized that if Simons was her married name they wouldn't know the man he was looking for, but he took a chance and asked if they employed a Mr Simons. After a few moments it was confirmed that a Thomas Simons worked in the stores. It seemed they were in luck. But luck wasn't the right word, for Swift suspected already that Gracey wanted him to collect the man and take him to the morgue. 'No rush, son,' Gracey said, 'Still work to do here.' But despite his talk of work he remained anchored to the chair, his open coat flapping over the armrests and hiding most of it, so that it looked as if what supported him was his own weight.

In a few moments Burns returned with his notebook in his hand and a pencil stuck behind his ear. 'I drew the short straw there,' he said, 'for we're all livin' in the last days and our friend's demise is just a sign that the trumpet's about to blow. But I think we're in clover for she says since the woman moved in about six months ago there's been plenty of goings-on – cars arrivin' at all hours, that sort of thing – and in particular a fella, youngish with black hair – looks a bit of a Teddy boy – comes a lot in a taxi. Stays over. Leaves in the morning.'

'He'll be the one, then,' Gracey said, as he started to put on his boots. 'Get Anderson and Ripley to check taxi firms if they remember bringin' someone to this address on a regular basis. Where they pick him up. If they need more help, get them to see the desk sergeant. Overtime if we need it.'

Swift rummaged again in the drawers but there was little that was personal. No address book, no photographs, just a couple of letters from a girlfriend working as a waitress in Liverpool. The contents of the house had a feeling of newness, of being recently chosen, but there were no receipts or hire-purchase agreements, nothing official or written. In her purse was a small amount of money and a photograph of presumably her as a small child. On the back was an address. Swift glanced to where Gracey and Burns were sitting and slipped the photograph into his pocket.

After the doctor had come and gone the photographer arrived holding two wooden boxes by their leather handles. He was a small man and the felt hat he wore seemed too big for his head. The brim was curling and would have given it the look of a sombrero if it hadn't been for the white braiding of snow. He joked with Gracey and Burns while he set up his equipment and loaded the flashes, but after a few moments they moved into the kitchen to escape the endless acrid splurge of light. Swift watched him do the angles, listened to his inane commentary about the snow and the difficulty of reaching the scene, then turned his back slightly and looked at the photograph. The girl was maybe about ten years of age and on a swing. Smiling as her momentum carried her backwards, her legs tight together pushing the air, her arms stretched above her head and holding the chains. As he pocketed it again he turned to see Beckett carefully opening the front of her gown to expose one of her breasts. When he saw Swift staring at him, he raised the camera to his face as he said, 'For the catalogue. Nothing personal.' Swift didn't reply but left the room.

In the kitchen he asked Gracey if he could go and was told to phone for a car to collect Simons. 'Meet him at the morgue down at the Sand Quay,' said Gracey, 'We'll have her sent over there shortly. You take the car, then go back to the barracks afterwards.' When he opened the front door he met the snow-striped shape of Johnston huddled on the doorstep. 'Bloody hell, how much longer is it goin' to take?' he asked. 'It's brass monkeys out here. I'll be gettin' bleedin' frostbite if I'm here much longer.' 'Not much longer now,' said Swift, 'they're just waiting for Beckett to finish.' 'It'll be me needin' a doctor soon,' moaned Johnston, then he clapped his hands in an attempt to put some warmth into them and expel his exasperation. When Swift set off to find the car it struck him that given the choice he would readily have swopped jobs.

When he found the car it was a hump of white and he had to clear the windscreen, using his arms like giant wipers to scoop away great crusts of snow. As he got inside it felt like entering an igloo and a powder of snow followed him when he closed the door. He had never driven a car in snow before, and he didn't like it. Although on the pavements it was a couple of feet deep, there was a narrowing channel down the middle of the road where the wheels of cars and lorries had compressed tracks but if the snow continued to fall, even this would disappear. The car felt unbearably light to his touch as if at any moment it might slide one way or the other. He drove very slowly, avoiding using the brakes as far as possible. At intervals he passed cars parked at crazy angles or abandoned. There was an empty bus skewed into a drifting bank of snow, and before very long it was obvious that he wasn't going to be able to complete the journey by car. But he stayed with it as long as possible, then parked close to where he thought the kerb was and set out on foot. If anything, walking probably reduced the journey time and when he reached the city morgue there was no sign of Simons. He sat on a chair in a alcove off the white-tiled corridor and waited. A clerk from the office brought him a mug of tea and he cupped its warmth in both hands. About an hour later the same man told him that the body had been delivered. It took about another thirty minutes for the father to arrive.

He was a small man, made smaller by the height of the two constables who accompanied him. Under his sports coat he wore blue factory overalls and he carried a lunch-box. The worst was probably over, Swift thought – the man knew he hadn't been brought to the morgue to meet the living. Some-one else had broken that part of the story and Swift was glad. He stood up and thought of shaking the man's hand but just introduced himself instead and, as they followed the attendant, struggled for anything else to say. The two constables had not followed and he was conscious of the clack of heels on the stone floors when they were led into the deepening silence of the building. There was a smell of the man, maybe petrol or oil, some factory odour that clung to his clothes and skin. Whatever grief he carried looked cowed and subservient to the unfamiliar world of officialdom he had suddenly encountered. His face was blank, almost neutral in its expression. When they reached the doors Swift paused and said, 'I'm sorry about this but it has to be done. We'll not linger – better to remember the person as they were when they were alive. That's what I think, anyway.' The man nodded and tucked the lunch-box tight under his arm.

They had done a good job, probably the best that could be expected in the short time available. The sheet covering her body hid the terrible necklace she wore, and much of the terror Swift had seen earlier had somehow been drained away to be replaced with something that looked more like sleep. He felt relief. His gratitude. The man stood still, saying nothing at first, almost as if he didn't recognize her, and then looked away.

'Mr Simons,' Swift said, as the attendant replaced the sheet.

'That's her, that's Alma,' the man said, running the cuff of his jacket across his nose and mouth. He turned away and Swift thought for a second of putting his arm on the man's shoulder but as he hesitated he turned again and without looking at Swift asked, 'And somebody killed her?'

'I'm afraid it looks that way,' Swift said. 'We're pretty certain.'

'Why would anyone want to hurt her?' Simons asked.

'I don't know,' Swift answered, 'but I'm going to do my best to find the person that did it.'

'That's good,' Simons said. 'She didn't deserve that. Nobody deserves that.' He took his lunch-box from under his arm and held it in both hands like something precious. Swift shepherded him towards the doors, anxious for them both to move away from where the now hidden corpse still pressed its presence into their memory. Once outside, he led him to the chairs in the alcove and asked the two policemen to give them a few minutes. Simons looked cowed again, and when he spoke he sounded almost apologetic for the supposed inconvenience he was causing everyone. Swift tried to be gentle with him, and for a few seconds they spoke of only the snow, then slowly he started to ask about his daughter and her situation. But there was little that sounded particularly useful in the responses.

According to him, Alma had always been a girl who went her own way, lived her own life, didn't bother much with the rest of the family. He had separated from his wife, who was now living in Australia, while Alma's two sisters were in England. Simons had never even been to her house. She phoned him a couple of times a month at work, saw him at Christmas – that sort of thing. That was the way she wanted it and he went along with it. He didn't think she was working – the only job he'd been aware of in recent times was a period she'd spent working as a machinist in Gallahers. There was no husband, never was, but she always seemed to have some fella on the go, was his way of describing it. He didn't know where she got the money for the house. Nor did he know any of the names of her past or current boyfriends.

Simons sat on the chair and stared at the floor. Swift signalled to the constables at the end of the corridor. One of them was surreptitiously smoking a cigarette and when he saw Swift he stubbed it out under his foot. As they came towards them, their heels gnawed at the silence that had settled. Swift took the photograph out of his pocket and handed it to the man sitting beside him.

'What age was she when this was taken? he asked.

'Eleven or twelve – it was taken on a day out to Bangor,' Simons said, holding the snapshot against the lid of his lunch-box. 'The swings round at Ballyholme.'

'It's a nice picture,' Swift said.

'She was always smiling as a girl. Always up to something. You couldn't watch her but there wasn't any badness in her, no badness in her.'

'No,' Swift said, nodding in agreement. Then he turned the photograph over. 'Do you recognize that address?' he asked. Simons looked at it but shook his head. 'Can I keep the photo?' he asked. When Swift said yes, he opened the lunch-box, tipped what few crumbs were in it into the palm of his hand, placed them in the pocket of his jacket, then stored the photograph carefully in the box. As Swift watched the man follow the two policemen down the corridor, he stayed on his seat. After they had gone he took a piece of paper from his pocket and wrote the address down. While he did so, he saw in his mind the image of a young girl riding higher and higher on a swing. A girl with no badness in her. He sat stone still until somewhere deeper in the cavernous, echoing building, a door slammed.

When Swift arrived back at the station there were reporters standing in huddles close to the front desk. When he entered they turned to look at him and, remembering Gracey's in-struction, he prepared to rebuff their approaches. 'No com-ment' – that was what they said in films in situations like this but he was given no opportunity to utter it, as almost im-mediately the reporters turned back to their conversations. Behind the desk Maguire was bouncing on the balls of his feet and grinning from ear to ear. When he spoke, his tone was that of a genial hotelier pleased to see his establishment so busy.

'Nothin' like a murder for bringing out the crowds, Swifty boy,' he said, nodding and smiling at a new arrival and although no one had asked him anything, 'Please, gentlemen, as soon as we have any developments you'll be the first to know. Don't block the door, please.' Then, putting his hand to the side of his mouth to announce he wished to pass on a secret, he whispered to Swift, 'They're bringin' him in, any minute. No one can say that Gracey hangs about. It's probably only the snow that's keepin' them. They found the taxi firm that delivered him to the house – driver knows him and all. Works as a barman down at the Silver Crown. Here, Swifty boy, if you ever decide to murder someone, don't take a taxi. Get on yer bike instead.' Maguire laughed at his own joke, then repeated his plea that the station door be kept clear.

There was the sound of a car outside and the huddles of reporters turned into a tightly wedged scrum in their attempt to push out through the doors. Some of the lighter ones were flopped aside like little fish as they encountered the great wave of Gracey coming in the opposite direction. 'Stand back, now, we're comin' through,' Gracey's voice boomed, and in his wake Burns trailed the handcuffed figure of a man dressed in a white shirt and jeans, with a black leather jacket draped over his shoulders. His dark hair was oiled and quiffed. 'Can't answer any questions just at the moment, but as soon as we have anything you'll be the first to know,' Gracey said, stopping to wave Burns and his prisoner past him and through the doors that led to the cells. Swift followed and watched the suspect being placed in the interview room. Gracey and Burns came back out into the corridor and Burns lit a cigarette. The sudden smell of sulphur and smoke made Swift blink. He had been around Burns for a couple of weeks but it was only now he noticed the skein of nicotine on his fingers, the way he held the cigarette at a distance from his body between his thumb and forefinger, which made it look as if he was minding it for somebody else. Gracey put his fingers to his eyes as if they were sore, then towelled his face with both palms before ambling off down the corridor.

'Not much of a case,' said Burns, dragging at the cigarette. 'Not much of a chase.'

'He's confessed, then,' Swift said.

'He will, he will,' Burns said, 'just as soon as Gracey gives him the squeeze.'

'So he's denying it.'

'Of course he is. Fair enough – it's what they do. But stay around and watch, Swifty boy, watch Gracey give him the squeeze. Before the night's out he'll be singing like a canary. Signing on the dotted line and thankin' us for the opportunity.'

'The squeeze?' Swift said, remembering Gracey's eyes meeting his as he brought the truncheon down. 'Knock him around a bit, you mean?'

Burns laughed and smoke streamed from his mouth. 'You're a gag Swifty – been watching those American gangster films again? Gracey won't lay a finger on him – he won't need to. And if he was going to, he'd have done it long before he reached the station.'

'So where's Gracey now?' Swift asked, turning his head away from the smoke.

'Probably gone somewhere to put his feet up,' Burns answered. 'Nothin's goin' to happen here for a good while yet. All part of the game. Let the bastard sweat it out for a while. Let him stew in his juices. There's nothin' they hate more than starin' at those four walls.'

Burns suddenly dropped the cigarette to the ground and stubbed it out with his foot as through the doors came the

Head Constable. Swift silently blew the smoke away from the front of his face and stood straighter.

'Detective Constable Burns, I hope you're not trying to live up to your name. Not trying to burn down the station,' the Head said.

'No, sir,' Burns replied, standing to attention.

'Where's Gracey?' he asked

'Gone to the toilet, sir,' Burns said. 'It's the cold, sir.'

'And who's this standing at your shoulder?'

'Detective Constable Swift, sir – on probation.'

'And they put you with Gracey, then. You could learn a lot, son – some of it you'll be better forgetting, though.' Swift nodded but didn't know if he should speak or not. The Head Constable pointed to the door of the interview room with his blackthorn stick. 'So the boy's in here?' he asked. 'Is he our man?'

'Guilty as hell, sir,' said Burns.

'That's good. I want it all tied up nice and clean – no loose ends to unravel in court. I'll give the press boys something to run with in the morning papers,' he said as he turned back down the corridor. Halfway along he paused and turned. 'Any more progress on that Reynolds case? The paintings ever turn up?'

'No, sir, not yet but I'm still working on it,' Burns said.

'Well keep on – Reynolds is an important man. Need some progress soon.'

When the swing doors shut behind him Burns cursed him under his breath, then looked for the cigarette he had stubbed out. 'Bloody memory like an elephant,' he complained, 'never lets you forget that he's on your case. Thinks it keeps you on your toes.' Swift was impatient to see the suspect but didn't feel able to simply walk into the interview room without a better reason. He watched while Burns opened their office door, sat at the table and started to write up his notebook, then followed him in. 'What was that old biddy's name from next door?' Burns asked. Swift told him, then asked about the man they'd just brought in and Burns, glad of the excuse to give up his writing, set aside his pen and leaned back on the chair. 'His name's Johnny Linton – he's a barman in the Silver Crown. Used to play in some dance band till they split. He's been knockin' round with her for about six months. Bit of a pretty boy – younger than her. Cried his little eyes out when we said she was dead – impressive he was, I'll give him that. Admits he was there last night, admits they had a row but strangely enough wants to insist that she was hale and hearty when he left. I'll enjoy watchin' Gracey givin' him the squeeze. The bastard deserves it – he's a fuckin' nancy boy.'

Burns went back to his writing, screwing up his face and staring at the ceiling while he sought to remember the details of his earlier interview. Gracey entered, pulling up his trousers and checking his flies. 'Listen, Swift,' he said, 'this might take some time and we've all missed our teas so what about nippin' round to Spence's and bringin' back three fish suppers? I'd send one of the men but you know what Maguire's like. What do you say? My treat.' He threw a crumpled pound note on the table, then sat down opposite Burns. As Swift looked at the money Gracey added, 'Salt and vinegar, plenty of vinegar.' Swift hesitated, then picked up the money but paused at the table before asking, 'Does Linton have a cut or scratch on his face?' Gracey and Burns looked at him. Burns snorted. Gracey said, 'Now, Swifty, what did I say about lookin' for clues and all that kind of stuff? And as far as I know, he doesn't, so I suppose he didn't do it and we should let him go.' 'I was just wondering,' Swift said, 'that's all. She could have broken her nails on some part of him other than his face.' 'Maybe we should inspect his dick,' Burns said without taking his eyes from his writing.

When he returned Swift tried to hide the embarrassment of his parcel as he walked through the flagging gaggle of reporters, but the smell seeped out from under his coat and identified the contents to everyone. Maguire raised an eyebrow, then busied himself writing in one of his ledgers. When Gracey saw him he said, 'Good man, good man,' then ripped open the wrapping of newspapers. Swift handed him the change and when Gracey asked him why he hadn't got anything for himself said he wasn't hungry. 'Suit yourself,' Gracey said plucking a piece of his fish and cramming it in his mouth, his fingers soon shiny with the heat and grease. 'Can I sit in during the interview?' Swift asked. He watched Burns hold a fat yellow chip level with his head then lower it into his mouth like a seal being fed a piece of fish. 'So long as you don't say anything, that's all, don't distract him. And when I say, leave and stay left,' Gracey answered.

It seemed to take the two men a long time to finish their meal. He watched them wipe their hands on the papers, saw the smear of ink it left on their skin. The room stank of the chips, damp wool, the rubber of their boots and the day's sweat. Swift started to feel sick.

'Have you ever felt passionate enough about a woman to kill her?' Gracey asked.

'Have you ever just felt a woman?' Burns added.

'A woman nearly killed me once,' Gracey said. 'Back in the fifties during the IRA campaign. A good-looker she was, too. Walked into Hastings Street barracks, cool as ice, and left the suitcase. We were lucky we didn't all go up. The boy on the desk said she had this real invitin' smile.'

'Invitin' you to Hell,' said Burns, licking his fingers.

'OK,' Gracey said, taking off his overcoat, 'let's get the job done.'

When they entered the interview room Gracey dismissed the uniformed constable and Burns sat on his chair with his notebook ready. There was only one other chair, so Swift went and stood in the corner. The room had no furniture other than the chair and table where Linton sat, his arms stretched across the bare wood. Gracey didn't take the seat opposite him but stood slumped against the wall, his head angled and, it seemed, looking at Linton with only one eye. For about a minute he didn't speak, as if he was waiting for someone else to start. When he began it was with a series of staccato factual questions uttered in a low monotone which suggested he wasn't particularly interested in the answers and required Linton to state his full name, his address and work place, how long he had known Alma Simons and so on. Swift watched Linton answer, saw his nervousness, his apparent desire to be helpful. The oiled sheen of his thick quiff of hair contrasted with the hollow pallor of his skin, and there was something finely honed about his features that made his facial movements seem almost feline. It was a face that was unmarked except by his present fear and his blue eyes flicking constantly round the three faces, searching for what they were thinking, or for some glimmer of a sympathetic disposition.

There was another long pause in Gracey's questions and then he moved himself slowly off the wall and sat down at the table and looked Linton in the face for the first time. 'Listen, son,' he said, 'there's only two roads stretchin' in front of us now and you need to decide which one you're goin' down. Now I've been sittin' in this chair for enough years to be able to tell you that the shortest and least painful road is always the truth.'

'I didn't kill her, Mister, honest to God I didn't kill her,' Linton said, his voice warping and wavering.

'No, son, don't talk, just listen to what I'm saying to you now, for I'm trying my best to help you, because it's my job to reach the truth and it doesn't matter how long that takes and you have to understand that nothin' ever stops me reachin' it. Look at me, son, look at me and listen to what I'm tryin' to tell you. Trust me, trust me with the truth, for it's the only way now for all of us, and if you tell me the truth I'm goin' to give you my solemn word that I'll do my very best to look after you, for I know you didn't mean to kill that girl and I'll speak for you.'

'Please God, I didn't kill her,' Linton said.

'No, son, don't speak, don't say any more,' Gracey said. 'Shush, son, shush now, just think about what I've said to you, just think about it.' Then he stood up and walked to the door, glancing at Burns, who closed his book and quietly followed. In the corridor Swift could see Gracey beckoning him. As he went to leave his eyes met Linton's, just for a second, but long enough to see the blue wash of fear and the first of his tears. In the corridor Gracey said, 'We'll give him twenty minutes, then go back in,' then ploughed a hand through his hair and muttered, 'I have a bad feeling about this one. Sometimes when they're as weak as this jessie there's nothin' to push against; sometimes they just lose their head and then they're charging round like a headless chicken, talkin' nothin' but bloody gibberish.'

Swift went back to the office and on impulse phoned his father to check how he was. As always his father's voice was edged with suspicion, his tentative 'Hello' edged with an aversion to speaking to whoever had chosen to intrude into the privacy of his home. Yes he was fine and his daily had lit the fire and yes there was plenty of food in the house. But the roads were already closed, the village cut off, so there'd be nothing in or out until the thaw started. The conversation lumbered awkwardly along familiar lines, stumbling into little drifts of silence. In the heart of one of these Swift thought of telling him that he was investigating a murder but hesitated and when Gracey and Burns entered the office said a hurried goodbye. The two men sat down at the table and for a while no one spoke until Gracey turned to him and said, 'There's no need for you to sit this out, Swifty – it could take a long time, so if you want to pack it in for the day that's OK.' 'I'd like to stay,' Swift said. Gracey shrugged and told him to suit himself.

When they went back to the interview room each of the three men occupied his previous position. Gracey had opened the collar of his shirt and loosened his tie, but everything else looked as it had twenty minutes before. 'So then, son,' Gracey said, 'what's it to be?' Linton stared at the table and repeated his innocence but in response Gracey said only, 'That's not what I wanted to hear,' then sat in sombre silence. In such silences Swift felt self-conscious, intensely aware of the slightest of his movements, the rustle of his clothes, even his breathing. He knew that Gracey used them to turn the screws a little more tightly, that under their icy weight words sometimes tumbled out in a desperate desire to escape the unbearable strain. At times Swift started to imagine his own guilt, turned in on himself the way a hellfire preacher confronts each of his listeners with the terrible burden of guilt. Truth was presented to Linton as his only route to redemption, the only way to ease the pain, his one opportunity to put things right. But Linton wasn't buying this escape and he sat at the table shaking his head slowly from side to side, locked into a rhythmic denial of Gracey's appeals.

Gracey stood up and walked to the side of the table, then collapsed his bulk so that his mouth was close to Linton's ear. 'Fuck you, Johnny boy,' he whispered. Linton ducked his head as if he expected the words to be followed by a blow but none came. What came was the squeeze. The only thing that Swift had ever seen that bore any resemblance to what he now witnessed was a cat playing with a mouse. There was the same leisured infliction of damage, the pleasured tossing and turning, the brief teasing moments when the possibility of escape seemed on offer. It began with Gracey asking Linton how long he'd been 'ridin' her, then moved to detailed questions about their sex life that made Swift squirm. How often, the where and the when, the how, what she liked, and when Linton failed to answer, or claimed he couldn't remember, Gracey painted some possibilities for him, each one more lurid and grotesque than the last. To every question there had to be a response and every question pushed Linton deeper into humiliation and self-loathing. Swift felt the dryness in his throat, and his hands pressed against the lime-green walls of the room which always looked as if they were wet. It was the colour of the slime in the boy's hair he had helped pull from the water. He felt sick again. He thought of his father padding round the empty house of his retirement, his slippered shuffle almost silent and of the snow pressing down on the roof and against the windows like a stranger seeking admittance. He still had a room in the house, the same room that had been his as a boy, high up under the roof. Why did the house always seem too big? Why had he believed as a small boy that other people lived in it besides his mother, father and himself? Invisible people who slipped in and out of the shadows, moved mysteriously and malevolently through the empty spaces. One day the house would be his, one day he would be his father and then he thought of the twisted body of Alma Simons waiting for him to find it and he shivered into the present.

'Maybe you weren't givin' her what she needed,' Gracey was saying. 'Maybe she was givin' it to others besides you – was that it? Couldn't bear the idea of somebody else givin' it to her, givin' it better than you – that it, Johnny boy?' And Linton was shouting 'No' and his face was a mixed stream of tears and mucus which made him look like an hysterical child who needed a parent to come and hold him. Then the voice dropped to a whisper and Swift had to strain to hear Linton say, 'I loved her, I loved her,' before he lowered his sobbing head into the pillow of his arms. But there was no respite and it went on for another hour until Gracey stood up and wiped the sweat of his exertion with his handkerchief. He was wheezing a little and he dabbed the corners of his mouth while he looked at his watch and told Burns the interview was suspended. Swift stood listening as Gracey lumbered down the corridor and banged the office door closed. He hesitated a second, then without looking at Linton he, too, was gone.

In the harsh light of the cell Linton's face seemed to have collapsed in on itself, his eyes shadowed and darkened, his cheeks scooped hollow and drained of colour. They had taken his laces and the belt from his trousers and he sat hunched on the concrete shelf of a bed with his legs pulled up tight. He didn't look as if he'd slept much and occasionally he shivered, but Swift wasn't sure if it was from the cold or from what memories afflicted him. It was still very early and there was little prospect of Gracey arriving for a while yet. There had been more snow during the night and even to reach the station would be a long, difficult struggle.

He offered Linton the mug of tea he had brought and looked

at his hands as he reached out for it. Were these the hands that had choked the life out of Alma Simons? He didn't know and he thought of the child on the swing, pushing back against the air, her hands holding on to the chains, the smile on her face. Swift knew he shouldn't be in the cell with Linton, that Gracey would be very angry when he found out, but for some reason he didn't care any more. He was angry himself now, but didn't know why. Was it the way he had been treated by Gracey? The way Linton had been treated? That a woman was dead? Or was it something else, something he didn't fully understand? He wondered what it would be like to feel the living warmth of her arms, the slow giving of her love. In Gracey's mouth it had sounded coarse, sordid, the words he used seeking to strip away its dignity. Maybe it hadn't been like that, maybe it had been something completely different, the way Swift, in the quietness of his barracks bed, imagined it would be for him, when it happened.

'Did he send you?' Linton asked.

'Who, Gracey?'

'He's off his head,' Linton said. 'Why doesn't he ever listen?'

Swift sat on the end of the bed and stared at the opposite wall. It was painted the same lime green as the interview room. 'When did you first meet Alma?' he asked.

'I was playing in a dance band,' Linton said. 'She was at the dance. It was a big bill, there was a lot of waitin' around. It was the Orpheus – she claimed it was the best floor of them all. Has that spring.'

'Who was playing?' Swift asked.

'The Freshmen were headlining; the Kestrels, the Vernon Girls, Johnny and the Teenbeats. She got the idea that I was Johnny of that group – I went along with it for a while until she realized. The next night she was there at Milano's. I left her home – it went from there.'

'Did you kill her?' Swift asked, still staring at the wall. The wall in his bedroom had wooden panelling. When he was a boy he used to imagine he saw images in the grain of the wood – people's faces, an Indian tepee, the wings of a bird. Sometimes he saw the lines as rivers flowing to an invisible ocean.

'I never killed her, I would never hurt her. Never hurt a hair on her head. She was the best thing ever happened to me.'

Sometimes in his bed facing the wooden panels and under the sloping roof it felt as if he was sleeping in a box. Sometimes he had a recurring nightmare that someone was hammering down a lid on this box – he tried to shout but he had no voice and then there was darkness and he knew that if he didn't break out he would suffocate.

'We had a fight that last night. I wanted her to come away with me – I thought that was what she wanted, too. We'd talked about it all the time. I had it all arranged, had fixed up a job in Glasgow through a mate. Then she told me she wasn't goin', said it wasn't possible any more. We rowed but honest to God I never touched her. I've never ever touched her – not like that, not like that.'

Suffocating would be the worst way to die – so slow, with each desperate struggle only using up the very thing you needed to survive.

'She told me it was over, that I had to go. I had the boat tickets in my pocket – I showed her them but it didn't make any difference. She told me I had to go.'

'What time did you leave?' Swift asked.

'About half nine. She really wanted me out of the house.'

'Which way did you leave? Front or back?'

'Back. She has this nosy old cow of a neighbour. I left through the yard.'

'You still have the tickets, then,' Swift said.

'No, I don't,' Linton said. 'When she put me out I'd lost the head and I threw them at the back door, them and the ring she'd given me. Stupid thing to do. Like a bloody child. But I wanted her to come away with me – I wanted it so bad.'

'What sort of ring?'

'Gold, snake-shape. Only thing she ever gave me and I threw it away.'

'Where did she get the money to pay for the house? – she wasn't working,' Swift asked.

'She said her father had bought it for her. He owns a couple of shops, has a bit of money.'

'Did you ever meet him?'

'No,' Linton said, 'She didn't talk much about him. Her mother was dead – killed in a car accident long time ago.'

'Did you know she was pregnant?' Swift asked. He had seen the doctor's report twenty minutes earlier. About two months gone.

'She wasn't pregnant,' Linton said, as if Swift was trying some new way to trick him. 'We were always careful – always. She wasn't pregnant.'

Swift didn't reply but stood up and looked for the scrap of paper he carried in his pocket. 'Do you recognize this address?' he asked. Then when Linton shook his head he hammered on the cell door for the duty sergeant. As the key turned in the lock Linton, too, stood up and said again, 'She wasn't pregnant. I would have known. She wasn't pregnant.'

When Swift went to the front desk, Maguire gave a long litany of towns and villages cut off by the snow, of impassable roads, of search parties. There were power lines down and army helicopters having to be used to take supplies to remote areas. One had also flown in to ferry a doctor and midwife to a woman about to go into labour. Even burials were having to be postponed because they couldn't dig the frozen ground. Snow ploughs were getting stuck in ten-foot drifts, the Belfast–Dublin express had collided with a local train at Lisburn station, injuring eight people. Maguire recited it all wide-eyed, pleased by the authority his information gave him. 'It's like the North Pole out there, Swifty – there's never been anything like it. Well maybe '47 but I don't think it was half as bad as this,' he said shaking his head. 'It's a bloody blizzard blowin' out there. The Corporation has a thousand men, a hundred mechanical units, tryin' to keep the main roads open and they've put out a radio SOS for more volunteers. They've opened an office down the unemployment to recruit those on the dole to help out.'

'No signs of Sergeant Gracey yet?' Swift asked.

'Probably snowed in – you might have to go round to dig him out, Swifty boy. And the airport's closed. He hasn't phoned in, but then there's exchanges out of action as well.' As he spoke, a line of constables filed in and Maguire pointed to the pile of long-handled shovels in the corner. 'Right, gentlemen, I want the front of the barracks cleared and the pavements along the front, so put your backs into it and get crackin'.'

'I didn't join to be a bloody navvy,' Johnston said out of the corner of his mouth as he took the shovel handed to him.

Swift watched the men trundle out of the barracks, some of them poking each other with the shafts of the shovels as they went. There was one shovel left. He went and lifted it. 'Goin' to help out? Good man yourself,' Maguire said, then tried to tune out the interference he was getting on the radio. Swift nodded, but when he got outside he walked past the group of constables, who were already using the shovels to scoop snow at each other. As he hurried on he heard a voice shout, 'Goin' to build a snowman, Swifty? Hey, Swifty, what's the difference between a snowman and a snow woman?' He stared ahead as if he hadn't heard. 'Snowballs!' He didn't turn round but carried the men's laughter in his ears while he walked the single track that furrowed the middle of the road. On either side were banks of snow at waist height and higher. It made Swift feel as if he was traversing an unending mountain pass and, although the snow had stopped falling, the wind whipped up the light surface and stung it against his face and eyes.

When he had left the barracks far behind he took his woollen scarf from the pocket of his overcoat and wrapped it round his neck and the lower part of his face. All around him the city was transformed into something only partly recognizable. Familiar landscapes were smoothed and rendered indistinguishable and everywhere a great weight of white pressed down on the buildings, layering and shadowing them into an echo of each other, and the snow had a shiny brilliance to it that the grime of the city had been unable to consume. Sometimes, already, the weight of snow had proved too much to bear and some wooden roofs had collapsed. But as he walked past a humped-back bridge of nose-to-tail cars, Swift felt none of this weight, for the snow had given him a temporary release from the predictable and an escape from the deadening shadow of Gracey, and its sudden offer of infinite possibilities made him wish it would stay for ever.

All schools were shut and tribes of boys roamed the tundra, pelting passers-by and spotting windows in unbridled rowdiness. A gang of them stood on a street corner and when they saw his approach bent down to gather ammunition, but he put his head down and hurried by as the volley of missiles plopped harmlessly into the banks of snow. In some of the streets he passed, there was a narrow channel cut down the middle of the street and from it tight pathways to each door in the terrace. At the end of one of these streets was a breadserver's van with people queuing to buy something from the van's extended drawers. Many of the women wore shawls over their heads like a scene in a remote village in the depths of rural Ireland.

When he reached Alma Simons's street he approached the house through the entry. He had to use the shovel to dig away the snow from the door into the yard so that he could open it wide enough to squeeze through. The snow was knee deep and each step pushed his boot down to the frozen base. As he walked to the door he felt he was walking on a great iced cake which crumbled and crunched under his weight and he wondered if his intention was mere foolishness, but he dropped the scarf from his mouth so that he could breathe more freely and then marked the immediate vicinity of the back door into a series of gridded squares, about a yard square, with the point of the shovel.

Moving the snow was a slow, frustrating business because he couldn't simply dig it in deep scoops but had to skim and scrape each of the marked squares, removing every new layer into a corner of the yard which he could only hope didn't hide what he was looking for. While he worked, his mind constructed a score of potential reasons why his search might ultimately be futile but he kept going, all the time hoping that the lull in the fall of snow would last long enough for him to finish the job. It was in the third grid, when his arms were already getting sore and the stream of his breath smoked the frozen air, that he found them. The tickets were in a sodden cardboard envelope which turned to mush in his hands but

even then he could distinguish the ink-bled name of Larne–
Stranraer and he took a small bag from his pocket and slipped
what remained inside. So many thoughts were swimming
round his head that he couldn't catch hold of them and he
went on scraping in the snow in an attempt to put them in
some order. Linton had told him the truth about the tickets,
but what did that mean? Only that he did have a reason to kill
her, driven by his anger and disappointment. He tried to think
it through as he continued to work the shovel, the rhythm
calming and directing his thoughts. If Linton had murdered
her, was it likely that he would have left through the back
door, then stopped to throw the tickets into the snow? Even
for a man in panic this seemed unlikely. But what if he'd
thrown them after a row on the doorstep when he'd arrived,
then forced his way inside and killed her? While he was in the
house a fall of snow could have covered them and made it
impossible to find them on his way out – that was a possibility.
The tip of the shovel scraped against a glint in the snow. He
bent down, took off his glove and delicately picked up the ring
with his thumb and forefinger. It was as he had imagined it
from Linton's description, and he rubbed it dry with the end of
his scarf, then placed it in the breast pocket of his shirt.

The snow had started to fall and he was pleased by its timing,
knowing that it would soon remove the traces of his work, and
he helped by back-filling where he had cleared. But there were
still too many unanswered questions for him to feel sure about
anything. Suddenly he had a feeling of being watched and,
gripping the shovel more tightly, he spun round and faced the
yard door but there was only the strengthening drop of snow.
Then he looked up and he saw Mrs Graham standing watching
him from her back bedroom window. Her eyes were blanched
out behind the glass and she was cradling something to her

chest. Something black. It was Alma Simon's cat. He raised his arm to her but she stepped back from the glass.

When he knocked at her door it took a long time for her to answer. It wasn't somewhere he wanted to be but there were questions he had to ask and he thought it best to get it over and done with.

'You're not looking for another body?' she asked, her eyes wide and staring.

'No, no more bodies, Mrs Graham,' Swift said. 'Just looking for evidence.'

'I hear you've got the man who done it,' she said. 'It makes me shiver just to think about it. I could hardly sleep last night turning and turning it over in my mind.' The cat sleeked into the room and rubbed itself against her legs, then went to a cardboard box by the side of the fire and settled on the towel bed. 'I felt I needed to give it a home – there doesn't seem anyone else. Couldn't have it starving to death. He's really settled well so I must be taking good care of him,' she said, preening herself and watching her new acquisition with obvious pleasure.

Swift thought of the cat moving across the dead body of Alma Simons and stared into the fire. Something made him put his hand inside his coat and briefly pat the ring, and then he thought of the white swell of her breast that Beckett had uncovered. He imagined him at that very moment in a dingy dark room that smelled of chemicals and sweat, staring at it as it slowly emerged from the striated swirl of fluid. Holding it up to see it better. Part of his collection.

'That Mr Burns is a very nice man,' she said, moving her reddening shins back from the heat. 'Said I'd been very helpful, said I'd helped them solve the case. I have a good memory for things, all right.'

'That's what Mr Burns said about you,' Swift answered. 'You've been a very big help to us, all right. He wanted me just to check a few small things with you, just tidy up a couple of wee things. You've been very patient.' She nodded and placed her hands on the armrests of the chair, as if bracing herself for a physical effort. The fire cackled and rushed into a momentary blue flame. 'The man you described to us came mostly by taxi, isn't that right?' Swift asked. She nodded again. 'But you didn't see him leave the night of the murder.' It was important he got it right in his own head. 'So what was the time you heard the fighting?'

'It went on a long time,' she answered. 'About shortly after ten o'clock, I think it was. Lasted maybe half an hour or more before it went quiet again. But there'd been shoutin' earlier as well, about nine – I've told Mr Burns all this. He wrote it all down in his book. I was making a cup of tea in the kitchen when I heard a rumpus. I felt I couldn't leave the cat outside to starve in weather like this – do you think they'll let me keep it? It's settled so well, as you can see.'

Swift told her that it was very kind of her and that he thought it would be all right. Then he asked her all the questions he had worked out the night before, paring them down to the bare essentials, anxious not to provoke impatience or confusion.

'So sometimes Mrs Simon's visitors stayed all night?' he asked, conscious of the indelicacy.

'Well, I'm afraid so,' she said. 'I can't say anything else, for it's only the truth. And if we're telling the truth, maybe the end she came to was the terrible punishment that comes to all sins. God is not mocked.'

'How did you know they'd stayed all night?' he asked without looking towards her.

'Well, wasn't the car still there in the morning.'

'The car? Not a taxi?'

'A car,' she said, patting the armrests as if beating out the rhythm of truth. 'Not a taxi. Bold as brass.'

'And do you remember the type of car?'

'Now, I don't know about cars.'

'Big? Small?'

'Quite big. Black car, I think.' She sighed as if the effort of memory had tired her.

'You ever see the driver?' Swift asked.

'Not exactly, but it must have been the man I described to Mr Burns, the one you've arrested.'

'That's right,' Swift said, 'That's right. You've been very helpful.' He stood up to go. The cat was an unbroken black ring which revealed no seam where head joined tail. 'And just one last thing. Who sold the house to Mrs Simons?'

'Sold the house? No one sold her anything – it's a Corporation house. Last family left to go to England. And who'll ever want to live in it now I don't know. Gives me the shivers just thinking about it.'

It was snowing again, a dogged, sullen fall, with no sense of joy or surprise. Swift knew he would have to return to the barracks and his spirits sagged as he imagined what would await him. At the end of the street, he hesitated, then turned back towards the entry and returned to where he had worked earlier. Already the new layer of snow had skirmished out most of his earlier traces. He stood tight against the wall where he could not be seen from next door and watched it fall. All the curtains of the house were closed, just as they had been the first time he had seen it, but now only darkness seeped through the thin material. He wasn't sure, he wasn't sure but there was something that pushed him on. There was fear, too, but this time it was edged by something else, a feeling of anticipation, the tremble of excitement that pleasures a child when it confronts the very thing that seeks to frighten. He felt the key in his pocket, the key he had taken from the drawer in the barracks, and its coldness stung him into movement.

After he entered the kitchen he locked the door behind him and stood listening. It seemed as if that great weight of silence was still pushing down on the house, pressing itself into every room, every cupboard and corner, seeping so thickly that he felt he could almost stretch out his hand and touch it, the way he had touched the falling flakes of snow. He stood still for a moment, afraid that he, too, would be smothered by what was freezing everything around him and he shivered from a coldness that he hadn't felt outside. There was a musty smell, spreading like spores into the empty spaces, and through it drifted the vestiges of cigarette smoke and perfume. Swift understood about empty houses. All his life he had known them. It was what he had returned home to each day after school. To a house that was already too big. His mother worked as the receptionist in his father's surgery and it was several hours before she returned home. His mother never wore perfume, or if she had he couldn't recall it. What she brought back was the scent of the surgery, the medicinal, something he imagined was the amalgamation of everything that formed her day. It clung to his father also – it was what they shared. But in their absence the house was his, whether he wanted it or not, and so he came to know it in a way that he couldn't when it was shared with others. And if he treated it with respect, brushed it only lightly with his hand, it would tell him its secrets – the things it kept from him as he slept in his wood-panelled room under the roof. Sometimes he would take off his shoes and climb under the great mountain of blankets and eiderdown that was his parents' bed, always resisting the temptation to slip into the danger of sleep but at times flirting with it, only pulling back at its very edge. He wondered what it felt like to feel his mother this close, this warm, and sometimes he imagined her whispering things into his ear – little pulses of love that fluttered across the white starched pillowcases like moths. Afterwards he would smooth and straighten the sheets, careful above all to erase the faint impression of his head on the pillow.

It was Alma Simon's bed he now lay on. The scent of her was everywhere and for a second it made him feel as if he was in a meadow filled with wild flowers. He imagined the sun warming his face. She had brought a picnic, all pretty and planned with care. He lay on his side and pushed his head into the pillow. Into her lap. Now there was no sense of time, only boundless space and air that could be breathed, and afterwards they'd walk and she'd know that he would give her something different from all the others, that in return for her love he'd provide and take care of her. Real care, so that nothing bad would ever happen to her again. Once as a boy he'd found a tiny feather from the eiderdown sticking to his jumper. He'd been more careful after that – it was the sort of thing his mother noticed. He put his hand in his shirt pocket and pulled out the ring, then placed it on his finger. But he knew enough about houses to know, too, that they were faithless, and that for every secret it had told him there were a score of others that it took perverse pleasure in hiding. So it was no good then as he lay awake, straining to hear the whispers and even the shouts that came from down the stairs, the house would never let him hear them clearly, never fully let him grasp their meaning. He put his hand under the pillow and pressed it to his ear as if listening to all the seas of the world inside a shell, and wondered what secrets this house kept from him.

Just as he had done all those years ago, he closed his eyes and waited for the slow, almost imperceptible approach of sleep, then started himself awake just when it seemed he would be touched by it. His mouth was dry and his throat a little sore. Sleep was an enticing pleasure and for a second he thought of not resisting it, but there were other things that invited him and after replacing the ring he got off the bed and straightened the covers, slowly smoothing away every crease or wrinkle. Then for the second time he opened the narrow wardrobe. The door stuck a little and he had to pull it, so when he opened it the half a dozen dresses quivered on their hangers and moved towards him. He calmed them, then, as if turning the pages of a book, let his hand linger on each of them for a moment, feeling the material between his finger and thumb. Cheap cotton prints all of them but to his touch they felt strangely beautiful. She liked blue. She must have looked pretty in this with its sailor collar and pleated skirt. The type of dress that might be worn to the seaside. Maybe that was where they went for their picnic, their day out, and he imagined a couple huddled together in a small car parked facing the sea. As she stares out at the white-combed sea he lets his fingers touch the wave of her hair, then gently he moves it from the nape of her neck and he bends his head towards it. The sound of a key in a lock. Turning. He felt in a second as he had when he knew it marked the return of his mother and so he threw the wardrobe door closed and the rattle of the hangers was their plea not to be shut away again. It must be Burns or Gracey and anxious to put on his uniform, his outer self, he shouted that he was upstairs, but there was only the sudden banging of the back door and when he hurried down the stairs there was no one there. As he stood in the open doorway, staring at the scurry of footprints that had spumed across the yard and disappeared into the entry, a little flurry of snow fell from the roof and landed on the sleeve of his coat. For a second before he brushed it away, the thin tremble of white seemed to flutter like a feather.

As soon as he entered the barracks Maguire winked conspiratorially and summoned him with an exaggerated flick of his fingers. Swift watched him move to the side of the desk and wondered if he ever went home, or had any life other than in this place and his seemingly endless job of guardian of the entrance. He gestured Swift closer while he rested his weight on the wooden counter, as if what he had to say could be transmitted only by the lowest of whispers.

'Listen, Swifty, I don't know where you've been but Gracey's lookin' for you and if I were standin' in your shoes I'd get along there quick. And he's hurt his neck shovellin' snow in his yard – tryin' to clear a path to his coal bunker – so he's like a bear with a sore head.'

Swift pushed through the swing doors, rehearsing his story as he went. He could hear Gracey's voice coming from their office and there was the sound of coal being rattled on to the fire. Swift hesitated, then pushed the door open.

'Well, well, look what the cat's dragged in,' Gracey said as he moved the thick stump of his neck from side to side and rubbed the back of it with the great towel of his hand. 'Nice to see you grace us with your presence, Swift. Now, would you like to tell me where the hell you've been and just what you think you were doin' talkin' to Linton this mornin'?'

'I thought I should look in at him, seeing you were delayed, Sergeant Gracey, and mindful of the state of mind he was in. When I spoke to him I had concerns that there was a risk of him attempting to injure himself,' Swift said, staring at the slumbering grey-smoked fire.

'Don't give me that shite, Swift, son. Do you think I came up the Lagan in a bubble? That nancy boy hasn't the balls to hurt himself and what was he going to do – beat himself to death with that oily quiff of his? So let me guess: he blubbered on your shoulder, told you how much he loved her and that he didn't do it.'

'Yes, Sergeant.'

'Shut your trap. I've got my eye on you, Swift, son, and I don't think I like what I see. So no doubt you fell for all his fuckin' fairy stories and told him you believe him.' Burns sniggered into his mug of tea. 'And you can shut up and all,' Gracey said, jerking his head in anger and then wincing at the pain. 'So, Swifty, if Johnny lover boy thinks he's found someone dough-brained enough to believe him and who encourages him to keep spewin' out all those lies, I'm not goin' to be best pleased with you. And when I'm not best pleased, you better look out.' Gracey paused to squirm his neck into the pillow of his shoulders. 'For I'll have you out there traipsin' the streets lookin' for missin' dogs.'

'There was someone in Alma Simons's house, someone with a key. They ran off before I could see who it was,' Swift said, abandoning his prepared story of being called to help out with an accident in the snow.

'And what the frig were you doin' round at that house? – no don't answer that for I know already. And after me spellin' it out for you in black and white. Mister Burns go and check the prisoner, me and Swift need to have an urgent discussion.' Burns stood up and as he passed behind the bulk of Gracey he looked at Swift and sawed his hand across his throat.

When he had gone Gracey sat down on one of the chairs and

dropped his head back over it so Swift could see the sagging folds of his chin and his eyeballs slowly draining white. He thought of the open razor that had glinted on the grimed floor of the bar toilets and for a second wished he held it in his hand. Gracey righted himself again, then stared at Swift as if seeing him for the first time.

'Swift, from the moment I met you, I could see you were a snotty-nosed little twat with your education and your head full of half-baked ideas from too many films and detective books. A regular little Sherlock Holmes who thinks that on the basis of five minutes in the job he's got it cracked. Well let me tell you this, son, that while I might not have any fancy certificates hangin' on my walls, I've thirty years of puttin' scumbags like Linton behind bars. And I've done big murder cases – not like this poxy murder of some tart, but cases where they flew over boys from the Met to show us how to do it and I've wiped their arse and wiped their eye, so don't you think that you can play clever bugger with me, for I won't have it. Do you understand? Not for a second.'

'Yes, Sergeant.'

'Now, you hand that key into the desk and under no circumstances are you to go anywhere near that house again. Is that understood?' Swift nodded. 'And don't even look sideways at Linton or you're finished. Now piss off out of my sight before I say any more.'

'Where should I piss off to, Sergeant Gracey?'

Gracey stumbled to his feet, knocking his chair over, and the sudden movement flapped a swirl of smoke from the fire. 'To the fuckin' North Pole for all I care,' he said, his frog-cheeked face pulsing red, 'and try to be smart with me and I'll crack your jaw. Report to Maguire, see if he wants any snow shovelled.'

At the desk Swift looked at the Occurrence Book. It was the familiar story of minor accidents, call-outs to help doctors reach patients, checks with old people, abandoned cars and lorries causing obstructions, complaints about hooliganism. A swan had been trapped in the ice-bound Lagan near Balfour Street and a rescue party in a rowing boat had to break the ice foot by foot. Caretakers of public buildings were constantly being sought as burst pipes flooded building after building. Police Land Rovers with supplies of food were being sent to cut-off villages. Up on Divis Mountain at the transmitting station, a rescue party finally reached the engineers after they had been stranded for two days. There seemed no end to it, and the great fist of snow that held the whole country in its grasp showed no sign of relenting. Even Maguire seemed a little morose as he watched Swift read the ledger.

'You got a bollockin', then,' he said. Swift nodded without lifting his eyes from the book. 'Don't take it to heart, son, there's not many in this barracks hasn't had one of those from the same man. Hurtin' his neck hasn't helped – you were a bit unlucky there. Still, no bones broken. Look on the bright side, Swifty, for sure, doesn't it beat shovelling snow?'

Swift moped about the barracks until his shift ended at six. He balked at the prospect of another evening trapped there, with only the radio for company and his mind turning over Gracey's words like little pebbles in his hand. He had already contemplated some of the possibilities for his future but found no clear way forward: he couldn't ask for a transfer and the only option was to accept defeat and request a return to uniformed duties. To do that was to spend the rest of his career shovelling snow. To jack it in altogether was to admit defeat, and that prospect left a bitter taste in his mouth, made worse by the knowledge of how self-satisfied it would leave his father, his instant prediction confirmed. As he wrote up his journal on his bed, he listened as the twangy guitars of the Shadows' 'Dance On' jangled out of someone's tinny radio, but while he pondered what to write for the events of the day, his mind turned more and more to the flurry of footprints scurrying acoss the yard. Heavy prints, bigger than his own and wide-striding. He had followed them out of the entry until they blurred and vanished in the criss-crossed mesh of the street. Big enough to be Gracey's. He twisted the delicious prospect in his head, weaving it towards a public denouement, hearing the click of the cuffs when they shackled those thick wrists. He remembered that Gracey had said her face was familiar, that somehow that morning he had hurt his neck. Running, maybe. The radio was playing 'Bachelor Boy'. But now the voice was laughing at him, at his pathetic, stupid ideas, at the single bed he slept in, and he remembered lying on Alma Simons's with his head pressed to the pillow, her scent all around him. He thought of the white swell of her breast, the fire of her fingers and toenails. A bachelor boy until your dying day. He turned over on his side and tried to shut out the stupid, sneering voice. He'd have asked her to come away with him – not somewhere like the black back streets of Glasgow, but somewhere far away from this place where there'd be the wash of sunlight and the sweep of space. Maybe even as far away as America.

He had to get away from the barracks. There was somewhere he had to go, and after he checked the address he had written on the piece of paper, he slipped it into the back of his journal, then put on a second pair of socks and as many other pieces of clothing as he could find. Walking was the only means of travel now. Almost instinctively he touched the ring which was still in his breast pocket. The only way out was down past the front desk and he tried to hurry, hoping that he'd make it without comment, but Burns was there with another detective. Money and a parcel were changing hands. Maguire was nowhere to be seen and when Burns saw him he stuffed the notes into his back trouser pocket and called after him, 'Hey, Swifty, are you doin' a Captain Oates – walkin' out into the snow to give your mates a better chance of survival?' 'I may be some time,' Swift said without looking back at him.

The cleared pavements were black-skinned with ice, making them more hazardous than where the snow remained un-cleared. Great, jagged teeth of ice, jutting from guttering and leaking pipes glittered like frosted fairy lights. Swift had gone only a little way when there was a power cut and all around him plunged into a sudden rush of darkness, leavened only by the seep of light from a full moon and a nervous scatter of stars. He wondered whether he should turn back but thinking of the alternative made him press on, and, taking his torch from his pocket, he shone it ahead as he walked. The ridged banks and wind-blown terraces of drifted snow seemed shrunk tight and enveloped by a blue membrane which trembled in the smear of light. Each step he took echoed with the gritty scrunch of freezing snow in the eerie silence that had settled on the city, while the few people he met flitted noise-lessly in and out of the shadows like hooded monks.

The street directory he had looked up had given the name of the occupant as Ernest McGrath and his occupation as un-employed. It made him think about the Simons house again. There was something strange about what he had found – it was as if she had just appeared in that space, because there was nothing that anchored her to it or established her relationship with any part of it. And it was almost as if someone had sifted out everything that connected her with the outer world. There wasn't a rent book or any receipts, no visible means by which she supported herself. She appeared to hang suspended in a kind of limbo world where she didn't work, she didn't sign on and there was no obvious network of friends. He turned it over and over in his mind as he walked. A phone with no book of phone numbers, a boyfriend who seemed to know so little about her.

As he walked his breath streamed in front of him, his breathing heavier as his pace slowed. Deep drifts of snow had swept against gable walls and advertising hoardings and, everywhere his torch shone, glittered and winked coldly back at him. He was deep in the mire of back streets where from every window shuffled and whispered the lull of candlelight. Some of the terraced streets had cleared pavements with the road left untouched, others had the dug spines he had seen earlier. They all had open curtains and the tiny front rooms were like little grottoes which flickered thin shards of yellow into the night. He wasn't sure what he would say when he found the house and he knew there was a high chance his would be a wasted journey, but it felt like one more step he had to take. Eventually he reached the address he was looking for, and when he did he switched off his torch and stood in the shadows.

Squirms of candlelight fluttered against the glass and there was the glow of a fire flitting and fidgeting in the room, but he couldn't distinguish anyone inside. He checked the number again and knocked at the door. He knew immediately that the man who stumbled to the door had been drinking and he peered out as if he couldn't see who had just knocked. 'Mr McGrath?' Swift asked, looking at the stubble-flecked face that stared through him. The man was unsteady on his feet and held to the door frame for support. He was wearing layers of clothes that frothed out over each other with a belt across his waist to hold it all in place, giving him the ragged appearance of a scarecrow.

'Hell's bells,' the man said, 'you must be desperate, to be out on a night like this. Must be far gone for you to be thumpin' the door in the middle of this fuckin' winter wonderland.'

'I'm desperate, all right,' Swift said, already piecing things together in his head. He wished he had a hipflask in his pocket to offer as a ticket of admittance.

'So you're here on business?' the man asked as he stared up and down the empty street. 'I can always tell, no matter what, I can always tell.' Swift nodded, the man lurched a little, then steadied himself and wordlessly signalled him inside. He followed into the jittery, smoky front room, which stank of stale beer and something similar to the smell of a wet dog. The man he assumed to be McGrath flopped into the chair closest to the fire and pushed his feet against the tiles of the fireplace. 'You didn't bring any drink with you?' he asked. 'Well, more's the pity, for you can't even get out for a jar, and if you do you're liable to break your neck on the way back or end up freezin' to death up to your uxters in snow.' He spoke to the fire but now he turned and leered at him. 'Well, who's been a dirty dog, then? Been dippin' your wick and got caught out?' He dropped his feet and they clattered against empty bottles. The light made his eyes yellow and his skin slippery and sallow like the grease from the candles. 'There's always a price to pay, son, for a bit of fanny and you better have it ready. Mrs McGrath doesn't do charity cases.'

'Shut your drunken mouth!' a woman's voice shouted, as like some spectre, she appeared in the room out of nowhere, 'Shut your mouth before I do it for you.'

'I was only tellin' the lad how it is, I was only—'

'Shut your bake now or I'll have the tongue out of your head!'

McGrath shrugged and lapsed into silence, occasionally holding up his hand as part of some silent defence. The woman was thin and wiry, the force of her words contrasting with her physical strength, and she turned to Swift and bristled herself tight and aggressive, demanding to know who he was and what he wanted. When she moved her arms, the shadows stuttered and fretted across the walls like the dark wings of a bird.

'Swift,' he said. My name's Swift and maybe you can help me.'

'Swift?' the man said sniggering, 'That's a good one – I'd say you've been a bit too swift, son. Rushed right in and now she's up the duff.'

'Who sent you here?' the woman asked, stepping closer to see him more clearly.

'A woman I know said you could help. I can pay.'

'How far gone?' asked the woman.

'About two months,' Swift said. He paused a moment, then added, 'Her name's Alma Simons and mine's Detective Constable Swift.'

Even in the trembling half-light he could see her face blanch with fear and her eyes blink and skitter round the room looking for an escape. McGrath slumped forward in his chair and gave a low moan before repeating over and over, 'God in heaven.' But she turned to him, telling him to hold his tongue, and her voice was hard again and in control. Swift knew already that the man was a surer bet but he knew, too, he had them both.

'We've never heard of any Alma Simons,' she said, folding her arms across her narrow chest.

'That's strange, for her name's been all over the news and on the front of every paper. You see, somebody murdered her.'

208

'We don't pay any heed to the news – we just keep ourselves to ourselves,' she said, shaking her head in denial of whatever he was about to put to her. A sudden draught made the candles flicker. Swift stepped into the middle of the room with his broadened shadow thrown on the bare screen of the wall.

'I think you better sit down,' he said, his voice low but strong. 'And no, I don't want you to say anything, because it's important that you listen to what I have to say, for there's only two roads stretchin' in front of us now and you need to decide which one you want to go down. No, don't say anything, just listen to what I'm saying to you. For you see, I already know all about the dirty little business you run here, but right at this minute all I'm interested in is Alma Simons. So what I need you to decide is which road you're goin' to go down. No, don't say anything but you need to know that the only good road for you both now is the truth – you need to trust me with the truth. And if you do that, I'll do my best by you.'

'Tell him, Arlene,' McGrath whispered, his voice thin and reedy and laced with pleading.

'Just shut up,' his wife said, 'just say nothin' and let me think. You start blabbing and you'll be sittin' in Crumlin Road.' The man's feet squeaked and clinked the bottles. 'Tell him, Arlene – he knows it already,' he said, turning to stare at her.

Swift's heart was drumming in his chest; he felt he was at the very edge, about to step over into the truth.

'The truth is,' she said slowly, 'we don't know anything about Alma Simons, nothing at all.'

'That's not what I want to hear,' Swift said, a rush of disappointment pushing out the words. 'And in case you aren't aware, for what you run here, there could be real heavy punishment. You're lookin' it right in the face.'

'She's tellin' you the God's honest truth,' McGrath whimpered, 'honest to God. We never even seen this woman, never even seen her.'

'She came here – I know she came here,' Swift said, trying to scatter and press his guesses into reality.

'She never came,' the woman said.

'I don't believe you.'

'She was supposed to come but she never did.'

'Maybe we should stop right now and start again down at the barracks,' Swift said. He felt it was slipping away from him and he let his anger rush him into whatever words scribbled across his mind. 'Maybe you've forgotten this is a murder case and that you're up to your necks in it. So just maybe she came here and there was an argument about the money – was that it?'

'The money was already paid,' McGrath said. 'Over the odds but he could afford it.'

'Shut your face!' his wife shouted, but when she tried to stand up Swift pushed her down again.

'She's tellin' you the truth. We never saw her. The money was paid but she never came. On the Bible, she never came. Listen, Mister, we take good care of the girls – don't just throw them back out on the street when it's over, like some do. It's the best for them in the long run. We take good care of all of them but this girl, she never came. Honest to God.'

'Who paid the money?' Swift said, going to stand over him. 'Who paid it?'

'Shut your bloody mouth!' she screamed from the settee, the thin wing of her arm beating into shadow.

'It's too late for that now,' Swift said, as calm as he could muster. 'Who paid the money?'

'Older guy, stank of money. I put the arm in for him lookin' down his snotty nose at us. It were us doin' him a favour, not the other way round. Drove a car. Big and fancy.'

As his wife fell finally silent, Swift dragged as many physical details from the man as his addled memory could muster. Wearing a suit and a hat, dark-haired, in his fifties, plenty of money. There wasn't much more. But it was something, something important, and then when McGrath's words drained away into a stammering repetition of the meaningless, Swift thought of what went on upstairs or in the back room and he shivered. He was glad she hadn't come here, so very glad, because sometimes he had found himself beginning to think of the child as his own. Their child. One of the candles puffed out with a final twist of smoke. There was nothing more to be done – the rest would wait for later – and he cautioned them with a promise that they'd be hearing from him again. He wanted to be gone, and as he spoke his final words the room suddenly surged with light, making his shadow collapse and the radio start to yammer. Like the flash of Beckett's camera. And although he tried not to look as he headed for the door, he knew that the photograph of what he had just seen had in that moment been added to his own collection and printed in his memory with all the force of its sordid misery.

As Swift returned to the barracks he was determined to have it out with Gracey and, for better or worse, put all his cards on the table. Things had gone too far to keep them secret and he tried to tell himself that after the initial shock Gracey might just be grateful, but the thought carried no conviction. What he had discovered didn't prove that Linton hadn't murdered Alma Simons, but it did place another man in the picture and that would have to be investigated. He rehearsed the moment of disclosure in his head and each time he tried to ensure that it was free of smugness or any outward sign of pleasure in having put one over on Gracey, but knew it wouldn't be easy to hide it entirely. 'Can I have a word, Sergeant Gracey?' he'd say, then usher him somewhere quiet in a conscious display of discretion. Or maybe he'd just arrive at the front desk and tell Maguire to summon him, tell him the case had taken a new turn and it would be in Gracey's best interests if he got himself to the station in double-quick time. Then for a delicious second he imagined by-passing Gracey all together and going straight to the Head Constable. But the flurry of pleasure these imaginings brought him was short-lived and soon edged with apprehension, as he remembered Gracey's earlier warnings.

So when he walked into the barracks, much of his earlier confidence had drained away and been replaced by a foreboding that left him nervous and uncertain as to how he should approach Gracey. After the night cold, the sudden heat of the station flushed his face. A couple of reporters were conferring over cups of tea and scribbling in notebooks. Three or four constables were getting ready to go out on duty and trying to think of as many last-minute checks as possible, in the hope that these would delay their departure. One flicked his torch round the walls while another fiddled with the buttons of his coat. 'Off you go now, lads,' urged Maguire, 'and don't be worrying – if you get lost we'll send the huskies out for you.' Swift stood aside while they filtered past and heard them draw in their breath, like men who were about to plunge into deep water. As he stood watching there was a heavy slap on his back that sent him stumbling forward a few steps.

'Out buildin' snowmen, Swifty boy?' Burns said, grinning from ear to ear. 'You're never about when things are on the boil.' Swift stared at him and saw the delight in his eyes. 'Well, none of us need be traipsin' round in the bloody snow any more and it's money in the bank for all of us. Maybe yer man'll even forget those paintings in the light of this.'

'In the light of what?' Swift asked, opening the top buttons of his coat.

'In the light of Linton havin' spewed his guts about an hour ago. Signed, sealed and delivered. Gracey gave him one blindin' hell of a squeeze and the bastard's coughed up and signed on the dotted line.'

'You mean he's admitted it?'

'You should be a detective, Swifty, you're so sharp.'

'Linton admitted it?' Swift asked again, fighting for breath.

'What's wrong? You're not tellin' me that you'd started to believe that little weasel's fairy story? God, you had, hadn't you? You've a lot to learn, boy,' Burns said, as he took a cigarette out of his pocket and fished around for a lighter. 'Just as well it wasn't all down to you, wasn't it? He'd be back walking the streets by now, laughin' his balls off instead of sittin' in that cell blubberin' like a bloody child.'

'So what did he say, then?' Swift asked, staring at Burns's brown-stained fingers as they struck the match.

'What do you mean, what did he say? I've told you – he coughed up, said he done it. Some sort of argument about her not goin' away with him. He was spewin' it out so fast I could hardly keep up with him. Shittin' his pants, he was. What she ever saw in him, I don't know. Bloody nancy boy. But listen, Swifty boy, there's more good news – Gracey says we're gettin' tomorrow off in lieu of all these hours we've put in. He's cleared it higher up, so you'll be able to get out your sledge and play in the snow to your heart's content.'

Swift watched him put on his overcoat and the way he

gingerly swapped the cigarette from hand to hand. After Burns had disappeared through the doors a thin curl of smoke still hung in the air. Swift felt a surge of anger but all he did was slice his hand slowly through it, trying to make it vanish.

There were no further falls of snow during the night but a heavy frost baked and crusted it into a brittle expanse of crystal. 'You know what will happen when this lot thaws,' Maguire said to him in the morning, when he saw him about to leave the barracks. 'There'll be such a flood that you'll need an ark to get up the road. It'll be like Venice out there, so don't be losing your boots, Mr Swift. Here, Swifty, do you know the world's worst job?' Swift shook his head. 'A bookie's runner in Venice. Do you get it, Swifty? Do you get it?' He nodded his reply, only to hear Maguire call after him, 'A sense of humour goes a long way in this job. Keeps you sane – you should remember that, Swift, son.'

The sun reflected so brightly off the frozen snow that it dazzled his eyes and for a second he had to shade them with his hand. The whole world seemed smoothed and polished into a fierce glitter which was veined and flecked with glints of blue and yellow. Underfoot it felt granular and crisp, lisping and squeaking as he walked. More of the main roads had been cleared and the snow thrown to the sides in thick, brown-crested waves. Swift lifted his face and felt the sun touch his skin. Perhaps it was the beginning of the end. Part of him didn't want it to be true, for when it was over he would be back in a familiar world whose predictability already threatened to crush his spirit. And he would always associate her with the snow. The two of them together, safe and warm, sheltering in the wilderness, cut off from the world and locked together in an embrace of love. The sun brushed his face lightly like the touch of her hand. Her breast white as the snow and veined with blue. And her love only for him, not shared with anyone else. Just for him.

By the time he reached the City Hall he was sweating lightly and feeling suffocated by his layers of clothes. The air was still cold, but in comparison with the past days there was a noticeable rise in temperature. Things felt as if they were loosening, beginning to stir and unlock themselves from the tight grip that held the city, the whole country, frozen and still. There were more people about and it looked as if they were beginning to reclaim what had been taken away from them, but it was unpredictable and after the snow it wasn't possible any more to feel secure about what lay ahead.

The great green domes of the City Hall had shed their thin skein of snow and glistened in the sun but everywhere else was edged and layered in white. Every ledge and balustrade was badged and shadowed by crests of snow, and the building stood behind the white-cloaked statue of Queen Victoria like a giant wedding cake ready to be cut. Swift walked round to the rear and took directions to the office he was looking for. After walking in snow the tiled corridors felt intensely solid under his feet and his rubber boots felt clumsy and out of place amidst the polished wood and elegant Victorian formality. He had made enquiries already and they had all led here. It was her house he was thinking about. At first he had thought Mrs Graham had been mistaken when she had said it was a Corporation house, but he had checked it out with the local housing department and eventually found that it was, but that no one had been allocated to it after the departure of its former tenants. It was as if Alma Simons had simply walked in the front door and lived there without anyone knowing about it.

The woman behind the partially open frosted glass could see him but made no attempt to acknowledge his presence or deal with his enquiry. He knew that the allocation of houses in the city was a convoluted and murky business, where deals were done and strings pulled by those small-time politicians and their confederates who found themselves with the luxury of permanent power. He knocked on the glass, causing the woman to lift her head but make no other move. He knocked again and this time she opened the glass a few more inches and peered out at him. 'We're closed,' she said. 'You'll have to come back in the morning.' She was about to close the glass again when he blocked it with his arm. 'Excuse me!' she said, her face tightening into thin furrows of anger. Without moving his arm he pulled out his warrant card and showed it to her, watching as she stared at his face.

'You don't look like a policeman,' she said.

'I'm a detective and I want to speak to someone about one of your houses,' Swift said.

'Have you filled in an application form?' she asked, still inspecting him.

'I don't want a house. I'm part of an investigation into a murder and I want to speak to someone who can answer some questions. So if you could find someone, I'd be grateful.'

The word 'murder' seemed to galvanize her into action and Swift watched her whispering in the ear of an older man who sat at a desk in the corner of the office, then point back at him. A few seconds later he was ushered into an adjoining room and shown to a seat. The man was in his late fifties and the shoulders of his black suit were sprinkled with a fine fall of dandruff which made it look as if he'd just come in from the snow. When Swift explained what information he was seeking, the man wrote the address down on a piece of paper and stared at it, as if he might find the answer by looking at it. 'So you want to know who lives at this address,' he said. 'That shouldn't be too difficult.' His voice was superior, smug, confident that such details were easily available to him, and still staring at the piece of paper he phoned through the details to someone in another office. As he sat waiting, he glanced at Swift and fingered the edge of his desk as if he was lightly playing a piano. 'A murder case?' he asked. 'That girl who was strangled – the one in the papers?' Swift nodded. The envelopes on the desk were all addressed to a Mr Johnston. Past the man's head he could see out through a window and for a second he thought it was snowing again but realized that it was little flurries disturbed from higher parts of the building. 'A terrible business,' the man added, attempting to fill the silent wait for the requested information. Swift said nothing. He had already learned from Gracey how effective a weapon silence was in putting people at a disadvantage. A few minutes later the woman who had dealt with him earlier returned with what looked like an account book and pointed at some of the lines with a pencil. The man nodded as if he understood, then flicked the pages backwards, keeping the original place with his finger.

'Our records show, Constable, that the house has been empty since the last family – the Gowdies – gave it up. About six months ago.'

'A woman called Alma Simons has been living in the house,' Swift said. 'And it's Detective Constable Swift.'

'I don't think that's possible Detective Constable Swift,' the man said, using his finger to underline the information. 'There's no current occupant listed – you can see for yourself if you like.'

Swift didn't move but said, 'The records are wrong. Alma Simons has been living there for six months. Living in that house until someone murdered her.'

'I can't see how that's possible,' the man insisted. 'She can't simply have walked in off the street and taken up residence.'

'It's beginning to look as if she did. Did she pay rent?'

'The house is definitely listed as empty so there won't be any record of her or any payment of rent.'

Swift felt an impulse to lean across the desk and brush the dandruff off the man's shoulders. He felt as if he'd reached a dead end. Through the window the sky looked blue and quickened into life. It was almost the same blue as the ledger.

'Why would a Corporation house sit for six months in Belfast when there's a waiting list as long as your arm?' Swift asked, the words in his mouth almost before he'd thought of them.

The man blew a thin stream of breath through his tightened lips and shifted on his chair. 'I couldn't give you the answer to that,' he said, closing the ledger and holding it tightly in both hands.

'Is it normal practice for a house to sit unallocated for that length of time?' Swift asked, stretching his hand across the desk.

'No, it wouldn't be normal practice. Not unless the house was deemed dangerous or in need of urgent repairs.'

'The house didn't kill her, Mr . . . Mr Johnston. The house wasn't dangerous. And another thing, would it be normal practice for a young unmarried woman to be given a house in preference to those on the list with families?'

'In normal circumstances, no, but sometimes there might be special circumstances.'

'And what would those special circumstances be?'

'Well, it's quite a complicated business,' Johnston said, holding the journal to his chest like a breastplate, but making no effort to elucidate.

'I'm told that it's often quite simple,' Swift said, 'that it's often who you know.'

'I don't know anything about that,' Johnston said. 'And I'm not sure that it's a proper thing for you to be coming here and saying. What did you say your name was?'

'Detective Constable Swift. And I'll not be troubling you any longer. I can see you're a busy man.' As he stood up he glanced down at the little slivers of damp his boots had left on the floor. He felt the stir of malice and as he was about to leave he paused at the door and asked, 'Did you ever meet Alma Simons, Mr Johnston?' then merely nodded at Johnston's flushed denial, before stepping into the corridor.

He had gone only a few steps when he remembered that he had never been in the City Hall before and, with nothing better stretching ahead of him on his day off, decided to take a look at the front entrance. There was a wedding party in the corridor, obviously just come round from Cleeland's in Great Victoria Street to add the grandeur of the building to their photographs. The bride and groom's cheap-looking suits were embellished by bits of fern in silver paper. There were only five people in the group and the absence of parents and family made Swift guess it was a mixed-marriage job. As he followed he saw Johnston come out of his office, almost colliding with the newlyweds, then scurry on down the corridor. He followed at a distance, tucking in behind the spill of laughter and back-slapping. They were going to have their photographs taken on the great white marble staircase, and while he shadowed them and kept Johnston in sight, Swift felt a sudden sadness that he wasn't the one walking with his new bride and somehow that he had been cheated of that moment. Maybe for ever. Despite the cheapness of their outfits, the poverty of the wedding, they had something which he had never known and which echoed his steps with envy and regret. He patted the ring that he still carried in his shirt pocket and something made him stop and put it on. She'd have the best wedding dress that money could buy – he'd buy her more things than anyone had ever given her, and she'd cry and say that no one had ever treated her as well as he had. But it wasn't just the things he'd give her – he'd be more gentle than any man she'd ever known and the love she'd feel for him would wipe away the memory of every other hand that had ever touched her.

They reached the great entrance and the sweep of marble stairs that looked as if they had been brushed coldly by snow. The bride and groom posed stiffly, momentarily chastened and made small by the arch and thrust of space and their laughter swallowed by the remote silence of the building. Johnston was on the stairs, his back bent with the speed of his steps and his face down, so he almost collided with a man coming in the opposite direction. This was evidently the man Johnston was looking for, and at his beckoning they went and stood together at the top of the first flight of stairs. But when Swift moved forward to get a better look, a tap on his shoulder made him start and spin round. He found one of the wedding party sheepishly holding out a camera towards him. 'Would you take a photo for us?' the man said, and Swift nodded. As he waited for them to sort out their positions he studied the dark-suited figure bending towards the smaller Johnston. He had placed one of his arms on his colleague's shoulder as if to steady him. He heard someone call, 'Everybody say cheese!' and raising the camera he focused on the group's self-conscious pose and then, as their smiles stiffened, took the picture. 'Thanks!' the groom shouted but as he walked towards the camera Swift raised his hand to stop him, saying, 'Just one more to be sure,' and then before they could rearrange themselves he focused on the two men at the top of the stairs and, pausing only long enough to stop the shake of his hand, clicked as both their faces turned to look at him. It felt like a cheap camera but Swift prayed, with all the desperation of someone who didn't believe, that it would prove good enough to capture the scratches that flamed and scrawled down the man's cheek.

As he knocked on the door, Swift realized that he was still wearing the ring and, slipping it off, squirmed his hand inside his coat and dropped it gently into his shirt pocket. There was no reply so he knocked again, this time with more urgency. From inside he could hear the sound of a radio or television. He blattered the door with his fist, then, while he waited, felt in his coat pocket to reassure himself that the camera was still there. It hadn't proved as difficult to persuade the newlyweds to part with it as he had imagined it might; he told them that it was urgently needed in a police case and promised that their photographs would come to no harm. The hardest bit had been convincing them that he was a detective, but when he had managed that he had left them wide-eyed and bemused, with something else to talk about over their celebration drinks.

There was the rattle of a key in the lock. Something made him turn and look around but the street was empty except for a couple of children polishing and smoothing a slide in the middle of the road. Beckett looked even smaller than he remembered him. He was wearing a brown woollen dressing-gown, braided at the collar and tied in the middle by a tasselled cord. Even when he saw the identity of his caller he didn't open the door fully, but sought to fill the partial view into the hall with his body.

'You're not tellin' me that you've got another corpse on your hands,' he said.

'No corpse, just some photographs that need developing,' Swift answered.

'Did Gracey send you round?'

'Yes, he says he wants these right away. Needed urgently.'

'Bloody hell, this is a bit much. I'm just at my tea, watching the television. I'll bring them round in the morning,' he said, holding his hand out for the camera and starting to close the door.

'Gracey wants them now, says I'm to wait,' Swift insisted.

Grumbling to himself under his breath, Beckett reluctantly opened the door and nodded Swift inside. The house had a strange smell, something vaguely similar to that of a chemist's shop but infused with the stale smell of food and a mustiness that had a sickly, sweet edge to it. It felt like a house that had never had a window opened, and Swift tried not to breathe in the air as he followed Beckett down the narrow hall, which was strewn with cardboard boxes and suitcases. Ahead, in the kitchen, he could see a clothes-line strung from a hook above the back door and from it hung a string of shirts and underwear. The shirts looked as though they belonged to a child.

Beckett pointed him into the living room. It was a mess. Coats, old newspapers and magazines, bits of indefinable machinery, littered the chairs and floor. It looked as if there had just been a burglary. There was a plate of corned beef and mustard on a table in front of the television and a cup of tea. *Double Your Money* was on the television and Beckett went to the set and turned the sound down. 'A monkey could answer those questions,' he said. 'It's probably all a fix. I'm waiting for *Z Cars* to come on – it's not bad now. You can tell it's been written by someone who's actually talked to a policeman for more than five minutes.' He moved a pile of papers and motioned Swift to sit down. 'I'm just tidying up, sorting through some things.'

Swift nodded and stared at the silent screen. He hoped it wouldn't take long to develop the photographs. 'So what's so urgent about these pictures?' Beckett asked, examining the camera. 'He'll be lucky if he gets anything worth a shite out of a cheap camera like this.'

'It might be evidence in the Alma Simons case,' Swift said, trying not to look at the plate of corned beef with its smear of mustard.

'A good-looking girl,' Beckett said. 'Those shots I took came out really well. She could have done a bit of modelling if she'd had someone to tell her what to wear, how to present herself.'

'Someone like you?'

'I do a bit, a bit of everything. I've done some glamour work, sold some of it in London as well. I don't just take pictures of stiffs. But you need the girls, and there's so many cowboys about it scares a lot of them off. If you like, you can have a look while you're waiting. I can do copies of anything takes your fancy.'

Swift felt as if he was being sold dirty postcards or shown a mucky photograph in the school playground but he needed the photographs developed, so he nodded and watched Beckett open a sideboard drawer and take out a red-backed album.

'There you go, Swifty, son, that'll help put the time in. And not a scrubber in sight. Put some lead in your pencil for you.' Beckett laughed and left the room. Swift sat with the unopened book on his knees and listened to his slippered feet slither and press the stairs. There was the sound of a door being closed. He stared at the silent television screen for a few moments, then opened the album. The pictures were all similar in style and composition, with heavily made-up girls puckering and simpering to the camera in predictable poses of coy revelation.

Wide-hipped, wide-eyed flouncy girls in polka-dot or frilled swimsuits, equipped with little props, such as parasols or a beach ball, which were supposed to bestow an air of elegant informality. They threw their heads back as if a warm breeze was blowing through their hair and the facial expression was always a cute naughtiness that suggested anything improper was only in the eyes of the beholder. The girls weren't good-looking enough to be glamorous, and after a while the photographs merged into a repetitive oneness that was drained of everything except a tawdriness which began to repel him.

Some of the girls might have been pretty, but, by being pulled into the lens of Beckett's camera it felt to Swift that they had become sullied and he remembered the brown-and yellow-stained snow cast up at the side of the road. He thought, too, of the nicotine-stained fingers of Burns and it seemed to him that so many things in the world were gripped and stained by such hands. What was the way to break them free, to let them breathe the cleanness of the first falls of snow? With a shudder he remembered the sound of Brown's long, thin fingers being broken by Gracey's falling truncheon. There had to be some other way than that, but what it was he couldn't think, and as he set the album down on the floor he wanted to be gone from the house and all the other houses that marred his memory.

He looked around the room and was disgusted by it. He understood that rooms were lives and it sickened him to have his own touched by this. And there was something else, too, something that he couldn't stop his mind circling constantly round. Somewhere in this house there was another album – Beckett's collection – and in it, if it wasn't there already, would be a photograph of Alma Simons with the soft white curve of her breast exposed to the rapacious, consuming camera lens.

He looked round the room again. Above his head Beckett's footsteps creaked the ceiling. There was the sound of glass knocking against glass, of water running. Swift stood up and walked to the sideboard, hesitated a second then opened the drawers, but there wasn't another album or anything that looked as if it contained photographs. Part of him was glad. But he guessed that it was probably kept somewhere safe, somewhere higher in the house, and without seeing it he could smell the sickness contained between its covers. He wiped his mouth with the back of his hand and hoped it wouldn't take Beckett long to complete the business.

He sat down again and closed his eyes. He wondered if his father was managing all right and decided he'd travel down at the weekend. It was easier now to think of excuses why he didn't make it home so often, as he could always put it down to the shifts, but he didn't really need to tell any lies because his father made no comment on the irregular pattern of his visits. He hated sleeping in his old room – it always felt as if he was stepping back into a past he wanted to leave far behind. And there was a moment, always a moment when he lay in his bed in that wood-panelled room, when he remembered things he had tried to forget. It was his mother's long, slow illness which confined her to her room until she never came out, the short visits supervised by his father when he stood by her bed and she told him to be a good boy or work hard at school, or some other whispered encouragement. Her voice made him think of the ebbing sea or the wind carrying off winter leaves and he'd nod, then feel his father's tap on his shoulder which signalled that the visit was over. He never understood where her voice got its strength to shout at his father. At first he didn't believe that it was hers, but it broke again and again against the silence of the house as he lay in his bed and tried not to understand, but even as he did that an other part of him could not prevent the piecing together of the snatches, the repeated scorn of the words, and finally the unmistakable rhythm of pleading.

He was good at piecing things together. Even as a boy. Making things fit. But only in his head. As he sat in Beckett's chair he knew that for some reason he couldn't do it in his life, couldn't turn the knowledge of his need into something tangible or real. The more he tried, the more he felt wind-blown, hollow at the core, and he was frightened that into the hollowness was about to flood all the shit and sickness of the world in which he now found himself. He looked around him. From out in the street he could hear the whoops of the boys on the slide as they were released into the fleeting freedom of speed. Maybe that was what had made Gracey what he was: it had to be that. You looked at shit all day and eventually you were absorbed seamlessly into that world and maybe, too, that was how you survived it all. What was he going to do? Be sick in the snow, then cover it up? Just maybe Gracey had it right, just maybe it was the way you had to be if you wanted to survive.

He sat for what felt like a long time, slipping in and out of memory, trying to fix a better destination for his journey. Eventually there was the sound of a door opening and Swift stood up when he heard Beckett's footsteps on the stairs. The footsteps stopped. 'Come up, Swifty, they're still drying. But what these've got to do with the Simons case is beyond me. Maybe Gracey's losing his marbles. There's nothing there but some shots of somebody's wedding – a City Hall job by the look of it.' As Swift climbed the stairs he felt a rising nervousness and placed his hand on the banister to steady his steps and tried to breathe calmly. On the landing he saw Beckett disappearing into a room and he followed, pushing his way through a double curtain that brushed his face and smelt of must. It was a small room and everywhere was bathed in a red light. 'This is the nest, Swifty; you're lucky – not many people get in here,' Beckett said.

Worktops and cupboards lined three of the walls and a white enamel sink rested on a metal trestle. There was the smell of methylated spirit and the room was awash with buckets, funnels, trays and mixing vessels. While his eyes struggled to acclimatize to the light he almost tripped over a length of hose. A couple of films, weighted with clips at the end, were hanging from a line. The photographs were still damp but the images clear. 'They need a while longer,' Beckett said as, using a dry chamois leather cloth, he wiped the side of a film, beginning at the top and working downwards in a single movement. 'I've never known Gracey to make such a fuss over so little. You sure you got it right?' Swift nodded and stared at the half a dozen photographs, scanning along them until he stared at the sheen of the two faces on the stairs. The scratches were reduced to mere shadow but the face was clear.

'Charlie Newburn.' Swift started as he felt Beckett's hand on the small of his back. 'What's Gracey want with a picture of Charlie?'

'You know him?'

'Swifty, son, you're a bit of a hick from the sticks. Everybody knows Councillor Newburn – he's a bigwig down the City Hall. Has his finger in more pies than the likes of you and me will ever know. Good time Charlie – knows how to throw a party all right. I took the photographs for him at his do last New Year's Eve. Anybody who was anybody was there and half the women hanging out of their dresses, goose-pimples and all. He knows how to spend a bob or two. But why does Gracey want a picture of him?'

'I don't know,' Swift said, squirming from his touch. 'He didn't say. Can I take the photographs now?'

'What's the rush? They're not dry yet, anyway. Listen, while you're here I'll let you see a few of my shots from the catalogue. Some of my back work. Some of it you won't believe until you've seen it and even then . . . It'll make the hairs stand up on the back of your neck.'

'You're all right,' Swift said, shaking his head, 'I've got to get back with these or Gracey'll be giving out blue murder.'

'Hold your horses, son,' Beckett said, 'what's the rush? Gracey's not goin' to be jumpin' for joy when he sees those nothin' snaps. Wait till you have a decko at some of these. They're the type of shots the papers don't publish – know what I mean?'

Swift took a step backwards as Beckett came closer and tugged the sleeve of his coat. His red smear of a face was prised open by the raw slit of his smile. Swift could smell the sour stream of his breath. He took another step backwards, then over Beckett's shoulder he saw the pinned photograph of Alma Simons, her opened gown revealing her breast and he stared at it and then at Beckett's bloody eyes but he was deaf to what he was saying. And then something inside him was loosening and flapping like a flag and his hand was gripping Beckett's throat, pushing the bulging-eyed face back into the falling clatter of trays and bottles. He heard his choking, guttering gasps but it was only the shock of Beckett's fingers feathering his face that made him break his grasp. He watched him stumble backwards and sag against a metal cupboard, the red sliver of his tongue snaking from his mouth and heard what sounded like a child sucking air through a straw, then brushed Beckett's touch from his face and gathered up the photographs and the camera. As Swift turned towards Beckett he saw him draw up his knees as protection and hide his head. He brushed past him to pull the picture of Alma Simons of the wall.

'You're a fuckin' headcase!' Beckett shouted after him while Swift struggled momentarily with the double curtain. 'A fuckin' nutter!' His voice rose higher, then slid into a wheeze and as Swift hurried down the stairs he heard Beckett's feet scrambling over the broken glass and the last litany of his curses.

Swift took deep breaths of the night air, then stowed the photographs away inside his overcoat. He wanted to run but knew the frozen snow would be treacherous underfoot and he had already felt enough humiliation to last him a long time. As the glassy clutch of cold fingered his skin he walked quickly, his eyes flitting nervously about him. He wasn't sure what he should do next, but as he made his way through the glittery frieze of streets he felt certain that he was getting closer to that moment when he would find the person who had taken the life from her. The life, the love, that should have been his. But he knew, too, that he couldn't continue on his own, that he couldn't take things any further without help from above, and the only person open to him was Gracey. He swore under his breath and repeated the stream of words like a mantra. In the dark shock of sky, the stars seemed suddenly brittle and blown by the currents of the night.

When he reached the barracks he paused outside and tried to see if anyone was about, but it was impossible to be sure and after a few moments of uncertainty he pushed open the doors and walked quickly across the line of the desk. It wasn't Maguire behind it and he didn't recognize the face that glanced briefly at him. Then he was through the swing doors and into the corridor that led towards the barracks at the back. Gracey would be long gone by now, and he had at least until the morning to decide upon a course of action. He was already anticipating the comfort of his bed with the mound of extra blankets he had managed to borrow from someone newly transferred down the country. The lime-green walls of the barracks always sickened him a little and he tried not to look at them, staring instead at the tiled floor with its cracks and stains, so all that he saw was a sudden dark blur out of the corner of his eye as a massive hand clamped itself to the back of his neck and another pinned his arm behind his back, then propelled him along the corridor and burst him through a pair of doors which led into an outer yard. He recognized the wheezing breath that fanned the back of his head as Gracey's and even though he tried to dig in his heels to brake his momentum, the motor of Gracey's body steamrollered him into the middle of the snow, then flung him to the ground.

'I warned you, Swift, you little toe-rag. I warned you fair and square, you jumped-up little gobshite but you wouldn't listen, would you?'

Swift tried to stumble to his feet but Gracey's first kick caught him somewhere just below his ribs and sent him sprawling back down again. The snow spumed up against his face and when he winced with the pain, closed then opened his eyes, he had to blink away the droplets of water. One dim outside light cast Gracey's long shadow across the square of snow. Swift looked up at the buildings that formed the four sides of the yard but only a couple of yellow-lit windows displayed any sign of life. The shadow suddenly lengthened – he thought of shouting but was too frightened and ashamed to reveal the extent of his fear, but when he tried to scamper to his feet, a second kick laced into his ribs and he squealed at the sear of pain that left him feeling as if he had been stabbed. There was a slithery, damp wheeze before another kick rushed the air out of him and left him gasping like a drowning man.

'I should have kicked the shite out of you a long time ago – saved all this mess. Because, Swift, son, you're so full of it that you can't tell your arse from your elbow and the funny bit is that you think you know everything so much better than everyone else. Isn't that right? Isn't that right?'

As Gracey walked about him looking where next to inflict new damage, Swift tried to control his breathing and curl himself into a protective shape but he could hear Gracey's feet scrunch the snow close to his head and his eyes fixed helplessly on the mesmeric black press of his white-rimmed boots.

'I've had Beckett on the phone squealin' like a pig about being assaulted and blubberin' on about some photographs that I'm supposed to have ordered developed. And the fuckin' Head Constable chewin' the balls off me after a complaint from the City Hall. And the funny thing, Swift, is that you're the man they're all goin' on about and I don't know what's goin' on. Not a friggin' notion except you must have lost your bloody marbles and started to think you're the Lone Ranger.'

'If you'll let me explain,' Swift said, raising himself on to all fours like a dog, the snow burning the palms of his hands. 'If you'll let me explain . . .'

He saw the kick coming and moved his head quickly enough to feel it only graze the side of his head and clip his nose. He stared at the gouts of blood spotting the snow until another kick knocked him over on to his back and then Gracey was standing astride him and shouting, 'No, son, I don't want you to say anything, I just want you to listen,' but Swift pushed himself up on his elbows and spat out, 'No you fuckin' listen, just for once you listen—' but before he could finish Gracey had grabbed him by the throat and was trying to shovel scoops of snow into his mouth. Swift tried to shake his head free but it was held in the vice of the grip and the snow was in his nose and in his eyes and he had to open his mouth to breathe and in the burning fear that he would choke he brought his foot smacking up between Gracey's legs. Instantly the grip was released and Gracey's breath streamed and croaked as if he was blowing up an enormous balloon and he staggered backwards, his hands vanishing inside the flapping folds of his thighs. In an instant Swift was on his feet and, as Gracey steadied himself, then charged like an enraged bull, curses streaming on the flaring smoke of his breath, he shook his head clear of the drip of blood and fixed his eye on the great black shape rushing towards him. Gracey was coming too quickly and Swift saw him stumble, then slip and slither, and suddenly he was out of control with all his weight thrown forward in a frantic attempt to find a balance. But as he lurched within arm's reach, Swift side-stepped and, clasping both hands like an axe, swung them down on the small of Gracey's back, sending him sprawling face down to the ground. His coat flapped up round his shoulders like a cape and for a few moments he was perfectly still before his arms and feet began to stutter and flail for leverage to push himself upright. For a second Swift thought of helping him to his feet as he walked towards him, but when he got close enough he kicked Gracey's legs from under him and, when his great weight flopped flat again, stamped as hard as he could on the broad open target of his back. There was a slobbering curse of pain, then a stubborn repetition of the attempt to push himself on to his hands and knees, but Swift responded with another full-force stamp which pushed Gracey down again and followed it with a kick in his side. Despite the energetic swing its impact felt muffled by the combination of overcoat and layers of fat.

'When I get up you're dead meat,' Gracey hissed, turning his face to stare up at Swift. 'You're fuckin' dead, boy.'

'But you're not getting up, are you? – you great tub of lard,' Swift said, but stirred by his anger Gracey tried again, only to meet the same result. He lay on the bed of snow and his breathing was heavy and broken, sometimes speeding up as if he was about to make another effort to get up. When Swift heard this he stepped closer and braced himself to dole out the same punishment. His own head was sore and every movement throbbed with pain, the legacy of Gracey's kicks. Gracey was mumbling an incantation of curses and watching him with one squirming, darting eye. To avoid it Swift moved constantly around him like a boxer circling his opponent. Once, out of nothing but malice, he kicked snow in Gracey's face then stepped back again as the scuttling eye fixed the full focus of its hatred on him, but he knew that he didn't have much time and that this would be his very last opportunity.

'Listen, Gracey, I don't know why but, I'm going to do you a really big favour and if you want to stop yourself making a complete arse of yourself, you'll listen to what I've got to say. It's about the Simons case and if you don't listen I'll go over your head and leave you looking like a complete wanker.'

'I could listen better standin' up,' Gracey said, squirming his shoulders.

'No, I don't think so. In fact, I think you're a man who's been listening to the sound of his own voice for so long that you've forgotten how to listen to anyone else, so just stay where you are and pin back your ears.'

'You're a brave boy all of a sudden, Swift. We'll see how brave you are when we're standin' face to face,' Gracey said, and he started to scramble off the snow, but Swift stamped him twice and then leathered him as if kicking a football. There was a violent mixture of curses and moans before Gracey collapsed to his former position and his breathing sounded as though he was swimming through the heavy swell of a sea.

'You're a brave boy, all right – kicking a man who's a bad back.' Gracey's voice sounded plaintive and Swift, forgetting his own pain and fear for a second, smiled. 'You know that assaultin' a senior officer will put the lid on your career before it's even started. After this they won't even let you catch stray dogs.'

'That'll make two of us, then,' Swift said, 'for I swear to God I'll take you with me. Now shut that bucket mouth and listen, for I'm only going to tell you the once.' He took a deep breath and stepped closer to Gracey's head where the thick white hair blended almost seamlessly with the snow. 'There was someone else involved with Alma Simons, someone who visited the house. And that someone was probably the father of her child – not Linton. I've checked it out. This man, who is older than Linton and has a car and money, had arranged for her to have an abortion – a back-street job. With a bit of a squeeze the McGraths will identify him. And did you never wonder about the house? How did a single girl get a house from the Corporation, a house she's not supposed to be living in? She paid no rent or anything. Don't you understand? Someone set her up in it, someone who was having an affair with her, probably the someone who killed her.'

'Linton killed her,' Gracey almost whispered, 'Linton killed her.'

'Linton loved her,' he said, then just managed to stop himself adding, 'but she didn't love him.'

'And what were you doing down the City Hall?'

'I went to find out about the house and when I was there I saw this guy, Charlie Newburn, a council bigwig' – Swift paused for effect – 'and he had scratches down his cheek.'

Gracey sniggered into the snow. 'Maybe he's been playing with a pussy cat,' he said. Swift felt it was going nowhere and that maybe it was time to give up trying. Thin skiffs of wind-blown snow drifted from the roof above. 'So how's it going to look for you when I prove that you got the wrong man?' he asked, giving it one last effort and firing the words close to Gracey's head. But his frustration had driven him too close and suddenly an arm shot out and grabbed his leg above the ankle. Immediately he tried to break the grip by stepping backwards but Gracey's weight anchored him to the spot and his furious attempt to stamp his fingers with his free foot only resulted in a slip of balance which Gracey exploited by giving his leg a fierce tug, tipping him on to the snow. Then Gracey was scrambling to his feet and scuffling and lolloping across the snow like an enormous bear and as Swift jolted himself upright he realized he was too late and before he could brace himself the full force of Gracey carried him backwards and smacked him into one of the doors. His head bounced against the wood and then, as he started to slither to the ground and Gracey tried to pull him upright by the collar of his coat, the other door swung open and a yellow stain of light flushed across the trampled, puddled snow. Swift turned his throbbing head to see the Head Constable and a range of other men crowding out of the corridor into the yard. Some were in uniform, others in their work shirts with braces sagging by their sides.

'What in the name of God's going on here?' the Head shouted.

'Just a bit of horseplay, sir, letting off a bit of steam,' Gracey said, helping Swift to his feet and brushing snow off his coat.

'Constable Swift?'

'That's right, sir. Sergeant Gracey was showing me some self-defence moves I'd asked him to show me,' Swift said, feeling his nose with his hand and leaning against the wall. He had started to feel dizzy. Someone at the back of the group was trying to stifle a laugh.

'I don't like this sort of thing, Gracey,' the Head said. 'I don't know exactly what you think you were doing out here, but it doesn't go down well with me. You see me first thing in the morning. Now get out of my sight the pair of you before I have you both standing outside all night guarding the snow.'

He turned on his heel and after he had gone Gracey told the rest of the spectators to 'piss off'. As Swift stepped out from the wall his head began to swim and his legs buckled under him and only Gracey's grasp of his coat stopped him from falling. When he opened his eyes again he was lying on his bed in the barracks and staring up at Gracey who was standing above him with a pillow. He started to scream but Gracey's hand clamped itself over his mouth and his red flaring face broke into a rumbling laugh. Then Gracey slipped the pillow under his head, dropped his hand and winked a marbled eye at him.

'So, Swifty, you think it was Charlie Newburn done her in?'

Swift had bad dreams and in them she was passed through the hands of many men. They were all there, taking whatever they could get, then throwing her aside. Their faces leered at him – Gracey, Burns, Newburn – and in the background Beckett's camera flashed its laughter. Then she was pregnant with his child, and trying to find him she turned up at his parents' house and they let her in but then took hold of her and told her they would get rid of the child. She phoned him, desperation and fear breaking in her voice, but when he set out to drive home to get her the roads were blocked with snow – huge drifts that he couldn't see over – and her pleading for him to come hammered at his heart. He sat up in the single metal-framed bed and wiped his face with his hand. His ribs were sore and he needed a drink but didn't want to move or venture out into the cold so he turned on to his back and, with his arms stretched down his sides, lay perfectly still and after a while slipped into a shallow sleep that carried him through to the morning.

For the first time that he could remember, Gracey arrived for work before him and was sitting in their room, staring at the powdery grave of grey ash and cinders. Swift didn't know what to say, so he lifted the empty coal bucket and shovel with the intention of taking it outside to fill. Gracey didn't look at him but instead lifted the poker and smoothed the mound of ash flat.

'What do you think you're doin', Detective Constable Swift?' he asked, as the acrid smell of the disturbed ash stirred into the room.

'Filling the coal bucket, Sergeant Gracey.'

'And why would you be doin' that when we're about to go out?'

'Where're we goin', Sarge?'

'To see the McGraths. And have that photograph with you. The car's out the front. I assume you're up to drivin' and not likely to run us off the road,' Gracey said and when Swift clanked the bucket down and turned to go, he heard Gracey call his name. He turned to face him. 'God help me, Swift, you better be right about this,' Gracey said, then repeated, 'You better be right.' Swift didn't say anything but nodded to show he understood.

The snow on the roofs of the tallest buildings was the first to vanish, sliding and slipping into a melted wash and polish of tile and chimney, while the snow on the streets had started to blotch and frazzle, looking in places like the congealed white of an egg being fried in a pan. Almost all the city's main roads were now clear, although the shadowed web of side streets was still thickly wedged with compacted snow that would need several more days before it raddled into slush. Gracey sat as he always did in the car, holding the passenger strap the way a traveller might on a London tube and while they drove he didn't speak, so the only sounds were the throaty turn and labour of the cold engine and the fine slur of water under the wheels. Parts of the city had started to look like the manged coat of some polar animal, a mosaic of the frayed and thread-bare, meeting thicker sections of pelt. And it had become an older landscape, shrinking and tightening into its own memory, with the perfectly preserved history of feet and criss-cross of wheels, the snakeskin tread of tyres, frozen like fossils. The paw marks of dogs and cats, the frittery scurry of pigeons; all were printed on the yellowing scree of parchment.

Swift glanced at Gracey and wondered what he read in the world outside but his face was expressionless, angled to the glass, and for all his size it was only the thin wheeze of his breathing that defined his presence. The sound of his breathing, the whispery slur and spray of water under the wheels. Swift shivered at a sudden stab of memory. It was the sound of his mother and father talking in the bedroom below his, their voices at first like the fine fistle of paper and then snaking into his room on the rising tongues of argument. His mother's persuasion, her insistent pleading – it felt that they lodged inside his head and wouldn't ever disappear, or be touched by something that would warm and thaw them into nothingness. He shivered again.

'If you're that cold, turn up the heater,' Gracey said, turning to look at him. Swift turned it up just as they passed the front of a bakery and, as if caused by his action, a line of snow loosened itself from an upper ledge and flurried like a run of notes into the air. There was the whine and wail of an ambulance behind them and he steered the car to the side of the road to let it pass. 'Another friggin' broken leg,' Gracey said. 'Soon half this bloody city'll be in plaster. I wouldn't be surprised if they run out of the stuff – they're running out of just about everything else. Ever break any bones, Swift?'

Swift squirmed, imagining a truncheon breaking his grip on the steering wheel but when nothing happened, answered, 'Collar bone once. Fell out of a tree.'

'What do you call a policeman sittin' in a tree?' Gracey asked. Swift glanced at him and said he didn't know. 'Special Branch. You should have known that, Swifty.' Gracey shifted in his seat, then said, 'It's a joke, son, a joke. Your trouble Swifty is you take things too seriously, take everything too personally. Bad habit.'

The rest of the journey was silent apart from when Gracey pulled on the strap to raise one of his buttocks off the seat and farted, then said, 'Excuse the French.' Swift tried discreetly to wind down his window a little, as soon as he thought Gracey wasn't looking, then when they arrived at the McGraths's street started to fill Gracey in on their characters, but Gracey tapped him on the back of the head, saying, 'I know the pair, son. Know them better than I know you. And there's more chance of you crackin' your face with a smile than Ma McGrath spillin' the beans. But now he'd sell his granny for the price of a drink.'

'You know about them?'

'The whole world knows about them.'

'Then why haven't they been done?' Swift asked.

'Some people think of them as social workers. Anyway, Swifty, who knows when you might need a wee homer yourself?' Gracey chuckled at his own joke and squeaked the glass clean with the back of his hand. 'Without the McGraths there'd be even more bastards out there than there are already.'

At Gracey's order he parked the car right outside the house. Swift saw the net curtain twitch before he'd the engine switched off but it took McGrath a couple of minutes to open the door and when he did it was to reveal only a sliver of himself. Gracey pushed it open and as it swung backwards it clattered against McGrath, so when they gained their first full view of him he was holding a hand to his head like a plaster.

'Take it easy, take it easy!' he complained. 'There's no need for brutality. No call for it.'

'Shut your hole, Ernie, you're givin' me a headache,' Gracey said, walking past him into the living room and looking round it as if he had come to serve a condemned notice. 'Where's the lovely wife, then? Out buying new knittin' needles?'

'She's gone to stay with her sister. Down south.'

'Now isn't that convenient. She's not doin' a wee family favour, is she? Well, that's a pity, Ernie, for it leaves you holdin' the baby, if you'll forgive my unfortunate turn of phrase,' Gracey said, looking about as if he intended to sit down but then changing his mind and taking up a position in front of the fire.

McGrath slumped into an armchair whose headrest was worn threadbare and black. 'What's goin' to happen to us?' he asked, rubbing his head again.

'That depends, Ernie, doesn't it? Depends on you, really. Some men don't mind prison too much – they get used to it after the first couple of years. Pissin' in a pot isn't the worst thing in the world.' Gracey picked a newspaper off the table and flicked his eyes over the back page. 'You'd have plenty of time for readin', that's for sure.'

'What is it you want?' McGrath asked.

'Not very nice of Arlene to clear off like that, leavin' you on your tod, leavin' you to carry the can all by yourself.'

'What is it you want?'

'It's very simple, Ernie. You just look at a photograph and tell me if it's the boy who came to make the arrangements for Alma Simons, and I'll be inclined to think that missin' wife of yours is the villain of the piece.' Swift went to take the photograph out of his pocket but Gracey shook his head.

'I don't know now,' said McGrath, his eyes skittering round the room.

'It's OK, Ernie, you take your time. It's an important decision. Five years is a hell of a long time to go without a drink – for that's what you'll get if I stick you up before a judge. And I'd say that before you got out you'd just about be ready to drink that piss out of the pot.'

'OK, OK, but you'll do your best for me?'

'You have my word: Swift here is my witness and he's as straight as they come. Detective Constable Swift, show Mr McGrath the photograph.' Swift handed it to him and watched as he took the briefest of glances before handing it back, as if unwilling to hold it any longer.

'That's the fella. That's him.'

'That's very good, Ernie, very helpful of you,' Gracey said. 'Now my young colleague will just take a wee statement from you, and then there'll be no need for us to trouble you any longer and we'll be on our way.'

When it was done and they were back in the car Gracey told him to stop at the first phone so that he could get a couple of men over to arrest McGrath and get him to the station. 'We don't want him doin' a runner over the border, well, not yet, anyway,' he said. Swift couldn't help himself, couldn't keep it in any longer. 'So you think it was Newburn who killed her?' Gracey let go of the strap and turned his head to look at him. 'No, Swift, son, I don't think that at all. And if you hadn't got your head full of sweety mice you wouldn't be talkin' like that. Why would Newburn kill her? Sounds like he's gone to a great deal of trouble to set up his little love-nest. The perfect arrangement: what would he want to kill her for? My money's still ridin' on Linton. And I know all you great detectives like to have a motive, so I'll give you one, Swifty. Linton found out about the baby, about her sugar daddy and it did his spastic little head in and he topped her. Why would Charlie, who is a man of some property in this city, want to damage what he'd invested his time and money in? That's not how a businessman thinks. Shag rent – that's not a tap he'd be rushin' to turn off.'

Swift hated every word that came out of his mouth. He wanted to press his foot to the floor and drive his passenger into the nearest wall. He tried to steady himself by staring at the road ahead and gripping the wheel tightly. 'Maybe it was the other way round and he found out about Linton, that she was planning to go away. Or maybe it was because she wouldn't get rid of the baby – Newburn's baby. Maybe he saw her as a threat to him, of his wife finding out.' He fumbled the gears, then had to brake as he got too close to the car in front.

'Hell of a lot of maybes in there. And for such a great man for evidence you don't have much to back any of it up,' Gracey said, pushing his feet instinctively to invisible brakes. 'He's in the frame, all right. Burns and John Thomas are round at Graham's now with a photo out of the *Tele* and with a bit of luck she'll be able to identify him as a visitor. So we'll have a link between them that'll back up McGrath's statement, but we have nothin' that'll place him at the murder scene on the night in question.'

'But the marks on his cheek,' Swift stuttered. 'And he was the one who came to the house that time I was upstairs.'

'Marks on a cheek are a careless shave and you didn't see who that visitor was, did you?'

Swift shook his head and wished he was lying on her bed, about to drift slowly into sleep, drift into sleep and not hold back. 'Are we going to pick him up for questioning?' he asked as they drove along the embankment. The river was a skein and sparkle of ice over the black water below. He felt Gracey's hand resting on his shoulder and heard him telling him to park the car, so he pulled in opposite some trees which thrust their bare, knotted branches over the railings of Ormeau Park.

'Listen, son,' Gracey said. 'Maybe you and me got off on the wrong foot and whether it was your fault or mine hardly matters. Now, I'm prepared to say you did some good work, even if you went about it all wrong, and I'm prepared to say you've showed more spunk than I gave you credit for, but you're still wet behind the ears and there's a hell of a lot of things you haven't got a hold of yet. There isn't a stick of direct evidence that says Newburn killed her. This is a beaten docket, son, believe me.'

'But what about him trying to arrange an abortion for her? We've got him on that,' Swift urged.

'Pissin' in the wind there, Swifty. It'd come down to his word against Newburn's and that's a contest you aren't going to win. A soak with form against one of the city's leadin' lights.'

'But we could bring him in, turn the heat on.'

'Listen, son, stop takin' this so personal. It's a fuckin' beaten docket. You don't turn the heat on a man like Charlie Newburn – this isn't some back-street hood. This is a man who has friends, who has influence. Lawyers, people in high places.

Him and the judge, half the jury, they'll be in the same lodge – Orange, Masonic, it doesn't matter. The only heat'll be burnin' the arse of you, of us. He probably plays golf with the Inspector General for frig's sake.'

'So he just walks away from it?' Swift asked, staring at the river, where the ice was being broken by a widening thread of black water.

'His name's in the frame and we can talk to him, but we need more if we want to make anything stick and right now we don't have that. I've got people working on it, lookin' into things, but the question you have to ask yourself is if it's worth the shite that's goin' to stick to us if we get it wrong.'

'He killed her,' Swift insisted.

'You don't know that. I don't know that. And just maybe, Swift, I don't want to know it, either.'

'Can I go back to the house? Will you let me have the key again?'

'If you want, but what for?'

'Because there's something there that he came back for, something he was prepared to risk going back for.'

When they drove back to the barracks Burns was there with the news that Mrs Graham thought she recognized Newburn but couldn't be sure. She hadn't seen him the night of the murder and didn't remember seeing or hearing a car arriving at or leaving next door. Gracey greeted the news with a shrug and, as he sank into his chair and started to remove his shoes, repeated as if to himself, 'Beaten docket,' then told Swift to get the kettle on. While they drank the tea Swift listened to their slurps and Burns's moans about having to spend time with Graham, and watched him throw a piece of yellow printed paper on to the table. Gracey squinted at it over the rim of his mug, then asked what it was. 'Another tract,' Burns said. 'I've got a whole pocketful of them. Next time I think it's Swift's turn to be saved.'

'Maybe Swift's saved already,' Gracey said, and, without Burns seeing, turned his head to wink at him.

Swift spent the rest of his afternoon investigating a break-in at a church hall. Nothing had been stolen because there wasn't anything of value to steal, but there'd been some vandalism and things thrown about. It was probably the work of children and he had to work hard at generating any interest or enthusiasm for the job. After it was done he returned to the barracks and wrote it up. There was no sign of Gracey, and Burns had gone off to collect his suit from Nugent. He sat in the office with the fire smouldered almost to nothing and listened to the voices rippling through the station. It was getting dark but he didn't put on the light. Soon his shift would be over. He tried to think things through clearly, to lay them out in straight lines, but it all seemed to defy his efforts and tangle up again. There was the sound of men's laughter, the type of laughter that came with a shared joke. He listened to it fragment into tiny echoes through the corridors and warren of rooms and felt the weight of his loneliness. All his life it seemed that he had sat in places like this and listened to something that conspired to exclude him. He glanced round at the buckling shelves of manila files; each seemed to whisper words that he couldn't quite grasp and each was a tightly bound secret that would never be made known to him. Once, after it was all over, he had tried to ask his father about it, about his mother's breaking voice which he couldn't get out of his head, but the words that he would have had to use were too terrible in his head and it felt that if he were to give then shape, something would break and tear into more pieces than could ever be put together again. Sometimes when he looked at his father he couldn't help but wonder whether

245

what had been done was right or wrong. He didn't know, but it seemed important to know, important to be brought inside the truth, even to know that it was done in love.

His thoughts started to darken and shadow his mind. He stared at the sunken embers of the fire and it seemed to him in that moment that only her love could save him, but that very thing had been torn from him by Newburn's hands. He could have saved her if only he'd known, if only she had let him. None of the others knew how to do anything but take from her, but all he wanted to do was give her his love. His love and his protection. There was only one way left to do that and he wouldn't let her down the way all the others had let her down. He remembered the photograph of a child on a swing, happy in the perfection of the moment, her smile carrying her through the silent, trembling air. A beaten docket. He shook his head in denial of the words. Somewhere a chair scraped across a floor. Out in the corridor, where the walls were the colour of slime in a drowned boy's hair, footsteps bruised the tiles.

He waited until they had clacked into silence, then went to the black wooden box and smoothed the grain of the wood with his hand. The key was in Gracey's top drawer. It felt small and cold in his hand. He opened the box and lifted out the Webley .38, letting it nestle and balance in the palm of his hand, looking at it as if it was something he had never seen before. Ignoring the brown leather holster, he slipped it into the pocket of his jacket, then locked the box and returned the key. The door of the office opened and Swift stumbled back against the table in the middle of the room. The light was switched on, blinking the room into yellow light.

'Scare you, Swifty?' Burns said. 'Think it was the Bogie Man come to get you?' He was wearing a suit made out of the green tweed. 'Well, what do you think?'

'Very nice,' Swift said, angling himself away from Burns's gaze but when he glanced back at him, he saw that his colleague's attention was fixed only on his new suit.

'It's dead-on, isn't it?' Burns said, holding out his arms stiffly in front of him as if waiting to be handcuffed. 'I knew it would make a cracker suit as soon as I saw it. Thon Nugent knows his stuff; fits like a glove. Listen, Swifty, if you like I'll keep my eye out for you and if anything comes along I'll give you a shout. You can never look too good in this job.'

'You're all right,' Swift said. 'Thanks anyway.'

'That's your trouble, Swift,' Burns said, 'you can't let anybody do anything for you. Now, maybe Gracey's getting soft in his old age and he hasn't been able to get through to you, but there's things you need to understand. And one of those things is that this is a team and we look out for each other, so you need to stop actin' like you're General Custer. For it's Indian country out there all right and if you don't have somebody watchin' your back, you're goin' to end up gettin' scalped. Do you understand what I'm sayin'?' Swift nodded. 'I'm only tryin' to help you son – some day you'll thank me for it,' Burns continued, delicately removing a thread from his sleeve. 'And another thing – for frig's sake lighten up a bit, you walk round all day with a face like a Lurgan spade. Maguire says you've no sense of humour and he's bloody right. I'm tellin' you, son.'

Swift watched him squirm his shoulders into the suit and as he headed for the door he let his fingers feel and trace the cold outline of the gun. When Burns was about to step into the corridor, he called after him, 'Thanks, I appreciate that.' Burns paused to nod briefly, then disappeared into the corridor. But even though he had left, no stillness returned to the room and Swift felt the stir and echo of Burns rustle and bruise the air and in his head he carried the image of his yellow-stained fingers against the green of his suit. He wondered about Newburn's hands, shivered as he thought of reaching out to touch them, then from his breast pocket took out the ring and slipped it on his finger.

Later that night, as he lay on his bed in an empty barracks, he tried to read but the words wouldn't register. He thought of ringing his father, then decided to postpone it a little longer and instead opted to go for a walk, but while fastening his laces he heard the wheeze of Gracey's breathing and the heavy shuffle of his feet. 'That's it, Swifty, get your kit on – we're goin' out,' he said, collapsing on the end of the bed and making the metal ends rattle and squeal. 'We're goin' to see a boxin' match. You like boxin', Swifty boy?' Swift shook his head. 'Naw, didn't think it'd be your cup of tea,' Gracey added. 'You don't go in for the Marquess of Queensberry Rules, do you?'

'Depends who I'm in the ring with,' Swift said, reaching for his coat.

'Oh you're quare an' sharp, Swifty, so sharp you'll cut yourself one of these days. And tonight it's Charlie Newburn we're gettin' in the ring with.'

'You're bringing him in?'

'No, son, but we are going to see the great man, have a wee word. Maybe it's time we put out a few fliers. Know what I mean?'

As they drove down to the Ulster Hall, Gracey explained that there was an amateur boxing tournament scheduled and that Newburn had put up most of the cups and prizes. He was a big sponsor of boys' club sport. 'A spit in the ocean,' he said, 'from what he's rakin' in from a string of businesses across the city. And those are only the legit ones we know about. Likes to present himself as Mr Generosity and mostly when there's a camera about to record it. But do you know, Swift, what really gets up my nose about Mr Newburn?' Swift shook his head without taking his eyes from the road. A sooty, black crow of a coal lorry in front sullied the eyes as it pressed its shadow across the snow. 'The bastard never invites me to any of his parties.' Swift glanced at him but wasn't sure if he was serious or joking.

They strode past the doormen with a nod of Gracey's head and entered the hall, where the ring was set up close to the stage. At long tables close to the ring and served by white-shirted waiters sat the black-tie spectators under a wavering, fuzzy blue scum of cigarette and cigar smoke, while the ordinary punters stood a distance behind or hung over the upstairs balconies. There was a sulphurous smell, primed with dampness and sweat, and Swift flinched with disgust, then started at the sudden, ferocious roar of the crowd as the ring produced a burst of action. Gracey slumped his hands into his pockets and stared at the ring, his head bobbing approval, his blubbery shoulders beginning to duck and dive a little. In the ring two matchstick-thin teenagers bobbed and shimmied a circle of each other, their skinny arms weighted by the bulbous red swell of gloves, then at intervals launched a flailing, flurry of swinging arms as if in a fit, before tightening once more into a protective shell. Gracey's voice joined with those all around them. 'Get inside, ya boy ya! Lead with the left! Jab! Jab! Work the right!' Swift watched the back of his neck thickly tighten and wrinkle as he vicariously soaked up the punches being thrown. Then, when he turned his eyes to the ring again, he saw a slick of blood skite through the air like spray off a car windscreen. The crowd howled ever louder as one of the fighters closed in for the kill, pummelling the crouching head of his opponent until the referee slithered in between them to stop the contest. Gracey shook his head in disgust. 'What's he stoppin' it for when thon boy couldn't punch holes in a paper bag?' he said, then beckoned him down the aisle towards the rows of tables. When they got closer a steward held out his arm to stop them but Gracey whispered in his ear and they passed through, Swift following, as he sidled to a spot near the side of the ring and took up a position where they could see the faces of the men sitting at the front table. They had to stand aside while the two fighters were led past. Swift stared at the red weals and blotches on their bodies, the swollen purple clot of the loser's eye and the referee's red-stippled shirt. 'Always makes a mess when somebody's cut,' Gracey said, sticking his tongue out over his lower lip. When Swift looked along the line of front-row spectators he could see fine spots of red on some of their shirt collars and on the table cloths and then, as his eye ran the line, he saw Newburn lean forward to tip the ash of his cigar into a tray.

The red tracery of scratches had faded and thinned into darker lines but they were still there and he was glad that Gracey could see them, too. 'Steady, Swift, son,' Gracey said, resting the weight of his hand on his elbow, 'let the dog see the bone.' The announcer introduced the next fighters and two more skinny lads bounced up and down on the spot, shaking their heads from side to side like metronomes and shadow boxing. The men on either side of Newburn were laughing at something he'd said and the laughter ignited a flare of anger inside Swift's head. He held on to the pillar in front of him and heard himself spit out the word 'bastard' in a stream of bitter breath.

'Easy, son, easy,' Gracey said, patting his back. 'You sound like you're about to climb in the ring. Get it out of your system. But what makes it so bloody personal?' Swift smothered the only words that could answer his question and shrugged a reply. 'Sometimes it gets you this way,' Gracey said, pausing to point out the fighter Johnny Caldwell, who was standing at the side of the ring, 'but you need to be able to see the wood for the trees. Need to keep a clear head.' He tipped his hat to Caldwell, who replied with a little shimmy of shadow boxing. 'Now if he hits you, Swifty, you go down like a roll of carpet and you don't get up again. Tatie bread, son.' The bell rang and there was the instant squeak of boots on the canvas and the slap of glove on glove. Struck matches quivered the dark hall and a gauze of smoke drifted into the lights. Swift fidgeted with impatience as Gracey seemed to settle to watch the fight but after a few seconds he straightened himself and glanced over at Newburn. 'Okay, Swifty, let's go and see the man, but unless I tip you the wink I do the talkin'.'

He followed Gracey as he ambled behind the rows of tables, finding it hard to walk so slowly and almost tripping over Gracey's heels when he paused for a few seconds to watch the fight. Then he was told to wait while Gracey passed along the row where Newburn sat and he watched as Gracey leaned across the table, said a few words, then pointed to the side of the hall. When he returned to where Swift stood, indifferent to the brawl and spit of the ring, Newburn hadn't moved or taken his glance from the fight. Gracey read his thoughts. 'Patience, son, learn a little patience. He's comin', he just doesn't want to seem too concerned.' He flapped the heat away from his face with his hat and stared at the ring. About a minute later Newburn stood and buttoned his jacket, stubbed out his cigar, then made his way towards them. Each step he took registered him more deeply in Swift's consciousness as he took in the thick gloss of receding black hair, the broad shoulders, the faint yellow lines of age under his green eyes. His tie-pin winked in the light but Swift's eyes focused on the dark lines on his cheek and the swing of his hands. There was a roar from the crowd when a combination of punches bounced one of the boxers against the ropes and the stretch and strain of the canvas as the two bodies pummelled into each other.

'Sorry to disturb you, Mr Newburn,' Gracey said, 'but I was wondering if we could have a few words with you? Maybe somewhere private.'

'I don't know what this is about, but it isn't a very convenient time,' Newburn said, glancing back towards the ring. 'I'm giving out the prizes after this fight.'

'It shouldn't take too long, and by the looks of those two boys the fight'll go the distance. But if it doesn't suit we can call with you at home afterwards.'

'OK, but I don't have much time,' he said, glancing at a wrist where there was no watch. Gracey led him to a side door and into a corridor that ran the length of the hall. It was almost empty, apart from a tight huddle of men angled into each other who were exchanging money and slips of paper. Swift stood a few paces behind Gracey and slightly to the side so that he could see Newburn clearly and while Gracey apologized again for picking such an inconvenient time, Newburn's hand checked his black tie was straight, then slid out of sight into his pocket. There was the sound of coins being turned over. Swift listened as Gracey casually, almost uninterestedly, told him he was making enquiries into the murder of Alma Simons and wondered if he had ever met her, or had any information that might be of help.

'Alma Simons?' Newburn asked, his hand rubbing the end of his chin, 'I read it in the paper but the name doesn't ring a bell. A bad business, but what makes you think I might know her?'

'Seems she was livin' in a Corporation house, without

permission, like,' Gracey said. 'Just wonderin' if you'd ever come across her.'

'No, never heard of her until I read the name in the paper. But we're holding our own investigation to see how she came to be in the house. Bit of a mystery,' Newburn said, his eyes flicking towards Swift. 'Wonder you're not takin' photos of the fight.'

'Detective Constable Swift – bit of an amateur photographer.' Gracey said, smiling and shaking his head. There was a roll of laughter from the group down the corridor and swear words splashed about. 'So you've never met this woman Simons?'

'Like I said, never heard of her till I saw it in the paper. I don't go round visitin' every Corporation house to see who's livin' in it. And I'm goin' to have to go – I'm givin' out the prizes after this.'

Swift waited for Gracey to turn the screw a little but instead he brushed the crown of his hat and apologized for having disturbed his evening's entertainment. There was a burst of rabid baying from the hall and a collective intake of breath. Newburn turned to go, straightening his cuffs and smoothing the greying side of his hair. Swift instinctively touched the back of Gracey's coat as if to urge him forward but the broad mass of his back felt indifferent to his encouragement and it was only as Newburn was about to return to the hall, that he heard Gracey say, 'Mr Newburn, one last thing: do you know a woman called Arlene McGrath?' Newburn hesitated, one hand on the handle of the door, and then he looked past them down the corridor and shook his head.

In the car Swift clutched the steering wheel tightly in both hands and hunched over it in frustration. His hair touched the coldness of the windscreen. 'Just drive the car, son,' Gracey said as he picked his teeth with his fingernail. 'And get me home in one piece so don't be drivin' like Stirling Moss. And before you start shootin' off your mouth and tellin' me what to do, put the friggin' heater on, it's brass monkeys in here.'

'Is that it?' Swift asked, shaking his head slowly from side to side.

'For the moment it is. Suppose you think we should have stuck the cuffs on him right there and then?'

'No I don't, but I thought you would've pushed him harder than that. Maybe the way you pushed Linton. But then Linton's a nobody, easy to push around.'

'You're one sparky bugger but don't push it too far, Swift, I might not appreciate what you're saying. But because I'm supposed to be teachin' you the business, let me tell you this for nothing. Newburn's not goin' to start blubberin' into his soup just because you start to scowl at him and, whether you like it or not, right now we don't have enough on him to stand up in a court. And if you rush in like a bull in a china shop you'll blow everything to hell and end up nowhere.'

'So what do we do?' Swift asked, glancing sideways at his passenger.

'We do what we've just done – shake him up a bit, put the wind up him. Right now he's shittin' his pants back there, takin' a few more drinks to steady his nerves. Thinkin' of who he can call on to get him out of this mess. That's our best tack now. Hope he panics a little, does something stupid.'

'And if he doesn't?'

'Like I said, it's a beaten docket, and you should start to understand that before it does your head in any more than it has already. We don't have anything worth a spit in the wind says he ever set foot in that house.'

Swift glanced up at the sky, where a full moon suddenly

pressed its blue-scabbed face into the dark spaces between buildings. It was the same colour as the dying snow and its etiolated light made the city a vaporous, flitting ghost of itself. Gracey asked him if he wanted to go for a drink but he declined the offer and knew his answer had been the one anticipated. When they got close to Gracey's home, he told him to stop the car and said he would walk the short distance left and it felt to Swift that for him to see where Gracey lived was considered an intrusion, something that crossed the line that separated work and the private world. He realized how little he knew about Gracey. He knew he was married but not if he had any children or anything else that wasn't rooted inside the walls of the barracks. As he slowly levered himself out of the car Swift could hear the squeak and wheeze of his breathing, the stretch and gratitude of the bruised seat as it resumed its shape, and then on the pavement he stretched before leaning back in, filling the space with the red strain of his face. 'Only going to say this once, Swifty, and then maybe it'll register in that shitehouse of a head of yours. I don't give a flyin' fuck who Charlie Newburn is, or who he thinks he is, and best if you remember that.' Then he smoothed his white wave of hair with one hand and donned his hat with the other, leaving Swift to watch his shambling scurry into the distance.

He sat in the car for some time staring at the sky. He let his hand find the ring and put it on. It felt good when he wore it. And then carefully with the very tip of his finger he traced the barrel of the gun that still nestled in his pocket. The moon had hidden itself behind tall buildings which leaned against each other like a row of white-spotted dominoes, and as always Swift didn't want to return to the barracks. He thought for a moment, then turned the car and headed for the avenue off the Malone Road where Newburn lived, driving slowly and deliberately in the hope that it would help him shape his thoughts into some sense of order. When he got there he parked a little way from the house, turned off the engine and lights and waited. The car got cold quickly but he pulled up the collar of his coat and blew into his hands. A woman walking her dog was the only other person he saw during his wait and then, after he had sat for about an hour, he saw the headlights of Newburn's car swing round the corner and sweep into his driveway.

Swift got out of the car and watched from the shelter of a privet hedge as Newburn locked his car, then fumbled for the key to his front door. Before he could find it, the door was opened by someone Swift presumed was his wife and he got the briefest glimpse of a woman in a pink dressing gown and a lighted hallway. For a second he thought of knocking on the quickly closed door and saying he had some more questions to ask, of seeing Newburn squirm in front of his puzzled wife while he asked about his business arrangement with the McGraths. But he remembered Gracey's warning and so did nothing but stare at the curtained opulence of the house and its impenetrable aura of power and privacy which made him feel a momentary flush of insignificance, and in that feeling he understood, too, that Gracey's assertion of the need for better evidence was nothing but the truth. When he repeated the phrase 'beaten docket' aloud, it tasted like ash that he wanted to spit away. He glanced up at a bedroom window as a light made the room glow red behind its closed curtains and let his hand slip inside his coat pocket to feel the comfort of the gun.

At first he drove aimlessly, letting the currents and contours of the roads take him where they willed, but then, like a man trying to find something to weight and ballast himself, he started to think, to piece things together in his head. It was slow because there was so much and sometimes it trailed off in a tangle of loose ends but he forced himself to keep working through the maze, the mire of frenetic, frantic images that fluttered and twisted inside his head. And just maybe Gracey was right and Newburn would panic, in his desperation do something irretrievably foolish that would carry him inside a closing net. He clung keenly to this glint of optimism and when he turned his face to look at the moon it seemed frozen and stilled into a calm that lulled the snow-scabbed city to sleep. And he knew, without understanding why, that he had to do this thing before the snow melted and vanished into the memory of another time and place. It felt as if, if he didn't, the truth, the love she would have given him, would also melt and vanish into a world that he knew he would never be able to reach again.

Like a dog returning to its own home, the car seemed to know its own way, unaided by its driver. Parking at the end of the street in the shadows of a gable wall, he walked down the narrow entry, which was filled with the smoulder of moonlight. The frozen snow crunched into ice below his feet and announced his approach, no matter how lightly he tried to tread, and each step tightened and stretched his nerves. He shone his torch on the yard door and noticed how wrinkled and blistered the paint was. Just as the first time, it swung open at his push, and when he shone his light on the back of the house it glittered in the dark squares of the windows. In one half of the yard the snow had withered away into a pocked thinness and in the other the skirmish of frozen footprints was slowly slithering into a watery oneness. The key felt cold and small in his hand and when he shone the torch on the lock, he saw that his hand was shaking a little.

He locked the door behind him but didn't put on the light and as he stepped into the house its damp coldness filmed his face, but it was the stir of his fear that made him shiver and he clutched the torch more tightly, holding it stiffly in front of his chest while he advanced into the hall. Dark little runs and starts of shadows searched for shelter from the skittering intrusion of his light and as they fled he was conscious of the sound of his breathing and the inexplicable tremor of sounds that emerged from the skein and fabric of the house that seemed to gulf above him. Part of him wanted to run back into the space of the night, part to throw on every light in the place, but, hesitating for a second at the entrance to the front room, he took a deep breath and stepped forward. His light hit the mirror, waking it from its sleep to blink and stutter into fuzzy yellow flower heads of reflection. He tried not to look at himself uncertain about what he might see and as the damp seeped deeper inside him he played the torch round the room in slow arcing sweeps.

Nothing appeared to have changed in the physical sense but there was a feeling of time having slipped away, carrying him ever further from that moment when he had seen her for the first time and, like his thoughts about the snow, it brought a belief that time was inexorably separating him for ever from what he wanted to hold on to. He moved slowly about the settee like a ghost, his memories lighting its buttoned folds and sometimes he touched it – where her head had rested, where he remembered the stretch of her arm – to absorb what was beginning to fade from him. He let his hand touch other things – the edge of the sideboard, the cream tiles on the fireplace, the red-faced dial on the radio – and then he sat in the chair Gracey had sat in. For a second he switched off the torch and let the darkness sweep in around him like a night tide and there was a sweetness in it that made him reluctant to break away again.

But there was work to do and it was that knowledge which eventually pushed him from the chair and into his search. Despite what swirled inside his head, he did it methodically, area by area, room by room, looking in the places he had already rehearsed in his head. He kept scrupulously to the plan, going first of all back through the places he had already searched but coming at them from a different angle and all the time trying to detect a secret place where something might be hidden. It helped him to think of himself as a boy, remember the secret world he had lived in and the type of places he concealed things, but despite his meticulous search he found nothing, and the more he looked, the more the house confirmed his first impression of it existing in a limbo devoid of the personal accumulation that marked most people's existence. He left the wardrobe to the last and, as soon as he began to open its door, the metal hangers trembled into sound as if in a little trill of expectancy. The spray of light from the torch and the gentle brush of his hand quivered the dresses into a momentary life which made his heart beat faster as he inhaled what remained of her scent. Pretending only to calm them, he touched each in turn, running the cloth through the length of his fingers and then as something suddenly broke inside him, he buried his face in the blue dress that hung at the front.

She was beautiful when she wore that dress. Beautiful for him. He slumped on the bed, facing the open wardrobe and let the torch rest on the quilt. It was coming to the end. Soon the snow would be gone, a memory melted away into nothing, uncovering the old ugliness that had been transformed and freed from itself with the soft brush of its lips. Lips he would never kiss. It was coming to an end and there was nothing he could do to stop it slipping away. And what would be left of him? He shivered in the cold and felt the weight of his future settling about him. There was nothing he could do. It was over. So why wouldn't the voices leave him alone? He heard their broken trails of whispers snaking out from the shadows and the empty rooms below. He turned the ring on his finger hoping he might be able to step inside the shield of its circle, and laid his head on the pillow. Never loud enough to hear what they were saying, always just out of reach – that's what he told himself – the words crumbling and fragmenting before he could ever fully grasp hold of them. But now they were growing louder, more insistent, and he was frightened that they would form into the words he didn't want to hear.

He turned the ring again on his finger and then, dipping his hand deep into his inside pocket, pulled out the photograph he had taken from Beckett. He laid it on the bed so that the beam of light passed over its surface, and for a second wondered if the light could burnish it into life, but then moved it into the shadows. The whispers were louder now, rising up to his room on the break of his mother's voice and there was nowhere for him to hide. They pounded in his ears like the surge of a fierce sea and he wanted to scream for them to stop but knew there could be no respite. Take away the pain. Take away the pain. And the words are laced with a curse and slew of brittle words that make them break and break so the pieces can never be put together again. Take away the pain. You can do it. And maybe it's right and maybe it's the only way to take away the pain, the pain that can't be borne any longer.

Always cold to the touch but snug in the palm of the hand. As if it belongs there. As if it recognizes the hand that clasps it. His hand moved it through the beam of light and the barrel darkened into an inky blackness. He slowly shaved the stubble on his cheek with it, then pressed its ridged end along his cheekbone. Take away the pain. Please, please take away the pain. And the voice is pleading louder than he's ever heard it before and he doesn't know any more if it's his mother's voice or if it's his own. It flows about him and then it's inside his head and coiling tighter and tighter until it's more than he can bear and he lets his lips kiss the barrel and then he opens them and it's inside his mouth. His hand is shaking, tightening, for maybe it's the only way. The only way to stop the pain: the only way to finally step inside. To enter the world in a moment. Finally to enter.

It's the door. And it had to be in a dream of what had happened before because in his head a key was scraping in the lock and turning with the sound that he recognized. His hand trembled as he took the gun slowly and carefully out of his mouth and laid it on the bed, trying to still the breath that rushed from every corner of his being and wanting to burst into a shout that he knew he couldn't stop if he were to let it start. He seemed to step outside himself in the moment, to be watching and listening to everything he did and thought, and that feeling of detachment brought a flush of control that calmed him into thought. Part of him didn't want to touch the gun again but he made himself pick it up, and with the other hand switched off the torch. The last thing he saw before the darkness swooped around him was the light rustle of the blue dress in the wardrobe and it was as if she was stepping towards him and in the darkness he carried the print of that image. Stepping towards him with her open arms. Taking him home.

He stayed on the bed and did nothing but listen to the slight crease and press of feet below. There were hardly any sounds but, like a stone dropped in water, the presence of another rippled out through the house, and something was stirring and scratching at the silence. He prayed that Gracey had got it right, that this was the moment when panic had pushed Newburn into something stupid, and he prayed too, that he wouldn't make a mess of it, that he wouldn't let it slip through his hands as he had done before. But he had to be patient, for he knew that if it was Newburn he had come to find something, and if he could let him find it before he took him, everything could be right, everything brought to right.

He stood up, slowly and lightly balancing his weight and holding the gun down the seam of his trousers as if it was an extension of his arm. Whoever was in the front room was using a torch – sometimes the light skittered through the open door and into the hallway. There was the sound of a drawer opening and the contents being rattled about with rising frustration. As the noise of the search grew louder and more frantic, he felt his patience tighten into a panic that he would be left chasing shadows once more, and he began to edge step by step towards the top of the stairs. The concentration on moving silently made him suddenly feel frail, bereft of solidity, and he wished that his arrival at the foot of the stairs would coincide with the bulk of Gracey bursting through the back door, but he knew that he was on his own, that no help was about to arrive. It was down to him now.

The stairs seemed steeper in the dark and, pressing one hand to the wall, he moved down them step by slow step, trying to test each one before he gave it his weight. The wall felt cold, as if damp buried in the plaster was trying to break out and he saw a little flutter of his breath fan the air in front of his face. There was something that sounded like furniture being moved and for a second he hesitated and strange thoughts ran across his mind and in the mesh of images the person he was about to confront changed again and again. So once it was Gracey, his open overcoat flapping about him like black wings, and once it was Beckett, his eyes like a camera pushing and prying into every secret place. Despite the cold he could feel sweat in the palm of his hand as he gripped the gun. The light from the torch splayed out into the hall and back inside the room and then it was more than he could bear and almost tripping over a missed step he stumbled into the room and shone his torch into the face of the man standing there.

Newburn flung his hand across his face as if the light had stung his skin, but before he had it covered Swift saw the dark splay of lines on his cheek. Then, as he raised the gun with one hand, his hand holding the torch fumbled for the light switch but failed to find it at first and so for a second he had to move the light away from Newburn. 'Stand still or you're a dead man!' he shouted, his voice sounding strange and unfamiliar. When the electric light came on, it flickered a little before stuttering into brightness that hurt the eyes. Newburn didn't raise his hands but stood perfectly still, and Swift didn't know if the paleness of his face was caused by fear or merely the sudden wash of light.

'For God's sake put that thing down before you shoot me or shoot yourself,' he said, his body flexing out of its previous stiffness. His hand combed back through his hair as if he was suddenly conscious of looking dishevelled.

'Don't move unless I tell you.'

'Are you supposed to wave guns at people?' Newburn asked, slipping into an almost casual tone. 'I take it you know who I am?'

'Yes, I know,' Swift said. 'You're the man who killed Alma Simons. Killed her on the same settee you're standing beside.'

Newburn glanced at it for the briefest moment, then returned his gaze to Swift, and when he spoke the words were bevelled by a thin edge of laughter. 'That's a good one, son, I'll get a few laughs out of that when I tell it. Best one I've heard in a long time.'

'Will your wife be laughing when you tell her you're being charged with the murder of a woman who was carrying your child.'

Newburn's hand lightly touched the side of his mouth then pulled away as he said, 'Don't talk shite, son, no one's charging me with anything.'

'What are you doing here?' Swift asked, suddenly conscious of the need to ask the right questions, say the right things.

'I'm involved in housing in this city, as I'm sure you know already, and after your questions earlier I wanted to see the place where this thing happened. There's going to be an enquiry and I wanted to take a look to see if I could find any answers. Maybe it was morbid curiosity. But I think you should put that thing away before it gets you into trouble.'

Swift didn't move or lower the gun. 'And is that why you came here in the middle of the night with a torch? You can talk to me as if I'm a fool, if you like, but I know why you're here as well as you do.'

Newburn's hand circled his wrist. 'I don't know what you're on about but I don't think I'm saying any more to you without my lawyer, and I'd say that if you had a case against me you'd have charged me before this.'

Swift could feel it slipping away from him. The gun was heavy in his hand 'Why did you kill her?' he asked, stiffening his arm again. 'Was it because she was going to have the baby? Were you frightened your wife was going to find out?'

'I don't know anything you're talking about, but the word on the street is she was a whore. Had half the city sniffin' round her. So they say, anyway. I wouldn't know.'

Swift stepped closer and his hand holding the gun was

shaking a little. He felt his fingers tightening on the torch until he was holding it like a club and his trembling arm wanted to swing itself back and strike the man standing there, but he stopped dead and tried to steady his breathing. For a second it felt the beat of his heart was so loud that Newburn must hear it but he stood there at the end of the settee and stared impassively, if he were experiencing nothing more than a little inconvenience, a minor discomfort that would soon be rectified in the light of day. For some reason Swift flicked on the torch and watched as it shone on the arm of the settee in front of Newburn. It was where he had been standing when he had shone the torch on his face. In the seconds after he had smoothed his hair back. Because he had been bending over? Swift stared at the settee and when he glanced at Newburn, he, too, was looking at it. The last place. It had to be there. Whatever it was had to be there. With the gun he motioned him to move back and after he had stepped towards the sideboard Swift began lifting the seat cushions, feeling each one with his hand – something he had already done – and slipping his hands along the back of the settee where it met the seat.

'Lookin' for loose change?' Newburn said. 'If you're short of a bob or two, I could maybe help you out. It wouldn't be hard to fix things up.'

Swift made no response, except to glance at him every few seconds to check that he hadn't moved. The lights flickered. He found nothing. He set the still lit torch on a cushion as his hand continued to slide. It came to the arm where her head had been and his fingers felt nothing as they ran along the narrow seam, and then, as he turned his eyes to Newburn, he touched what at first felt like merely a pin or the head of a tack. Then prising the seam wider he shone the torch in and saw that what he had touched was the broken metal clasp of a watch. Taking a bunch of keys out of his pocket, he hooked the end of one through the broken links of the bracelet, and pulled it slowly out, as if drawing some silver fish from a dark sea. It must have come off in the struggle and then been pushed into its hiding place by the final twists and squirms of her body. He held it in his hand long enough to read Newburn's name engraved on its back and the date of its presentation from his colleagues in the City Hall. Swift threw back his head as something fountained and gurgled in his throat but as he did so the lights flickered again, then stuttered into darkness, and as he grabbed for the torch Newburn's fist smacked against the side of his head and sent him sprawling face down on the settee. A blow to the back of his head almost knocked him senseless, but even in the spinning, swirling blackness his hands held tightly to both the gun and the watch and as he tried to shake his brain clear, then stumbled to his feet, he heard the clatter of Newburn's feet bursting out through the back door. Like a dog emerging from water, Swift again tried to shake the pain from his head and straightening slowly, dizziness making the yellow shadows of the room flare, he searched for a balance, and despite the pain found himself smiling and repeating 'Yes' over and over again.

He stowed the watch in an inside pocket and shone his way out of the room, through the hall and into the kitchen. After the darkness of the house, the moonlight seemed to call him forward and he stumbled into the silver sheen of snow, holding the torch in one hand and the gun in the other. As he ran through the doorway into the entry, he slithered and almost lost his balance, but the surge of cold air and the rush of adrenalin started to clear his head and everything in his body felt alert and focused. Newburn had cleared the entry but as Swift broke into a run it felt as if his presence lingered in each step he took and the blue scrunch of snow was printed with the desperation of his flight. Then when he reached the end of the entry and carried on into the middle of the street, he was momentarily blinded by the scream of headlights as Newburn's car bore down on him and, after starting to raise the hand holding the gun towards the shadowy smear of windscreen, he let it fall again and flung himself into the bank of snow that smothered the kerb. The car passed in a black blur and, when it reached the corner of the street, slid and quivered for a moment as the wheels sought traction, then righted itself and vanished.

A few seconds later Swift was turning the engine of his own car and cursing it as it reluctantly kicked into life, but soon he was pushing the accelerator to the floor and making the gears squeal and complain. The main road was clear and he could see Newburn's tail lights in the distance but he felt strangely calm and all his concentration was given to driving – he had never gone so quickly and wasn't sure of what the car was capable. The road was still icy in places but there was no way of knowing where until it was too late, so he had to be careful to avoid too-sudden breaking and judge corners accurately. He was moving gradually closer, close enough for Newburn to see him in his mirror and his hands gripped the wheel more tightly. For a second he thought of Gracey and wished he was sitting in the car beside him, then in his imagination saw him as a humped shape under the tight press of white sheets and woollen blankets. He heard, too, the rattle and snuffle of his breathing, the creak and groan of the bed. Gracey was safe in the world of his dreams, and as he drove Swift momentarily longed for the weight, the ballast, he would bring to this moment, but while the engine roared and rasped in his ears he knew that this was the thing he had to carry through on his own. And as he watched the tail lights ahead he thought of the gun he carried in his pocket and constructed in his head the scenarios that would allow him to use it. Maybe it was only right, maybe it was the only way. Any other way and there was still the chance that Newburn would walk away. He remembered what Gracey had said about power and contacts and he knew no one else could know the goodness in Alma Simons that he knew. It was an unequal contest which maybe only the gun could bring to balance.

Blotched, snow-speckled buildings huddled along raddled roads of fading snow as he sped by. A vaporous blue light trembled from the coke-filled brazier of a night watchman on a building site. He knew already that Newburn wasn't heading towards his home but knew also that this was a man who had bolt-holes all over the city and a potential legion of helping hands. When Newburn's car was forced to slow at a junction he was able to reduce the distance between them some more. The moonlight stirred the city into pearly striations of light and made its thin thread of streets seem briny, aqueous, as if they had been washed by some beryl sea. And everwhere the city was asleep, blind to what hurtled through its streets, and Swift felt a surge of loneliness that eased his foot off the accelerator, but it was followed almost immediately by a new urgency. Everywhere he looked, the snow was beginning to stain and slither into nothingness. He thought of the nicotine stains on the hands of Burns. Soon the whole world would look like that, and then it would be too late. He had to do this thing while there was still time, and everywhere he looked time was running out.

The knowledge made him reckless and he began to push the car faster than was safe, his desperation driving him on and the sliding, skidding wheels were nothing more than little pulses on the very edge of his consciousness. A team of salters and gritters pulled back to the safety of the kerb as Newburn's car shot past them with a warning blast of horn and, as Swift passed, their faces were a pinched and cold-tightened frieze of confusion. In his head he heard the clack of their long-shafted shovels when they scattered their cargo across the road with a twitch and flick of their wrists, and something about their faces made him think of Alma Simons's father the day he had spoken to him in the morgue. He thought of him sleeping in some nothing of a room where the street lights outside flushed a soft burn of electric over his silent sleep and cradled the small photograph of a girl on a swing that leaned against his bedside lamp. Newburn charged his black car into the heart of the night, its rear swinging on corners and the tail lights staring back like the eyes of an animal sparked into fire. Swift blinked as if to break their spell and then opened his window a little to let the cold night air brush against the heat of his brain. It hissed and streamed against his face and the road ahead was a glittering swathe of light that called him on.

Soon they were moving out of the city and on to roads that climbed high above it and everywhere there was frozen snow cladding the slopes of fields. He tried to think where Newburn was heading, but couldn't, and in his rear mirror the city below was a shiver of glassy light, haloed by moonlight and stars. They came to a road junction and Newburn slowed to make a left turn, but had to brake to avoid a collision with a lorry. Swift pressed the accelerator and pushed his back into the seat as the car screeched forward with a piercing whine and he knew there was only one way now, and just as Newburn's car started to move again he hit it behind the back wheel, sending it spinning a half-circle and his own car into a skidding, shuddering halt. It took him a few seconds to jolt himself free from the car – his chest hurt where it had hit the steering wheel and he could feel the spreading dampness of blood through the ripped knee of his trousers – but he could still move and as he stumbled into the middle of the road he saw Newburn restart his engine and try to drive off. He ran faster but his feet slithered away from him on the polished sheen of the road and he fell. Then while he tried to prise himself upright he slipped again and this time he lay still and watched Newburn's car reverse towards him, only to lurch to a stop when the buckled rear wheel wedged itself tighter into the mangled metal of the wheelguard. It ground a few feet forward again but then limped to a final stop, and as Swift found his footing he saw Newburn jump from the car and run across the road to the entrance of a quarry dug out of the hillside.

Swift started to run but was slowed by a sudden surge of pain in his leg and he called after Newburn to give himself up, but as he momentarily paused to ease the pain he saw him vanishing through the haphazard and half-hearted fencing that skirted the entrance and sagged forward on lolling posts. Swift looked round for a house or a phone, for any source of help, but there was nothing and the city below seemed locked in its indifferent sleep. There was only his own help, and he let his hand grasp the Webley that still nestled in his pocket. Then, going back to his car, he gathered the torch, checked that it was still working and as he passed Newburn's car shone it into the driver's side. The keys were still there and he took them out and placed them in his pocket, then hurried to where he thought he had seen Newburn disappear through the fence, but when he reached the spot there was no gap to be found and he had to run the light of the torch along its length until he found the slit. In the light he saw that a flap of trouser hung loose at his knee and that what felt like a deep cut was still bleeding, but he squeezed through the gap without snagging his coat on the wire.

He switched off the light – it only served to pinpoint his own position – and let his eyes acclimatize to the moonlight. In front of him, cut into the gradient of the hill were broad steps of terraces littered with piles of rubble and antiquated pieces of machinery whose function was disguised by their coating of snow and the impossibility of determining where one piece began and another ended. There were tin sheds to one side and a series of wooden outbuildings that leaned against each other under a thatch of snow and everywhere the snow still lay thick and largely untrammelled as if no one had been there since the first falls, and the slow shift of moonlight made everything nebulous, vague and undefined except by what he was able to construct through memory and imagination. The scabbed and pitted side of the hill sheered steeply ahead like a cliff face and great trenches of scree swept down in tributaries of excavated stone. There was no sign of Newburn or any other trace of movement and Swift stood motionless in the shadow of an excavator, uncertain of what to do. It seemed dangerous and futile to start searching such a large area, cluttered with endless hiding places from where his quarry might emerge and attack. It was a lonely, deserted place and for the first time he felt the sharpening edge of fear. It wasn't a place he would choose to die. He tried to tell himself that Newburn was the one who felt fear and for the first time he took the gun out of his pocket.

He clambered on to the excavator and leaned against the driver's cab. There was a stab of pain in his chest – it felt as though he'd cracked a rib. His breathing was a rasp in his throat and sounded loud enough to carry across every crevice and trench of the quarry. He slowly scanned the blue-washed snowy terrain, searching for some sign of Newburn's presence but there was only the bitter swirl of a rising wind which made his face smart and skiffed fine lilts of snow from the white-capped peaks of rocks or the metal latticework of cranes. A bulbous, hunched rat crossed the open ground in front of him and made him shiver. He crouched down and waited – that was all he could think to do now – in the hope that, if he was patient and silent, Newburn's desperation would sooner or later cause him to make a run for it.

He scooped a handful of snow and pressed it against his knee. He wanted something cold against the pain in his chest but knew he had to keep warm. It felt colder all the time and he cursed himself for leaving his gloves in the car, as the metal of the gun burned his skin and made him move it from hand to hand every few minutes. His breath skipped and funnelled in front of his face no matter how hard he tried to stop it, and in his mind it smoked ever higher into a signal of his presence. From time to time he stood up and, holding on to the meshed grill of the frosted driver's cab, peered across the tundra, but the more he searched it, the more his eyes played tricks on him, and in the blue-shadowed dips and hollows he thought he saw the outline of a crouching man. On impulse he reached for a stone nestling in the teeth of the traction wheels and flung it into the opalescent tremble of light and, as it clattered off a rock, almost immediately felt the foolishness of his action, which in his memory turned him into a nervous child throwing stones at the suspected hiding place of a rat, the burst of bravado trying to disguise his fear that something might emerge.

As nothing but memory stirred from the re-formed silence, he clawed out his fingers to clasp the mesh of the cab and saw them clutching not at metal but at the eyes that stared at him through the frosted glass. As an involuntary shout burst from his lips, he stepped backwards and in that second the cab door flew open and smacked against his chest, knocking him off balance and sending him tumbling into the snow. Even with the cushion of snow, the breath rushed out of his lungs and left him sucking frantically for air like a drowning man. He had dropped the gun and the pain in his side was a sudden sear. He had dropped the gun and even with its black against white he couldn't see it. He scrambled in the snow like a dog trying to dig up something previously buried, his head jerking up and round for a sight of Newburn but as he found the torch and switched it on he heard the slap of running feet and knew his quarry was in flight.

The gun had fallen further away than he had thought possible and as he brushed the snow from its barrel he hurried round the machine and shone the torch after Newburn, whose heels squirmed up puffs of snow as he ran, his arms and legs flailing like cracking pistons, his head enveloped by a gauze of his breath. Swift called after him to stop and the words jittered high and shaky in his throat like birdsong and as he set off in pursuit he saw Newburn stumble and fall, then right himself, before setting off again with his feet bruising and treading the snow. He gave chase but the pain in his chest felt as though it might explode at any moment and throw him to the ground. He watched Newburn running higher, up the steps of terraces, but there could be no escape in that direction and then, saw him veer to the right, probably a prelude to an attempt to sweep round in a circle and back to the road. Swift struck out across the debris-strewn terrain in an effort to cut him off, and when he called out again his voice was stronger, the words ground out with the rhythm of his run. Newburn fell again and took longer to get up this time. Ignoring the pain, Swift put on a shambling, scurrying burst of speed and, close enough to see the terror in Newburn's face as he measured the closing distance between them, felt for the first time the beauty of the retribution he carried towards him.

Suddenly Newburn stopped and for a second turned full face towards him and as Swift blinked, it looked as if his black suit and his black hair were blanched and stripped of their colour by the summary fall of age, as if a fierce frost had reached down and grasped him in its hoary grip. And Swift blinked again and saw that Newburn was trapped by a polished swathe of ice that stretched ahead and blocked his escape. He, too, paused, and, trying to summon a final sustaining draw of breath, shone the torch towards Newburn but what it struck now was not his face but his back as he set off across the ice. Swift hurried towards the edge and watched the fleeing figure slither and struggle to stay upright and when he reached where the first thin reeds stuck up through the rim of snow, he drew the gun from his pocket and held out his arm until the final tremble had slipped away and his aim felt steady and true. Newburn slipped again, then clambered into new flight. The back of his coat was spangled and starred with wet and Swift closed one eye and tried to shut out the whispers that riddled the wind that streamed about his ears. Take away the pain. Over and over. Take away the pain. The only way. His finger cradled the trigger and he wanted the sound to block out all the others. Block them out for ever. The shot seemed to crack the night open and it echoed and echoed as if trapped for ever in the chambers of stone. He watched Newburn stumble then cry out as all around him the ice cracked and rucked into jagged splinters and for a second he thought his shot had killed him, but when he lowered his arm from where it had been raised to the sky he knew it was the thinness of the ice that now pulled him down.

He stood motionless while Newburn floundered in the water, his frantic struggles to escape only serving to shatter the blue membrane of ice and sending him stumbling deeper into the water. It came up to his waist and, if not deep enough to drown easily in, would prove difficult for an increasingly tired man to climb out, and there was a smear of blood where he had cut his hands in his futile efforts to break a channel free. His cries for help rose with the stretch and creak of the ice, each one more pleading than the last. Swift shone the torch across the ice, making it glitter like diamonds, then looked around for a piece of wood or a length of rope but the covering of snow made the search pointless and taking off his coat he strode calmly on to the ice, sure-footed and glad of the lightness that measured his steps.

By mid-morning the station had been become so crowded with reporters clamouring for information, that the Head Constable had told Maguire to clear them out into the street. The phones rang constantly and there was a whisper that the Inspector General himself was on the way. Newburn had been formally charged and was in the cells awaiting interview, while his solicitor was in the process of summoning bigger guns to take up the case and warning anyone who would listen of the dire consequences for all concerned in 'this ludicrous charade'. As he passed Swift in the corridor he had told him that 'his goose was cooked', that 'he was finished', but Swift had brushed him aside without reply, remembering Gracey's admonition that he was to say nothing to anyone. 'Play the dummy flute, son,' Gracey had instructed, 'and say nothin' to anyone. Don't even talk in your sleep. Court's the place we'll do our talkin.' A few minutes later he had followed him into the toilets and stood with his back blocking the door and for a second Swift had thought of that moment in Madigan's Bar, but this time there were only words of warning. 'If we frig this up, Swifty, we're tatie bread – it'll be over for the both of us and I'm not ready to collect me pension just yet. And you, you'll be out on your arse before your bum's even warmed the seat. Understand what I'm saying?' Swift had nodded as he washed his hands, trying not to look at the washed-out face in the mirror in which the only colour was the blue circles under the eyes. 'And another thing – get that bloody gun back in the box before you shoot someone and when they ask, say the thing discharged accidentally as you stumbled in the snow. Blame it on the friggin' snow.'

Now Gracey sat at the fire in their office and held out his hands towards it. Other detectives stood round the room waiting for him to give them instructions but he only stared silently at the flames and, from time to time, rubbed their heat into his hands. Burns entered and squirmed up to the fire. 'Bloody freezin' up that mountain,' he said to no one in particular. 'And Swifty, you didn't half make a mess of that car. Not so much *Z Cars* as pushbike for you from now on.' He winked at someone but no one laughed. Gracey ran a hand through his hair and blew a stream of breath through his lips. 'I still think Linton's our man,' Burns said as he shivered suddenly. Gracey angled his head to look at him, as if seeing him for the first time, but then turned his gaze again to the fire, spitting into its heart and making it sizzle.

'When are you going to interview him?' Swift asked, looking at the fire over Gracey's shoulder.

'No rush, Swifty boy. Let him sweat like everyone else. And God knows he needs to thaw out a bit yet before he works up one of those. So patience, young Swift, a bit of patience.'

'When it's the time, would you let me give him the squeeze?'

Swift asked, hearing his words spread through the sudden silence, until it was broken by Burns's loud laugh.

'Give Newburn the squeeze?' Gracey said, turning sideways on the chair while Burns's laugh collapsed into a snigger. 'Give Newburn the squeeze? Well, you've done everything else, so just maybe you should be the man to finish it off.'

'You can't be serious,' Burns said, glancing at Gracey and then looking round the room for support.

'OK, Swift, you can lead the way and I'll be ready to step in if you give me the nod. Just don't be threatening to shoot him if he doesn't give the right answers and Detective Constable Burns, I want you to get your arse out of that suit – you look like a friggin' leprechaun – and before you do that, sort out Linton and get him off the premises without him talking to the press. They brought him over from Crumlin about an hour ago.' Burns stood, as if drained of words, and as he turned to go Gracey called after him, 'And put the kettle on and see if you can rustle up a few sandwiches for Swift and me – this might take some time.'

Swift found a quiet place in the station and sat and planned everything in his head, working everything out, covering all the angles, preparing for all the possibilities and then when it was time headed down to find Gracey. In the corridor with the lime-green walls he met Burns leading Linton towards the back yard. Neither man acknowledged him and Linton stared only at the brown paper bag that held his returned possessions. His face looked thinner and his hair had been cut short. The smell of prison laced his steps. Swift stood and watched him follow Burns towards the back gate, then waited as the small door cut in the large metal gates was opened for Linton to slip through. Burns couldn't free the bolt and Linton turned for a moment and looked back. Swift's hand closed round the ring he held in his pocket as their eyes met. The only thing she had ever given him. He took a step forward and then stopped. The door was open and Linton bowed his head as he disappeared. He looked at the ring, at the fading snow. It was time. Gracey would be waiting for him. Then, as Burns locked the door again, he placed the ring on his finger and went inside.

A NOTE ON THE AUTHOR

David Park has published three novels *The Healing*,
The Rye Man and *Stone Kingdoms* and one volume
of short stories *Oranges from Spain*. He was the
winner of the Authors' Club First Novel Award,
the Bass Ireland Arts Award for Literature and a
twice-winner of the The University of Ulster's
McCrea Literary Award. He lives in County Down,
Northern Ireland with his wife and two children.

A NOTE ON THE TYPE

The text of this book is set in Linotype Stempel Garamond, a
version of Garamond adapted and first used by the Stempel
foundry in 1924. It's one of several versions of Garamond
based on the designs of Claude Garamond. It is thought
that Garamond based his font on Bembo, cut in 1495 by
Francesco Griffo in collaboration with the Italian printer
Aldus Manutius. Garamond types were first used in books
printed in Paris around 1532. Many of the present-day
versions of this type are based on the *Typi Academiae* of
Jean Jannon cut in Sedan in 1615.

Claude Garamond was born in Paris in 1480. He learned how
to cut type from his father and by the age of fifteen he was
able to fashion steel punches the size of a pica with great
precision. At the age of sixty he was commissioned by King
Francis I to design a Greek alphabet, for this he was given the
honourable title of royal type founder. He died in 1561.